DIS **HUGELY**

"HYP
—Orlando

"FAST MOVING."
—*Booklist*

"IMPRESSIVE."
—*Kirkus Reviews*

"TERRIFIC...
ROUGHAN IS A NATURAL."
—*Douglas Kennedy,*
author of The Big Picture

"A SUPREMELY HIP,
BRAZEN DEBUT."
—*Publishers Weekly*

SPECTACULAR PRAISE FOR
THE UP AND COMER

"THE UP AND COMER is a millennial, Wall Street version of *The Player*—a tale of a Yuppie prick who gets his comeuppance. Beyond the sheer speed and undiluted excitement with which THE UP AND COMER is told lies a cruel comedy of manners about overprivileged, spoiled New Yorkers.... Sleek entertainment and a malicious thriller: fast, nasty, jolting."
—Bret Easton Ellis, author of *American Psycho*

"First-timer Roughan knocks one out of the park with this satisfyingly lean and propulsive thriller.... An impressive debut."
—*Kirkus Reviews*

"If F. Scott Fitzgerald had written 'The Perils of Pauline' and set it in contemporary Manhattan, the result might well be the brilliant THE UP AND COMER. With pitch-perfect ear and dialogue for days, Roughan has written a funny, smart, and start-to-finish riveting chronicle of life as it is lived among upwardly mobile young Americans. A killer first novel, as entertaining as it is authentic."
—Jerry Stahl, author of *Permanent Midnight*

"A supremely hip, brazen debut.... As Roughan wraps his crafty plot around some impressively tense moments, the novel morphs into an engaging, cinematic page-turner."
—*Publishers Weekly*

"A screamer. Fast, fun, and dead-on compelling. A great ride of a book."
—Robert Ferrigno, author of *Heartbreaker*

more . . .

"Wry, self-deprecating wit . . . has a hypnotic charm."
—*Orlando Sentinel*

"Great characters . . . an entertaining and very contemporary examination of how far a man will go to protect the life he's so happily settled into."
—*Ridgefield Press*

"What makes this thriller so good is the narrative voice . . . elegant writing, fine dialogue, and deft jokes at the expense of lawyers and Manhattan society."
—*Tatler* magazine

"An irresistible page turner. . . . The plot is fiendishly brilliant and tautly woven. . . . Roughan's book crackles with wit and sharp dialogue, yet there is a dark, serious undercurrent that keeps you riveted on several levels."
—*Greenwich Time*

"Roughan has an ability, like Donald Westlake, to combine comedic elements with serious matters. . . . I was howling with laughter while almost falling off the edge of my seat. At the same time, Roughan plots so well, and so simply, that in the end everyone gets what they deserve. Well, almost everyone."
—Bookreporter.com

"A wonderful decline-and-fall story for our well-heeled times . . . written with great rude brio. . . . Roughan is a natural. He tells a story with deceptive ease, making you compulsively turn pages . . . and he captures, with spot-on accuracy, the dubious underside of anyone who believes 'careerism' is a noble calling. This is a terrific debut."
—**Douglas Kennedy, author of *The Big Picture***

THE UP AND COMER

HOWARD ROUGHAN

WARNER BOOKS

An AOL Time Warner Company

WARNER BOOKS EDITION

Copyright © 2001 by Howard Roughan
All rights reserved. No part of this book may be reproduced in any form or by any electronic or mechanical means, including information storage and retrieval systems, without permission in writing from the publisher, except by a reviewer who may quote brief passages in a review.

Cover design by Diane Luger
Cover photo by Tony Stone/Alan Delaney

Grateful acknowledgment is made to reprint portions of "My Way." English lyrics by Paul Anka. Music by Jacques Revaux & Claude Francois. Original French lyrics by Giles Thibault. © 1967 Societé de Nouvelles, Editions Eddie Barclay, © 1995 renewed. © 1969 Chrysalis Standards, Inc. (BMI), © 1997 renewed. International Copyright Secured. All rights reserved. Used by permission.

Warner Books, Inc., 1271 Avenue of the Americas, NY, NY 10020

Visit our Web site at www.twbookmark.com.

An AOL Time Warner Company

Printed in the United States of America

Originally published in hardcover by Warner Books.
First Warner Books Paperback Printing: September 2002

10 9 8 7 6 5 4 3 2 1

For Christine,
who reads me like no other

Acknowledgments

Laura Tucker for her intelligence, wit, and that most endangered species of personal traits: the willingness to take a chance.

Richard Curtis for simply being the consummate professional.

Rick Horgan for his ever keen insight and always cool demeanor. A brilliant combination for which I'm eternally grateful.

Jamie Raab for walking into the room and effortlessly reciting lines back to me. No quicker way to my heart.

Jody Handley for her amazing comprehension and gifted perspective. So good while so young is so unfair.

Harvey-Jane Kowal and Betsy Uhrig for their perserverance in the epic battle to protect the English language from my seemingly endless attempts to butcher it.

Nancy Wiese and Erika Johnsen for going to the ends of the earth for me.

Scott E. Garrett for his most informed counsel and trip to the dentist.

Elaine Glass for her unyielding spirit and contagious optimism.

Also, Stephen Schaffer for his incredibly vast expertise. Mike Lewis for being so generous with his time and wisdom. Paul Weinstein for always being able to help, book included. And Ralph Pettie for being the first teacher who encouraged me to write.

Finally, John and Harriet Roughman. My right from wrong, true measure of trust, and forever my foundation.

THE UP AND COMER

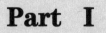

Part I

ONE

The four of us were having dinner together, as we so often did. It was at the Grange Hall down in the West Village. There were Connor and Jessica, Tracy and me. Connor, never one to instigate a conversation let alone dominate it, was nonetheless center stage.

"I realized the other day," he began, his narrow eyes darting back and forth among us, "that we're all at the age now where we can really only rely on our instincts and intellect in order to succeed." Connor stopped for a moment, presumably to let the supposed magnitude of this statement sink in. He continued: "When you think about it, from the ages of, like, twenty-eight to . . . oh, let's say thirty-four, we're all kind of just out there without a net. I mean, when we're older than that, odds are we'll have collected enough experience—personal, professional, what have you—to get our asses out of almost any jam. And when we were younger, let's face it, nothing really too significant was expected of us, precisely because we didn't have any experience. But those in-between years—right now—that's when we're really on our own."

I remember watching Connor finish that last sentence, the way he deliberately reached for a packet of sugar as if he were testing out an artificial limb. I remember because it was at that precise moment that I wish it had occurred to me: *I should probably stop fucking his wife.*

TWO

"Absolutely incredible!"

Tracy stood before me, loaded shopping bags in hand, a smile ear to ear. She'd been gone a good six hours.

"Back so soon?" I said, barely looking up from my Sunday *Times*. But it was clear there wasn't enough sarcasm in the world to burst my wife's bubble. She just ignored me.

"Everything fit; everything I tried on fit me like a glove. It was like karma . . . clothes karma!" Tracy said with a giggle. "That's what it was!"

Now hold it right there. Were this most anyone else's apartment and the same scene was being played out, odds are the guy in my shoes would start huffing and puffing about how much this little shopping spree was going to set him back. Some heated words would be exchanged, followed by a full-blown argument that in turn would give way to any number of tantrum-related activities such as kicking, screaming, or heaving a vase across the room.

But this wasn't anyone else's apartment, this was our 3,500-square-foot penthouse loft in Chelsea, paid for in cash by my father-in-law, Lawrence Metcalf, as a wedding gift two years ago. Which is not to say I married for money. No, I married for *a lot* of money.

So when Tracy would go four figures deep into Bergdorf's or Bendel's, or, on this particular Sunday afternoon, Saks Fifth Avenue, I, Philip Randall, couldn't really give a shit. It wasn't our money she was spending, it was Daddy's, and you didn't have to be the sharpest knife in the drawer to figure out that whatever moral or self-esteem issues one might have with that, it simply wasn't worth acting on them. Period.

"Philip, if you want me, I'll be in the bedroom."

That was code, of course. It meant Tracy wanted to have sex. As if wealth wasn't a blessing enough unto itself, it so happened that spending money made my wife horny. Really horny. And the more she spent, the more horny she got. It actually made for an interesting post-coital ritual. We would finish up, and depending on whatever it was she had let me do to her and how much she had been into it, I would try to guess how much money she'd just spent. Once, on a whim, she bought herself a Cartier Pasha watch at Tourneau. It was the only time we ever had anal sex.

"That was at least three G's," I gasped, rolling off her.

"Two thousand," she gasped back. "Though not including tax."

(Truth be told, I wouldn't have rated it much more

than a couple hundred, however, I had learned early on to always come in at a higher number.)

Tracy got up from the bed and headed for the bathroom. I watched her. She was still very thin, as thin as when we first met four years ago. Her breasts were not large, but they were round, a nice shape. Occasionally, after too much to drink, she'd talk about getting implants, though I knew it was something that she'd never do.

"Oh, guess who I bumped into?" came her voice from the bathroom.

"Who?"

Tracy reappeared in her robe. "Tyler Mills," she said.

"No shit."

"Yeah, he remembered me and everything. Of course, I didn't have a clue who he was at first. He looked horrible, though."

"Funny how a suicide attempt will do that to you," I said. "Where'd you see him?"

"Outside of Saks. He was standing by the doors."

"By himself?"

Tracy nodded.

"What'd you talk about?"

"Nothing, really; I asked how he was doing and all that. It was— Oh, on second thought, he did say something strange; well, not really strange, just kind of weird."

"What was it?"

"He said he hoped to be talking to you soon."

"You thought that was weird?" I asked.

"It was the way he said it, like it was something that you might not want to do."

"What, did he say that?"

"No, I got the sense that there was more to it, though," she said. "Do you know what it's about?"

"Not a clue."

"Anyway, I gave him our number as well as your one at work. That was okay, right?"

THREE

There are probably more lawyers in Manhattan than in any other city in the world. I say *probably* because I've never really taken the time, or more accurately, had the inclination, to find out for sure. Statistics like that are just assumed by New Yorkers out of sheer egocentricity.

Many of the lawyers I know say they wanted to be one at an early age. Often it was because they had a parent who was one, or in some instances they'd been influenced by a character who was one on television or in a book they had read. I'd bet *To Kill a Mockingbird* alone is responsible for over a hundred lawyers in this country easy. No matter what the influence, though, the mere thought of there being a bunch of pubescent types walking around knowing they want to be lawyers has always seemed to me to be ludicrous. Always will.

As for me, I didn't know I wanted to be one until my last year at Dartmouth. It was no great epiphany or anything like that, and there was hardly any deep soul-searching involved. In reality, it was on account of a lame classroom exercise in a poli-sci course.

We were doing a simulated United Nations conference in which every student represented a member country. Given the current political context of the time (a diminishing Cold War, budding capitalism, blah, blah, blah . . .), the objective was to advance your country's interests as best you could. I represented Hungary. I kicked ass.

I managed to persuade the voting majority in the class on every initiative I introduced. No matter what dissenting argument was presented by another student, I ripped it to shreds. It was pretty wild, and the most amazing thing about it was that it was also pretty easy.

When the class was over, there must have been six or seven other students who came up to me to tell me how well I had done, and practically every time they made some comment on how I'd make a really good lawyer. One guy, who I'd never even said as much as hello to, asked me if I planned to take the LSAT. *The LSAT?*

Just like that, people saw something in me that I'd never seen for myself. I was skeptical at first—there were, after all, a fair number of dimwits in the class—but the more I thought about it, the more I thought they could be onto something. Maybe I could make a good lawyer. Besides, it wasn't like there was anything else shaping up for me to do. French lit may have been a fun major and a good way to get laid, but even I knew there was no way to make a living from it.

I took that LSAT, scored a Reggie Jackson (44), and got accepted at the University of Virginia School of Law. I concentrated on criminal law and memorized a whole bunch of crap over the course of three years. When the recruiting season started, the only thing I knew for sure was that I wanted to work in Manhattan. I got three offers.

Then one day a professor pulled me aside after class and told me that Campbell & Devine was looking to hire an associate. It was like being tapped for a secret society. They were a small Manhattan firm with a huge reputation. The Green Berets of law. Having roomed with Jack Devine in college, the professor said he could arrange an interview for me. Not to piss on myself, I told him, but why me? Because you're exactly the kind of son of a bitch he's looking for, he said. It was one of the best compliments I'd ever gotten.

I don't remember the flight up to New York. I couldn't tell you if it was good weather or bad. I'm pretty sure I ate, though your guess is as good as mine when it comes to what. The only thing I remember was sitting down across from Jack Devine, a huge leather-inlaid desk between us, and him holding my résumé in the air . . . and then ripping it up. Slowly.

"We won't be needing this now, will we?" he said with a hint of melodrama. He let the pieces of paper fall to the desk. I could've sworn they fell in slow motion.

The interview lasted five minutes. It consisted of one question and one request, neither of which had anything to do with law. Or so I thought. The question, which came first, caught me completely off guard.

"Philip, why are manhole covers round?"

Damned if I knew. Though I had a sneaking suspicion that wasn't the answer Jack Devine was looking for. So I sat there and stared at him. At least that's what it surely looked like to him. What he couldn't see was a guy's brain scrambling for its life to deliver something, anything, that would seem plausible. Finally, without even knowing it, I blurted out an answer.

"Because the holes are round."

Jack Devine sat there and stared back at me for a moment. Then, he let out with a huge bellowing laugh. It was like a thunderclap.

"Because the holes are round!" he yelled. "Fuckin' A! Donna, you gotta hear this one."

A big-haired brunette in a tight skirt appeared all curvylike in his doorway. Staten Island, without a doubt.

"Because the holes are round," Devine said to her with a "get a load of this" staccato.

"Good one," Donna said, looking at me with a trained smile before walking away.

Hell, I'm on a roll, I thought. What's next? Why's the sky blue? What's the difference between AM and FM? The mating habits of horseshoe crabs? Bring it on, Jack!

He brought it. "You see that pen?" he asked, pointing at a Bic sitting atop a nearby credenza. "I want you to sell me that pen."

There was no hesitation on my part this time. Though a little knowledge can be a dangerous thing, a little confidence can do wonders.

"*Sell* you the pen?" I began, getting up and walking over to the credenza. "Shit, Jack, you can *have* the pen!" I picked it up and tossed it on his desk. "And there's plenty more where that came from."

Three days later I got a phone call back at school from Donna. She told me to hold for Jack. Deleting the constant flow of "ums" I uttered, the conversation went something like this:

JACK: You big on summer vacations?

ME: Not necessarily.

JACK: Good answer. The job starts June first, it pays
           a hundred fifty thousand, and if you don't pass
           the bar on your first try you're fired. You can
           give me an answer now or let me know by to-
           morrow morning. Any later and the guy who
           actually knew why manhole covers are round
           gets the offer.

ME: I'll talk to you in the morning.

At 9:01 the next morning I called Devine and accepted
the job. He welcomed me aboard and told me to prepare
to be great. That was five years ago.

———————

"Morning, Philip, how was your weekend?"

"Great," I said. "And yours?"

"It sucked."

My secretary, Gwen. Candid to a fault.

I had once been at this law school wine-and-cheese
party where this guy with a tan, some senior partner at
a firm in Miami, was bending my ear about the dos and
don'ts of the legal world. Most of it was forgettable, except for one thing. He said no matter what I did, no matter how many rules I bent or truths I stretched, never,
ever hire an attractive secretary. The temptation, he said
with a mouth full of Gouda, would prove too great a dis-
traction. It seemed to be an insightful observation. Even
more so when I learned that his second and third wives
could each type better than eighty words a minute.

So I made sure Gwen was unattractive. Actually, her

parents made sure of that. I simply made sure that she worked for me. Gwen was fat, had acne scars, and her hair was even thinning. (Okay, so I went a little overboard.) But damn if she didn't know how to cover my ass.

"The Devine One was looking for you," she said, following me into my office. "He came by twenty minutes ago. I told him you were at a deposition."

"Good save," I told her, looking down at my watch. Nine-thirty-five. Where did I think I worked, an ad agency? I started to head back out the door.

"Don't bother; he only wanted to make sure you could sit with him this afternoon at two," Gwen said.

"Any details?"

She shook her head. "No, just two o'clock in his office."

"Tell Donna to let him know I'll be there," I said.

Gwen went back to her desk and I settled into mine. The offices of Campbell & Devine were on the thirty-first floor of the Graybar building, right smack in the middle of midtown. It was an okay area to work in, I guess, though I'd never had anywhere else to compare it to.

After sorting through a couple of files in between long stares out my window, I got up and closed my door to make the call. After two rings, Jessica picked up. We exchanged hellos. Then we got down to business.

"I can't today," she said in a super-hushed tone. As an ad sales rep for *Glamour* magazine, Jessica was subject to the virtual-office concept and the lack of privacy that went with it.

"Aw, c'mon," I said.

"No, really," she continued, her voice trying to sound more earnest, "I've got a presentation this afternoon and we've changed around some of the charts. Everything's a mess. I've got to get it in order."

"Bring the stuff," I said. "I'll help you."

She laughed. "Yeah, right."

"Seriously, I will."

"Philip, I—"

I interrupted her. We had a rule about not using our names, especially on her end. She broke it regularly.

"Sorry," Jessica whispered. It was all the leverage I needed.

"Listen, I'm busy too," I said. "I just really want to be with you today, that's all. We'll keep it to an hour, max." I could sense the tide was turning. "I'll bring lunch, chicken Caesar wraps from Piatti Pronti."

"And a diet peach Snapple?"

"And a diet peach Snapple," I repeated back. Victory. "See you around twelve-thirty. I'll be the early one."

FOUR

Jessica Levine was born, raised, and will probably die in New York City. Depending on your opinion of Woody Allen movies, that's either a blessing or a curse. Her father lost a battle with cancer when she was six, a precarious age as far as someone's memory goes. One time when we were lying in bed together she began to cry over no longer being able to recall how he smelled. She knew it was a sweet smell, not flowery or anything like that, just somehow sweet. Only suddenly she could no longer smell it. Mere weeks ago, she said, she needed only to think of him and breathe in to remember. Now nothing. Another casualty of the distance the advancing years were putting between her and her memories of the man.

Her father had been a successful financier and, as one might have expected, very well insured. So Jessica, her mother, and her younger brother, Zachary, had carried on very nicely in their duplex on Park Avenue. As Jessica would tell it, her mother suppressed her grief by joining practically every committee for the arts there was in the city. Consequently, Jessica grew up going to any-thing and everything that featured a curtain, velvet ropes, or raging homosexuals.

She was pretty, not turning-heads pretty, rather the kind of pretty that seemed to develop slowly before your eyes. I tried to explain that to her once by comparing her to a Polaroid snapshot. I don't know what I was thinking. Let me get this straight, Jessica said, what you're saying is that at first I'm an out-of-focus blur? Okay, not the best analogy, I assured her, switching im-mediately into my backpedal mode. She understood, though. She always understood.

Affairs may be first and foremost based on sex, and yes, there was barely a time that Jessica and I were alone together that we weren't proving that point. Nonethe-less, there was something else going on. It was as if the two of us both lived our lives dreading the thought that one day, with death imminent, we would look back and ask ourselves with a defeated sigh, *"Was that all?"* Ours was a greedy generation to begin with, and she and I still seemed to want more than most others. We were two driven individuals for whom the idea of being self-ish wasn't such a bad thing. In short, we were to each other what our spouses had turned out not to be. Kiss-able ambition.

Logistics. When the affair first started we had to pick a place to rendezvous at. We discussed renting a small studio, but the more we talked about it the less it seemed like a good idea. Having to sign a lease, nosy neighbors, and the prospect of one day having to hear, "Honey, what are these keys for?" were way too much to handle. No, a hotel would be the better choice, we decided. But which one? Jessica suggested the Paramount. I suggested that we'd have less chance of being discovered if we confessed on *Nightline*. The idea, I reminded her, was to not have to worry about bumping into friends and acquaintances. The hotel didn't have to be a dive, it merely had to be a little out of the way.

We settled on the Doral Court, off Lexington on Thirty-ninth Street. It was one of those places that you'd never know was there unless someone pointed it out to you. It was clean, conveniently located for both of us, and had all the pretensions of being discreet.

We never walked in together and we never left together. The way it worked was like this. One of us, usually me, would be "the early one." This meant that I would go ahead and get the room (using my corporate Am Ex, of course, with the monthly statement being mailed to me at work). Once in the room, I would call Jessica at her office and let her know the room number. Ten minutes later we'd be between the sheets.

Two, maybe three times a week this would happen. At Jessica's office she would claim that she was taking lunch. At my office, where eating at your desk was the norm, I claimed to be going off to the gym. I even carried a gym bag around with me.

To some people, I imagine, this would all seem a little paranoid. Then again, those people have probably never had an affair. The odd thing was, all the precautions had become more than two people making sure they wouldn't get caught. They had become part of the attraction. Simply put, the secrecy was a turn-on. It made the bond between us stronger. And yes, it made the sex better.

———————

I picked up lunch for the two of us and headed over to the hotel. Checking in had become almost comical. The day shift had obviously come to recognize me, and it wasn't too long before they figured out what was going on. Naturally, they pretended not to know, and in doing so had turned somewhat robotic in their actions. They would smile and say all the pleasantries required of them, but their movement was stiff around me, and all of them avoided making unnecessary eye contact. All of them, that is, except for Raymond.

Raymond, as his name tag read, was a young black guy who stood out not because of his skin color but because he seemed actually to enjoy his job. While his coworkers all wore the faces of opportunities missed, Raymond walked around like he had grabbed the brass ring. He was tall and lanky, with a shaved head and a diamond stud in his left ear. I had little doubt that his supervisor had checked some handbook when he first started to see if male employees were in fact allowed to have an earring.

Not only did Raymond know what was going on, but he let me know that he knew. It was a look. A slight smile combined with a tilt of his head as he would hand me my room key. It wasn't as if he was trying to embarrass me. If anything, it was more like, *Hey, man, does she have a sister?*

Raymond didn't check me in this time, though. It was Brian. He was new to the hotel and had only been working there a couple of weeks. This was the second time he had waited on me. I pictured him at the coffee machine in some backroom being clued in by another employee about me and my nooners. Did he laugh? Did he want to know more? Or did he simply nod, not really giving a shit? Perhaps Jessica and I were just one of many affairs that were going on in the hotel. Maybe there was a whole parade of indiscretions passing back and forth in front of these guys. It was a big city, after all.

"Here's your room key, Mr. Randall. Enjoy your stay."

You bet I will, Brian.

There's a weird sense of anticipation when you walk into a hotel room for the first time. Even when you basically know what it's going to look like. A bed, a bathroom, a television, a desk or table of some kind. Except now it's suddenly your bed, your bathroom, your television, your desk or table. At least for the night. Or in my case, just an hour or so in the afternoon.

First things first, I headed straight for the phone and dialed. One ring.

"This is Jessica," she said.

"Room four-oh-six."

"Okay."

We both hung up and I leaned back against the headboard. I was a terrible waiter, regardless of whether or not the wait was for something good. My parents (we'll get to them) maintained that it was because I was born nearly a month premature. The pattern was set, they said—it made me a restless child who in turn grew up to be a restless adult. While that's a little too simplistic for my liking, I will concede that from the womb to my marriage, I perhaps wasn't much for the feeling of confinement.

I checked my watch. Twelve-twenty-seven. I opened my gym bag and took out my toothbrush and a tube of Colgate. Improved oral hygiene: the unintended benefit of having an affair.

I checked my watch again, this time with better breath. Twelve-thirty-two. I started to pace, something I did a lot, and when that didn't cut it, I sat back down. I grabbed the remote and turned on the television. A soap opera appeared. A very good-looking woman was telling a very good-looking man that she couldn't take it anymore. She didn't say what the "it" was that she could no longer take, but she looked really serious. Time was you couldn't pay me to watch this stuff. Way too ridiculous. Now it didn't seem so far-fetched.

Finally, a knock on the door. When I opened it, Jessica came bursting in with an angry huff.

"My boss is such an asshole!"

"What happened?" I asked her.

"She's an asshole, that's what happened. I'm the top producer in the entire group, and the bitch reshuffled my accounts around without consulting me first. I can't fucking believe her; it's like she can feel me breathing down her neck!"

"You know, if I wanted to hear complaining I've got a wife I can call," I wanted to say but didn't. "That sucks," is what actually came out of my mouth. Not that that did any good. I don't even think she heard me. I'd never been too adept at knowing when to keep talking and when to shut up around a woman, especially an angry one. I was pretty sure, though, that this was a shut-up moment. So that's what I did. I stayed quiet. Turned out I was right. After steaming for a little while longer, Jessica abruptly stopped.

"Oh, god, I'm sorry," she said with a guilty smile. "It's just that it made me so angry." She started to walk toward me. "I didn't even say hello, did I?" Before I could decide if it was still a shut-up moment, she kneeled down and unzipped my fly. Hello.

I've been intimate with two Jewish women in my lifetime, neither one of whom had any problem performing oral sex. So much for that theory.

I returned the favor to Jessica. Then, after concluding with the good old-fashioned missionary position, we broke open the sandwiches and promptly lost track of the time. Before we knew it, it was ten of two. *Shit!* I had ten minutes to get my ass back to the office and meet with Devine. In thirty minutes, Jessica had to be showing those newly arranged charts of hers to some media slugs at Young & Rubicam. We both dressed in a panic. Were there an Olympic event that involved buttoning a shirt while simultaneously doing a video check-out from a hotel room, I would've surely gotten my face on a Wheaties box.

Like I said, normally we would stagger our exits as

we did our entrances. Then again, normally we weren't scrambling around like extras in a monster movie. One after the other we came flying out of the revolving door to the hotel. It was a minor breach in our security; well worth it, I thought, given the circumstances.

FIVE

I came running into the reception area of Campbell & Devine at a minute past two. There was an unmistakable taste of chicken Caesar wrap working its way up my throat. I stopped to catch my breath. As I stood there panting, Josephine, the firm's receptionist, looked up from her magazine. She nodded toward my gym bag, a puzzled expression filling her face.

"You sure are in lousy shape for a guy who works out so often," she said.

I laughed, hopefully not too nervously, and headed back to my office.

"Buzz Donna and have her tell Jack that I'll be by in a minute," I said, passing Gwen.

Most of the time I returned showered after being with Jessica (hygiene aside, remember I was supposedly at the gym). But on those rare occasions that I couldn't, I would resort to the drawer. The Drawer. Any guy worth his salt has one; any woman for that matter too. A desk drawer filled with the essentials of personal grooming in case you should need a touch-up during the day. Me, I kept it simple: cologne, breath spray, floss, hair gel, a comb. All of which I grabbed and used very quickly while proving once again that the most important item hanging on my wall was not my law degree but the mirror behind my door. With every hair back in place and the smell of sex overpowered by Bulgari for Men, I emerged from my office and made my way toward Devine.

———————

Thomas Methuen Campbell, the Campbell in Campbell & Devine, was a distinguished-looking man with a serene gaze. At least that's what the huge portrait of him in our offices depicted him as. Had I known him, Devine once told me, I would've discovered that his placid exterior was merely a facade. For in fact, beneath it lurked a far darker man.

According to Devine, Campbell was the last of the great sons of bitches, with a soul that would make even the devil blush. When he died of a heart attack in the fall of 1992, the funeral was mobbed. Ten percent were apparently there to mourn, the rest showed up to make sure he was really dead. There was much to be said about his prowess as a litigator, his ability to make opposing counsel seem weak, and his penchant for getting a jury to eat out of his hand. And through bits and pieces, I heard almost all of it from Devine.

Originally, the firm was Campbell & Associates, started by Campbell in 1972 after he left the partner track at Silver, Platt, Brown & LePont. He took one client with him, a small outfit called Procter & Gamble. At the time, Monsieur LePont swore that he would get his revenge on Campbell if it was the last thing he did.

As it turned out, the last thing LePont did was to fall down in his shower a year later and kill himself. In the greatest of ironies, he slipped on a bar of soap. Ivory, of course: P&G's flagship brand.

In 1976, Campbell hired Devine fresh out of the University of Vermont Law School. By that point, there were six associates practicing at the firm, all of whom had law degrees from Yale, Harvard, or Stanford. Upon introducing Devine to his colleagues, Campbell announced, "Ladies and gentlemen, I would like you to meet your control group." A lesser man might have been embarrassed, perhaps even insulted. Devine, on the other hand, told me that he thought it was the funniest fucking thing he'd ever heard.

After a few apprentice-type years, Devine went on to what could only be labeled as one hell of a winning streak. He possessed the same ruthlessness as Campbell in the courtroom, the difference being that he did it with a smile. As a team, they were good cop—bad cop at its best, and while the sign on the door may have read Campbell & Associates, to everyone on the street they were soon Campbell & Devine. So it was only a matter of time before Devine asked to make it official. He had a good case, and if there was one thing that Campbell always respected, it was a good case.

With apparently little resistance and even less fanfare, Campbell bestowed the title of managing partner on Devine in 1988. In doing so he asked for only one concession in return. That when Campbell eventually passed on, Devine would agree to face every tough decision with the following question: What would Campbell do?

It was a very clever man's stab at immortality.

"How is the Devine Gatekeeper doing today?" I asked Donna, smiling straight back to my molars.

She barely looked up from her computer and waved me in like a third base coach on Xanax.

In an article in the *Wall Street Journal* a few years back, a reporter had described Jack Devine as "Patton with a legal pad." Despite the fact that Devine had no military background and didn't conduct himself in a manner that suggested he did, the description was dead-on. The most obvious reason was the physical similarities between the two men. (Though I've always maintained that Devine actually resembled George C. Scott in the role of Patton more than he did Patton himself.) What really made the moniker stick, however, was more intangible. It was twofold, really. First, Devine, like the famous general, possessed the kind of leadership qualities that demanded greatness from others. Be it out of fear or respect, you never wanted to let Devine down if you reported to him. Never. Second, and a logical extension of the first, was that when it came time to do battle in the courtroom—or any room, for that matter—there were few other men if any that you'd want leading the way.*

---

*A revealing footnote to all this: when he read the aforementioned article, Devine's only reaction was to point out that given the infamous slapping incident that tainted Patton's career, the reporter had left himself dangerously open to being sued for libel.

Devine was on the phone when I entered his office and he motioned for me to take a seat. It was the same seat in front of the same leather-inlaid desk I had sat in when he first interviewed me five years ago. What wasn't the same, or more appropriately, what had developed, was our relationship. Although he had no children of his own, I'll spare you any father-and-the-son-he-never-had analogies. Let's just say the guy must have seen something in me that reminded him of himself. From the get-go it was clear that my doing well was very much a reflection on him.

Fortunately, I didn't disappoint. With Devine as my mentor I rather quickly established myself as a real up-and-comer. Small firms rarely made title distinctions among associates, but Devine did. You came in as an associate. If you did well, you would eventually become a senior associate. From there you either became partner or *of counsel*, the common equivalent of "close, but no cigar."

After three years, I was made a senior associate, the fastest that had ever happened in the history of the firm. Said Devine to me on the day of that promotion, "Philip, I've always believed that the title catches up with the man. In your case, that the title had to stop and puke its brains out a few times along the way from exhaustion should only make you feel that much prouder."

I smiled, apparently a little too broadly. Devine let me have it.

"That said, if you let this go to your head, you'll be one young, sorry-assed, out-of-work senior associate."

Back in his office, Devine was now raising his voice

into the phone. "Listen, Bob, I don't give a shit what some damn jury consultant is telling us. Dumbing down the twelve is not the way to go." He rolled his eyes while apparently listening to Bob's response. Then it was his turn again. "What would I do if I were you? I'll tell you what. The first thing I would do is start trying to be a lot more like me!"

He hung up the phone and gave it the finger. Looking over my way he muttered, "Good weekend?"

"Yeah, you?"

"Don't ask."

"Why, what happened?"

Devine snarled. "The bitch got caught DUI."

I knew he was talking about Mrs. Devine, though I wasn't about to appear so quick on the uptake. Bitch or no bitch, she was still my boss's wife. I gave him an "I'm not exactly sure who you're talking about" look.

"Nice try, Philip," was his response. Nobody could see through bullshit better than Devine.

"Had she actually been drinking?" I asked.

"Shit, yeah! Broad daylight too. She was at some champagne brunch for the wives at the club, a little too much champagne. On the way home she dialed direct into a telephone pole."

"Is she okay?"

"She's fine," he said. "Though the same can't be said for the car."

"Totaled?"

"Practically." Devine began to shuffle some papers on his desk. It was his way of getting down to business. "So guess what you get to do?"

And to think I thought we'd simply been making small talk.

He continued: "You get to represent her."

"I do?"

One of his thick eyebrows went up. "Why, you don't want to?"

"No, I do. It's just that I thought—"

"You thought that I would do the honors."

"Yeah."

"Philip, I've represented cousins, uncles, a brother-in-law, you name it. Every fucking twig on the family tree. There's one exception, though. I'll never represent someone that I'm sleeping with . . . wife or otherwise. Do you know why? Because it would jeopardize my objectivity. You follow?"

I followed.

Devine leaned in. "You're not banging my wife, by any chance, are you?"

I loved this guy. "Ah, no, I don't think so."

"Good. That means you'll be able to keep your objectivity. The only thing I'll ask is that you make it, and I stress, as quick and painless for her as possible. Any questions?"

I folded my legs. (It had become my way of getting down to business, though I wasn't sure anyone had noticed yet.) "Just a few," I said, knowing full well that Devine hated questions.

I asked, "Did she call you from the station?"

"Right in the middle of the Yankees game."

"So what happened?"

"I made sure she declined the Breathalyzer in favor

of a blood test," he explained. "The more time for the alcohol to metabolize the better."

I nodded. "That must have made the cops happy."

"Tickled," he said with a short laugh. "Nothing like having to waste two hours at a hospital, not that the extra time ended up helping. She still came in at point one six."

"What about the heel-to-toe?" I asked.

"Said she thought she was pretty wobbly."

"Was she wearing heels, maybe?"

"Good question; find out," he said.

"I don't suppose you want her coming by the office?" I asked.

"No. I'll set up a lunch for the two of you, and she can fill you in."

"You don't want to be there?"

"Do you think I should be?" he asked slowly. A trap if I ever did see one.

"I'd prefer you not be. I wanted to make sure that's okay with you."

"It's fine," he assured me.

"Off on a tangent here, you don't have any interest in going after the country club, do you?"

Devine smiled. Nothing made him happier than a lawyer looking into every angle. "Nah, the club is the one place left where a pariah is appreciated for who he is. I don't want to lose that. Besides, they're indemnified up the wazoo."

Donna buzzed in to tell him he had a call. Someone from the district attorney's office.

"I've got to take this," he said. "Would later this week be good for the two of you to have lunch?"

"Sure," I told him.

"Great. I'll let you know for certain." Devine reached for the phone, and I turned to leave. "Oh, and Philip?"

"Yeah?"

"Not a word about this to anybody."

"About what?"

SIX

Dwight was in rare form.

"So I'm screwing this girl the other night," he began, "and we're going at it like porn stars." He paused and took a quick drag off his cigarette. "So I decide to turn her over and do her from behind, right, when all of a sudden she says to me, Don't you think that's a little presumptuous of you? And I say, Don't you think that *presumptuous* is kind of a big word for a five-year-old?!"

We all laughed. There was a fine line between sick and funny and Dwight Jarvis had pitched his tent there a long time ago. We had met through Connor (who knew him as an undergrad at Michigan), and he was the perfect example of one of those friends you'd never have if not for another friend. By day he was an investment banker, by night an aspiring alcoholic.

Welcome to guys' night out. Mind you, we'd never use such an overwrought cliché to describe our evening, but when you got right down to it, it was just us guys, it was definitely night, and we were out. Out of our minds, to be exact. Due in no small part to the plethora of cocktails we'd had to kick things off at the Monkey Bar. In addition to Dwight, Connor, and me, the group included Menzi.

Joseph Paul Menzi was his full name, though as was often the case with Italians, everyone called him by his last name only. He was tall, around six-four, with jet black hair that recently had begun to recede. Ten years and twenty fewer pounds ago he had been the starting tight end for the Dartmouth football team. (We're talking huge hands; I once saw him palm a watermelon outside a Korean deli.) Menzi was the youngest of nine children and by far the richest. He reveled in it. Despite numerous explanations, however, his parents still had no idea what someone in arbitrage really did. Come to think of it, neither did I.

So there we were, riding high atop the food chain. Four guys with far too much disposable income and far too much expendable energy for having worked all day. Oh, to be young, handsome, and wealthy in the city that never sleeps.

After a few more rounds, Dwight slammed back the last of his bourbon, barely finding the table again with his empty glass. "Who's hungry?" he demanded.

A fast cab ride later, he was leading us all into the Gotham Bar and Grill, making a beeline for the maître d'—a tall, thin man with indented cheeks undoubtedly caused by years of sucking up to celebrity types.

"Franklin, party of four, please," Dwight announced.

The maître d' glanced up and quickly performed a once-over on us. There are something like fifty-six different muscles in the human face, and not one of them on this guy's flinched. Looking down again, he extended his index finger and began scrolling down the reservation book. "Franklin, Franklin . . ." he mumbled as the finger slid all the way to the end of the page without stopping. Mildly pleased, he informed us that he didn't seem to see that name anywhere.

"Sure you do," said Dwight. "It's right here." With that, Dwight took his right hand out of his pocket and placed it on the reservation book. When he removed it, Ben Franklin's face on a hundred-dollar bill was staring up at the maître d'. The effect was nearly instantaneous.

"Oh, yes," said our new best friend, his hand promptly removing the evidence. "I believe we can accommodate you." He motioned to a D-cup in a size-two dress. "Gentlemen, if you would follow Rebecca, she'll show you right to your table."

Hell, we would've followed Rebecca off a cliff if that's where she'd led us. When we got to the table—a corner one, no less—she extended her arm like one of those prize girls on *The Price Is Right*. As we all sat down, Dwight couldn't resist being a dick.

"You wouldn't happen to be on the menu tonight, would you, darling?" he asked.

"Fuck off," she wavered.

And that was that.

We ordered every appetizer on the menu and an '88 Mouton Rothschild at $600 a bottle. Then we unwittingly began to play Top That, a kind of revolving game in which one of us initially regales the others with a story of sexual conquest or testosterone-laden athletic achievement only to have everyone else try to top it. In other words, I'll take heavily embellished bullshit for a thousand, Alex.

After eating and listening to Dwight's tale of the two nympho nurses and the turkey baster last summer on Nantucket, I'd had enough.

"I've got to make a call," I said, getting up.

The pay phone was downstairs by the rest rooms. Guys' night out was one of the few times I could call Jessica at home without having to worry about Connor picking up. I began searching for a quarter in my pocket.

"Your friend is an asshole," said a voice.

I turned around to see Rebecca sneaking a cigarette off in the corner.

"Excuse me?" I said.

The girl who'd seated us walked over and folded her arms across her chest. "Do you hang around with him by choice, or are you required to as part of some cruel punishment?" she asked.

"Who, Dwight?" I said. "Aw, he's not so bad once you get to know him."

"Like that'll ever happen."

Good one. I smiled and Rebecca extended her hand.

"Rebecca," she said.

"Philip," I replied, grasping her hand with a slight squeeze. She had curly, long black hair, a dark complexion, deep-set eyes. At least a catalog model if not the occasional runway. We stood there for a moment saying nothing. I couldn't tell if she had simply been making polite conversation or was now waiting for me to ask her when she got off work. Turned out to be a moot point. She spotted my wedding band.

"How long have you been married?" she asked.

"About two years."

"Two years, huh?" Her mouth broke into a grin. "Do you love her?"

Interesting question.

"As a matter of fact, I do," I lied.

"Good."

She tossed her cigarette and walked away, but not before one of her breasts brushed against my shoulder. The girl really knew how to make an exit.

I regrouped and plunked a quarter into the pay phone.

"Hello?"

"Hi, it's me," I said into the phone.

Jessica's voice came back, "I hate it when you do that."

"Do what?" I said.

"Say, *It's me,* as if there's only one it's me in my life."

She was right. "Sorry."

"This is so weird, you calling me when the two of you are out together. I don't know if I like it."

"I suppose it is a little unfair of me," I admitted.

"Try a lot," she corrected me. "So are you boys all behaving?"

"For the most part," I said.

"Is Dwight smashed yet?"

"You have to ask?"

"I hate him when he drinks."

"That would mean you hate him period."

"Can't you guys do one of those intervention-type things with him?"

"We're hardly the models of sobriety," I reminded her.

And so it went for a couple more minutes. Meaningless chitchat that gave us an excuse to hear each other's voice.

"So what are you doing?" I asked.

"Trying to figure out how my life got this way," replied Jessica.

"Sorry I asked."

"Am I going to see you tomorrow?"

"I suppose that could be arranged," I said.

"Gee, don't do me any favors, stud."

I laughed. "I'll call you in the morning."

"Okay."

When I got back upstairs to the table, Connor was sitting there by himself.

"How's she doing?" he asked as I sat down.

I panicked for a second. "What?"

"Tracy," he answered. "I assumed that's who you were calling."

"Oh. She's fine." *Phew.* "So where are the guys?"

"Smoking cigars at the bar."

"You didn't want to join them?"

"Not really," said Connor. "Besides, I didn't want you to think we bolted on you."

"Thanks."

The place was still buzzing, and we both took a moment to soak up that unique spectacle afforded us by the patrons of a top-ten Zagat's restaurant. Beyond all the chemical-peeled skin, personal-trainer bodies, and salon-colored hair, here was the true battlefield of fashion. I had even coined a phrase for it: *waging wardrobe.* A little roving eye reconnaissance made it clear that on that night, despite some regiments of Hugo Boss and DKNY, the Prada and Armanian armies seemed to have the place pretty much surrounded. In my gray Brooks Brothers pinstripe, I kind of felt like Switzerland.

Eventually, I spotted a large table by the opposite wall. It had to be somebody's birthday. As I tried to figure out who in the group that somebody was, it occurred to me that there were probably two types of people in this world: those who hate having "Happy Birthday" sung to them in a restaurant and those who make the same claim only to secretly enjoy it. I determined that I fell into the former category and my wife, Tracy, definitely fell into the latter.

It was right about then that I started to sense that Connor's waiting for me at the table was about more than being polite. A few moments later he confirmed my suspicions.

Said Connor, "Jessica's been acting weird lately."

"Weird? How so?"

He drew a deep breath. In the time I'd known him he'd never been what you'd call forthcoming with his feelings. This was obviously very difficult for him.

"Things are different between us," he explained. "She's different. I don't know; it's like there's this distance. Even when we're having sex, her mind seems to be somewhere else."

"Maybe it's her job," I offered up. "You always tell me how intense she is about it. Or maybe there's something with her mother or brother, something that she hasn't burdened you with."

"No, it's not anything like that," he said.

"How do you know?"

"I just know."

I watched as a waiter brought a piece of cake with a candle in it to the large table across the way. I knew it was the bald guy.

"I think Jessica's having an affair, Philip."

I turned back to find Connor's eyes waiting for me. "You think *what*?"

"I think she's having an affair," he said.

"You're serious?"

He had never looked more serious in his life. The fact that he simply stared at me without saying a word in response was the biggest, fattest, most affirmative yes there was. He was dead serious. This was going to be tricky.

"Connor, how long have you and Jessica been married?" I asked.

"Ten months."

"That settles it right there. She can't be having an affair," I said with a reassuring smile.

"Why's that?" he asked.

"The gift rule, that's why. A couple can't start cheating on each other until everyone's had that first year to get them a wedding gift. Letitia Baldridge—you can look it up."

Connor didn't see the humor.

"You know, it could be Eric Johnson," he said, nodding as if he had put it all together. "We were at a party a couple of months back, and Jessica and he were talking to each other for a really long time. I swear to god, if it's him, I'll kill him. I'll get a gun and shoot the motherfucker right in the balls!"

"Jesus Christ, Connor, calm down," I said. "I don't

think you've got anything to worry about with Eric Johnson."

"Why not?" he asked.

"Trust me."

"I'm not in the trusting mood, in case you haven't noticed. Why couldn't it be him?"

"Because he's a Rice-A-Roni, that's why," I said.

"A what?"

"A Rice-A-Roni," I repeated. "You know, the San Francisco treat."

It took him a second.

"Eric Johnson is gay?!" he nearly shouted.

"Yeah, he made a pass at me last fall."

"Get the fuck out."

"Okay, maybe not, but Tracy did tell me that a friend of hers from school who knows him saw him at the Vault doing it with another guy."

"*Doing it* doing it?"

"I don't have the video, if that's what you're working toward."

Connor slouched in his chair. "Wow. Who would've thunk?" he said.

"Freud, apparently. Eric's the quintessential mama's boy, after all."

"Okay, so it's not Eric Johnson. It could be anybody."

"Or it could be nobody," I reminded him.

Connor had a "go ahead, keep trying to convince me" look to him. I went ahead.

"Connor, I don't want to play the lawyer on you, but everything you've told me here is pretty circumstantial. It's all stuff that you're perceiving. Now, you come home one night and she's humping the mailman, then we'll talk. Until then, even if she is being a little distant like you say she is, I really don't think it's anything to worry about. My bet is that it will pass. Hell, a little while after I got married to Tracy she was doing the same thing. It was like buyer's remorse or something. I'm telling you, a new marriage must be like a new house. It needs time to settle."

I looked at Connor. He seemed to be mulling it over.

"But what if she is having an affair?" he asked.

"What if, what if?!" I said, throwing up my arms. "What if Jack Kennedy had been riding in a hardtop and Teddy had the convertible, huh? *What if then?* My point is you can speculate all you want about what if, but the only thing that really matters is what is."

"What is what?" came Menzi's voice over my shoulder. He and Dwight had returned from the bar.

"What is the chance that you two single boys hook up tonight," said Connor, covering for us in surprisingly seamless fashion.

"Funny you should mention that," shot back Dwight. "It so happens that Menzi and I have made the acquaintance of two extremely lovely young Indian girls at the bar."

"Gandhi or gambling?" I asked.

"I wish they had casino blood," said Dwight. "Then we could marry rich and relax, kind of like someone we know?"

"Now who could that be?" said Menzi, scratching his head and getting into the act.

I feigned being hit and shuddered, "Ooh, that hurts."

"So you boys might get lucky after all, huh?" said Connor.

"It's in the Hefty," Dwight boasted. "And since you guys appear to be laying down the challenge, Menzi and I won't feel so bad about dropping you old married farts now like bad habits."

"Dead weight at age thirty-one," I sighed, shaking my head. "What went wrong, Connor?"

"What's that you say?" he replied in an old man's accent. He hit his ear. "Damn hearing aid!"

The waiter came and put the bill on our table. I picked it up and threw it in the air to Dwight, who instinctively caught it.

"Thanks, man," I said, getting up and falling in line right behind Connor, who was briskly making for the exit.

"Not funny!" I heard Dwight's voice tail off from behind us. I winked at the maître d', blew a kiss to Rebecca, and jumped into the cab outside that Connor had immediately hailed. All without ever breaking stride.

"Two stops," I said to the back of a turban. "The first is Nineteenth Street, between Fifth and Sixth. And the second . . ."

"Eighty-first, between Columbus and Amsterdam," Connor said, taking his cue.

The turban nodded and the cab sped off.

"One of these days I suppose we're going to have to pick up the tab," said Connor. I looked at him and shook my head. "Yeah, you're right," he followed up with quickly. "Screw 'em."

The two of us laughed, and it seemed to me that Connor had perhaps emerged from our conversation in a better place than where he had started. The big question was, would it last?

When I got home Tracy was fast asleep. I went into the bathroom, closed the door behind me, and jerked off to the mental image of a threesome involving Jessica, me, and a certain restaurant hostess.

And that was that.

SEVEN

Sometime during my teens, the exact year escapes me, I created in my mind a sliding scale of what I called—for lack of originality—Risk Factors. The scale numbered from one to ten. For instance, something like . . . oh, I don't know, crossing the Sahara on foot, was a Risk Factor 10. Shoplifting the Talking Heads' latest album, meanwhile, was a Risk Factor 1. Both were dangerous, of course, just not to the same degree. Ever since then, I'd used this scale as a quick and orderly way to assess all the risks that came along in my life. From there I could better determine which ones were truly worth taking.

After the night out with the guys I woke up the following morning with two headaches. One was alcohol induced, the other Connor induced. My affair with Jessica had suddenly jumped from a Risk Factor 5 to a Risk Factor 6. (By way of comparison, the prospect of having to defend my boss's wife on a DUI charge was a Risk Factor 4, tops.) Mind you, the affair was still a very manageable endeavor. What the previous night had done, however, was remind me that the whole thing was not entirely in my control. That's what worried me a bit. Clearly Jessica was not holding up her end of the bargain.

———————

So how does a guy who's only been married a year and a girl who still has her tan from a Caribbean honeymoon end up having sex together? It's about time I answered that.

Jessica and Connor were what we called CMFs. That stands for City-Made Friends. When Tracy and I first got married and settled into our loft in Chelsea, Tracy decided that it would be fun if we were to make friends with another couple that lived in Manhattan. The catch was that it couldn't be anyone we were introduced to, rather, we had to initiate the friendship ourselves. That, according to Tracy, was the "fun" part.

As well, it couldn't simply be the first couple we met. It had to be the right couple. Tracy insisted that we each first make a list of the three qualities that we wanted most in our new friends in order of preference. We'd then compare our lists and settle on one master list. I resisted the whole idea on the grounds that it was silly. Tracy told me to lighten up. The next thing I knew, the two of us were sitting across from each other at Capsouto Frères in TriBeCa, making out our lists between appetizer and entrée. There was no peeking allowed.

When we both had finished, Tracy wanted me to read my list first. I declined, reminding her that the plaintiff always went before the defendant. After a disapproving look and her announcement, "Here are the three qualities I desire most in our new friends," she read me the following:

1. Fun
2. Attractive
3. Without children

It was my turn. I cleared my throat and read:

1. Intelligent
2. Never done time
3. Don't call each other "sweetie"

After considerable debate, none of which is particularly relevant in hindsight, our master list ended up having one quality from each of our lists. It read as follows:

1. Attractive
2. Intelligent

The fact that there was now very little difference between our master list and the master race was not lost on me. Nonetheless, it represented a concession on both of our parts, the very definition of a marriage.

Then began the auditions. (Would you expect anything less?) Turned out, finding an attractive *and* intelligent couple living in Manhattan was not as easy as one might think. It took some doing, or more accurately, some dinners, as that was our litmus test. While Tracy and I scouted jointly, it was Tracy on her own who got results. After she would make the acquaintance of what always was the female half of a potential couple, she would arrange a dinner. That's when we could sit both halves of the couple down together and decide if they were friends material or not.

Sometimes you knew it wasn't to be even before you cracked the menu. Take this one husband-and-wife team from the Upper East Side, for instance. He was an actuary; she researched obituaries for the *New York Times*. I kid you not. Dudley and Martha Erdman, a.k.a. the human Sominex.

Then there was the close call of Alex and Cindy. Tracy had met Cindy after some Sunday-night lecture at the 92nd Street Y. Cindy seemed intelligent and while perhaps not a knockout according to Tracy, she had a lot of "attractive features." That same evening, the two of them shared a cab home together with Tracy dropping Cindy off at Sixty-ninth and Third. Before getting out they agreed to a dinner at Cafe Loup that Friday evening.

Walking into the restaurant, I begged Tracy to let me tell them that we were swingers so we could watch their reaction. If they were our kind of people, I pointed out, they'd appreciate the humor. Suffice to say, Tracy gave me her disapproving look again. Three bottles of wine later, though, I couldn't resist. It was perfect. After a scary pause, Alex and Cindy burst out laughing. Voilà! City-Made Friends. Check, please.

Not so fast. While we were splitting the bill, Tracy realized that Alex and Cindy had our phone number, but we didn't have theirs. So Cindy wrote it down on the back of a Banana Republic receipt and slid it across the table. It sat there like a grenade.

"Seven one eight? Isn't that, like, one of the boroughs?" Tracy asked, looking at the area code.

"Yeah, we live in Brooklyn," said Cindy, obviously not thinking twice about it.

Tracy: "But didn't I drop you off at . . .?"

Cindy: "Oh, that was my sister's place. We were staying there a few nights while she and her husband were on vacation."

To Tracy's credit, she didn't let her disappointment show at the table. In fact, as we got into the cab after saying good-night to our potential new friends, she'd been so polite, so enthusiastic, that I was fairly convinced that Tracy had already decided to overlook our self-imposed "must live in Manhattan" rule. Silly me.

"No dice," she said, staring blankly ahead through the cab's Plexiglas divider as we took off.

We both knew she was being unreasonable, an outright snob, to be more precise. We both knew I had every right to lay into her like nobody's business. And we both knew that when all was said and done, we'd still never see Alex and Cindy of Brooklyn ever again.

The CMF search lost some of its urgency for a while after that. Then about a month later, Tracy came home after work one day with the news that we had plans that Saturday night. As an occasional freelance graphic artist (and by occasional, I mean with the frequency, let's say, of rotating your tires), Tracy had landed a gig at *Glamour* magazine helping to revamp its layout. She explained that during an office party to celebrate some associate editor's birthday, she had met a very nice girl by the name of Jessica Levine. Jessica sold ad space for the magazine and was engaged to a software programmer.

"I really think these could be the ones," Tracy said to me while pouring a glass of wine. "It just seems right."

Saturday night, table for four, Zarela.

What I liked most about Connor Thompson upon first meeting him was his overall reluctance to the whole dinner. His general expression seemed to scream, *Who the hell are these two strangers I'm eating with? Furthermore, how well do I know my fiancée that she would arrange such a thing?* No doubt my sentiments exactly, had I been in his position.

Jessica, on the other hand, had good reason for being there. She told us that she was agreeable to the dinner because the whole "my friends/your friends" situation that every couple must cope with had really started to get on her nerves. Thus, the opportunity to make some "our friends," as she put it, was too good to pass up. Made sense to me.

Intelligent?

We didn't exactly exchange IQs, but Connor and Jessica both seemed to be pretty much on the ball, and if pressed, I'm sure could've each offered up a compelling literary quote or unique assessment of the military-industrial complex.

Attractive?

Connor was a decent-looking guy, albeit a little weak in the chin. Wavy black hair, a tad under six feet. Most notably, he had these ellipse-shaped eyes that at first glance made you think there was some Asian blood in him. (There wasn't.) He spoke in measured sentences and were it not for an easy laugh, could possibly have been perceived as being a little stiff.

As for Jessica, I refer you to my aforementioned Polaroid snapshot observation. Brunette, brown eyes, and from what I could tell at the time (and later confirm firsthand), a good figure. To be sure, I didn't look at her and immediately forget Tracy's name. Jessica simply wasn't like that. What she was, however, was perfectly nice, perfectly friendly, and as far as I could tell, perfectly engaged.

After about three margaritas at Zarela you're essentially feeling no pain. That's probably why the place continues to get such rave reviews year after year. Either no one can remember if they liked the food the following morning, or they were too numb at the time to actually taste it. As we all sat there licking the salt off the rims of our glasses and getting to know each other, it was clear that this wouldn't be the last dinner we'd have together, a notion that gained considerable momentum when early on Tracy said, "Before I forget, give me your telephone number so we have it." We saw that magical 212 area code Jessica wrote out on a cocktail napkin and knew it was all meant to be. Finally, at long last, City-Made Friends.

We skip ahead. While the four of us attended parties, saw exhibits, and did all the other NYC *de rigueur* in the months that followed, it was the dinners that became the staple of our friendship. They were always on the weekend, never at the same restaurant. If it was a Friday, we generally called it a night after the meal, citing fatigue from the work week. If it was a Saturday, however, the meal was merely a precursor to what would usually be a night of club hopping. For in addition to a taste for expensive shoes and bad teenage-angst television shows, another thing that Tracy and Jessica had in common was a love of dancing.

Which leads us to that fateful Saturday night.

Connor and Jessica had just returned from their honeymoon the previous weekend. After we looked at their pictures from St. Bart's over dinner at Gascogne, the girls decided that they wanted to go dancing at Vinyl. A downtown cab ride later, Connor and I were doing the white man's overbite with our wives, trying in vain to keep the beat.

Roughly around 2 A.M., Connor had had enough. Insisting that everyone else stay and have a good time, he shouted above the music that he was exhausted and was heading home. A quick glance told me that he wanted me to stay and chaperone the girls. I nodded and mouthed, "You owe me." He smiled and turned to give Jessica a kiss. Then he left.

From the bar I kept an eye on Tracy and Jessica as they did their best impression of the Solid Gold Dancers. Actually, they were both quite good. Hips gyrating, arms moving this way and that. To every single guy in the place, I'm sure they ranked extremely high as worthy one-night standers. That or a couple of very hot lipstick lesbians (even more of a turn-on, I suppose). Tracy had on a short skirt and one of those satin button-down tops. Jessica, an equally short skirt with an open white shirt under which she wore a skin-tight leotard kind of thing.

The two of them continued to dance with each other into the night. In between songs, excuse me, "extended dance remixes," they would come over and devour a round of drinks. By 3 A.M. they were loaded.

Getting two intoxicated women to leave a nightclub

when they didn't want to leave a nightclub was no picnic. Still, I persevered and ultimately prevailed, literally grabbing each one by the arm and leading them out to the sidewalk. We piled into a waiting cab.

"Uptown," I said to the driver, telling him our two stops.

"Wait, you can't let Jessica go home by herself," Tracy said with a slight burp. Drunk as she may have been, she still had her bearings. With the two of us living in Chelsea and Jessica on the Upper West Side, we'd be getting out of the cab first.

"Don't be silly," said Jessica.

Yeah, don't be silly, I was thinking, knowing exactly what Tracy had in mind.

"No, you don't be silly," Tracy countered. "Philip will stay with you to make sure you get home safe."

"I'll be fine, really," Jessica pleaded.

"Of course you will, because Philip will be with you to make sure," Tracy said, having what turned out to be the last word on the subject.

The cab pulled up in front of our building, and Tracy got out. She hugged Jessica good-bye and said, "Thanks, honey" to me.

"Eighty-first, between Columbus and Amsterdam," I reminded the driver. He sped off.

Manhattan was a strange enough sight during normal waking hours. After hours, it was a whole different animal. Stay out late enough and you were sure to see something to startle even the most jaded eye. That night it was the old man in the hospital gown.

On the sidewalk, out my side of the cab, was this grandfather type walking in nothing but a hospital gown.

What made it truly unique was that he had one of those admitting bracelets around his wrist. As he walked, he would occasionally look over his shoulder.

"Hey, Jessica, check this out," I said, motioning outside my window.

"Huh?"

"This guy, you've got to see this guy."

Jessica blinked a couple of times and leaned over to my side. The old guy walked past the cab while again looking over his shoulder.

"Holy shit, you can see his ass!" she said, giggling.

I looked again and sure enough, the old guy was shooting the moon. We both laughed. Jessica made a piglike snort and we both laughed some more. I caught the eye of our driver looking at us in his rearview mirror. In that instant I wondered what it must be like to make a living one-fifth of a mile at a time.

It was silent for the next couple of blocks. We stopped at a red light.

"Do you want to kiss me?" Jessica whispered.

I turned to her. "What?"

"Do you want to kiss me?" she whispered, only slower.

Honestly, I was floored. Sure, all guys determine whether or not they would sleep with a woman within the first fifteen seconds of meeting her, and sure, Jessica—even as an undeveloped Polaroid—had easily been a yes. Still, a lot of time had passed since those first fifteen seconds, and I hadn't thought about it again. Until that moment.

I began to stammer, "I, ah . . ."

"Because I want to kiss you," she said. Then she did.

She slid across the seat and began kissing me, pressing her body up against mine. I'm sure if I had told her to stop she would have. I didn't, though. I didn't want her to. Instead, as the good Reverend Jesse Jackson might have put it, I reciprocated, it escalated, and before you knew it, we fornicated. Not in the cab, however. No, our driver only got to steal glances at some heavy foreplay before dropping us off at the corner of Eighty-first and Columbus. The fare was thirteen dollars. I gave him a twenty and told him to keep the change. I winked at him. We both knew it was he who should've been tipping me.

Jessica and I started to walk toward her and Connor's apartment without saying a word. After we passed a couple of brownstones she grabbed my hand and led me down underneath a set of steps. *That's* where we fornicated. I lifted up her skirt and pulled down her underwear, letting it drop to the ground from around her knees. (I absolutely love that little two-step thing women do when stepping out of their panties.) Meanwhile, Jessica undid my pants and pulled down my boxers. Then the only words were spoken.

"Are you sure you want to do this?" I said to her.

She reached down and put me inside of her. I took that to mean *yes*.

So how does a guy who's only been married a year and a girl who still has her tan from a Caribbean honeymoon end up having sex together? That's how.

When we finished, Jessica finally spoke. "We'll have to do that again," she said.

While pulling up my pants, I looked at my watch. I should've been back home by that point. We quickly kissed and I ran to hail a cab. In all the haste, we were able to avoid any postinfidelity awkwardness. Though I'm not sure there really would've been any. Alcohol or not, the prospect of regret somehow seemed very remote.

In the cab back downtown, the one thing I head-gamed myself about was Jessica's sexual history. I remembered Connor once telling me that she hadn't had too many boyfriends before the two of them met. Given what had just transpired, though, that gave me little solace. Memo to self: get tested in a couple of months. Yeah, leave it to AIDS to make the notion of an unwanted pregnancy seem almost trivial. While I assumed she was, I never asked Jessica if she was on the pill. But hey, what's an abortion when compared to one's own funeral? As I leaned my head back in the cab, far enough that I could look straight up through the rear window at the night's stars, I thought to myself what an incredibly self-centered, every-man-for-himself world it was. And without a doubt, exhibit A was me.

With any luck, Tracy would've been asleep when I returned to our loft. Instead, she was up reading in bed.

"What took you so long?" she said, her eyes remaining on her book. She no longer seemed the least bit drunk.

"What a space, she couldn't find her keys," I said. It would've been a little tough to claim traffic at 4 A.M. The keys seemed very viable. Assuming they wouldn't be enough, though, I was prepared. "And I picked up the *Times* by their place," I added. Indeed I had picked up the paper, only it was after thinking for thirty blocks about how to handle Tracy should I have to. I told the cab driver to pull over at a newsstand on Forty-sixth

Street. "I got talking to the guy in the store; he was from Yemen. I asked him if he thought it would be a good place for us to vacation and he laughed like it was the funniest damn thing."

"He probably thought you were a weirdo," Tracy said, finally looking at me. For sure she thought I was a weirdo, which was fine by me. She could think anything she wanted to, so long as she didn't think I had just been fucking her friend Jessica.

I undressed, did a little postsex wash-down in the bathroom, and crawled into bed. "You don't think there's a Four Seasons in Yemen, do you?" I asked.

"I doubt it," Tracy said. She closed her book and turned off the light.

I walked up to the counter at the hotel. A familiar face was there waiting.

"Hi, Raymond," I said.

"Hey, Mr. Randall, real nice to see you again."

"You as well. It's been a while."

"Yeah, I know. I was taking some time off."

The way he said it, it didn't sound like a vacation.

"Everything all right?" I asked him.

Raymond scratched his ear, the one without the diamond stud. You could tell he was deciding whether or not to get into it. "It's my mother," he offered. "I was back home to see her. She's been kind of ill."

"I'm sorry to hear that," I told him, and I was. "Is she going to be okay, if you don't mind me asking?"

"Don't know yet. She found out she's got cancer of the stomach. Never even knew you could get it there.

She says it's the devil's doing, that he sees her as too much of a threat to him up here on earth. Pretty religious, she is."

"Well, if she's smart enough to know it's him, I would imagine the devil doesn't stand much of a chance."

Raymond laughed and told me he hoped that I was right. The entire time we were talking he was checking me in, his long fingers popping away at the keyboard of his computer. *Of course* I was there for a room. Raymond knew there was no need to ask.

I waited until after Jessica and I had sex that afternoon to tell her about my conversation with Connor the previous night. I knew that if I'd mentioned it to her before, there wouldn't have been any sex. For me, there was no such thing as thinking with the wrong head.

Jessica got out of bed and went to the window. She pulled back the curtains and stood there naked. In the sunlight that spilled in, she became a silhouette. A worried one at that.

"So he's onto us," she said.

"Correction. He's onto you."

"What's that supposed to mean?"

"It means you're obviously acting different around him and it's making him suspicious."

"I'm not, though," she said.

"You may think you're not, but you've obviously got a tell."

"A what?"

"A tell. It's a poker term. It means you do something that you're unaware of that gives away your hand."

She didn't quite follow. "What in the hell are you talking about?!" she snapped.

"Never mind," I said. "Listen, Connor was saying that when you're having sex it's like you're not there."

"So?"

"So, what I'm saying is, you have to get your head back into the sex, or at least make it seem that way."

"I don't believe this; you're telling me that I have to have better sex with my husband?"

I shrugged. "Fake the orgasms if you have to."

She put her hand on her hip. "What do you think I've been doing?"

I stopped and looked at her for a second. She instantly knew what I was thinking.

Said Jessica, "Oh, yeah, right, like I really wanted to take on a second acting job."

My ego back in check, I pressed on. "I know this all sounds weird and I know it can't be easy for you. The good news is, I went a long way in calming Connor down last night. I don't think it's going to remain a problem, I really don't."

My jury of one looked at me. She appeared to have come around to my point of view.

Then came, "Maybe we should just cool it for a while."

The way she threw it out there like it had been a bottled-up thought, it was obvious that she was barely paying attention to me. It pissed me off.

"Maybe," I responded. "In the meantime, now that every pervert with a telescope has gotten a good look at you, do you think you could close the curtains?"

Now we were both pissed off.

"Doesn't this *ever* bother you?" asked Jessica, raising her voice.

"What?"

"This! Us! What we're doing here. Doesn't it ever bother you?"

"I take it I should say yes. Is that what you want?"

A snicker. "What I want, or at least what I was hoping, was that for once you would express some guilt about what we've been doing. Maybe, dare I say, a little remorse."

"That would prove what?" I asked.

"For starters, that you're human," she said.

My turn to snicker. "You're making it sound like you're being made to do something against your will."

"Spare me the two-to-tango bit," she said.

"You might also want to keep in mind that it wasn't me who led us down beneath that brownstone the first time," I said.

"Oh, I see, so you're the innocent victim?"

"I didn't say that."

"You didn't have to. I guess my powers of seduction were too much for you to resist that night, huh? You poor thing." She was starting to lose it. "Don't you see, what I'm trying to tell you is that the only thing that bothers me more than my conscience is the fact that you don't seem to mind at all. Actually, it does more than bother me . . . it scares me."

I was shaking my head. "Grant me one assumption," I said. "That my not telling you about any guilt-ridden moments doesn't mean that they haven't existed for me. Yes, I'm human. Yes, I've had my doubts about this whole thing. Not to turn the tables, but you haven't exactly been forthcoming yourself. Maybe it was a game of chicken. Part of the reason I never said anything is because you didn't."

"If it's getting to the both of us, though, why do we keep doing it?"

"Force of habit?" I joked. I should've known better.

"See, that's what I'm talking about. It's like you're too fucking blind or arrogant to figure it out! This isn't make-believe, Philip, this is real, with real consequences. And you? You act like you're merely along for the goddamn ride!"

"Oh, Jesus, Jessica, give me a break."

"You want a break? I'll give you a break," she said.

Jessica immediately began to put her clothes back on. She said nothing more. I sat there in the bed and watched her. When she had angrily fastened the last button on her blouse, she picked up her purse and marched out of the room.

"Fuck you too!" I yelled as the door slammed behind her.

EIGHT

Lunch with another woman for a change.

Sally Devine strolled into Hatsuhana that Thursday at one-fifteen, as expected. The reservation was actually for one o'clock, but Jack had tipped me off that she'd never been less than fifteen minutes late for anything in her life. Consequently, I'd been waiting at our table for nò more than a few minutes myself when she arrived.

We'd met once before, at an office Christmas party that she and Jack had hosted at the apartment they kept in the city, though I wasn't sure if she'd remember me. The most I'd said to her that evening was "You have a lovely place here." Had the line to suck up to her as the boss's wife not been so long, I'm sure I could have made a greater impression.

Now here she was standing before me. "You must be Philip," she said, shuffling her Chanel bag from under her right arm to her left. A heavily bejeweled right hand was promptly extended to me.

"And you must be Mrs. Devine," I replied, getting up and shaking her hand.

"Please, call me Sally."

"Sally it is."

The short and stocky proprietor type who'd shown her to our table pulled her chair back for her. At first glance he kind of looked like a Japanese Buddy Hackett.

"A-ri-ga-to," she said to him as if repeating back to a Berlitz tape.

He nodded appreciatively and rested two menus on the corner of our table. With a slight bow, he turned and walked away.

Sally, once settled in, leaned over to me as if she had a secret. In a hushed tone she said, "Let me say right off the bat that I wish our meeting for lunch was under better circumstances."

I agreed, although it quickly occurred to me that had the circumstances truly been better we'd probably never have been meeting in the first place.

While Sally craned her neck this way and that to check out the clientele at the neighboring tables, I regarded her for a moment. At first glance she was a few years past her prime, though for a woman in her late forties she was giving aging a significant run for the money. She had auburn hair down to her shoulders, very alert eyes, and from what I could tell, a shapely figure. A face-lift was a definite possibility, although the only cosmetic surgery that was clearly evident was a nose job. The thing was just too perfect to be God's handiwork.

Her attention returned to our table. "This is my favorite sushi restaurant," she declared. "Did you know it once got a four-star rating from the *New York Times*?"

"I didn't know that," I said.

"I wish I had the chance to get here more often; I spend most of my time these days out in the country, you know."

"I take it you and Jack don't use your apartment here in the city much anymore?"

"Really the only time is when we're going to the theater or have a function to attend," she explained. "Of course, Jack uses it sometimes when he's working late . . . that or when he's screwing one of his girlfriends."

She said it so nonchalantly I almost missed it.

"Excuse me?" I said.

"You heard me," was her reply.

I was saved by a young waitress in a kimono. She asked us if we'd like anything to drink.

"Sake," Sally ordered.

"Vodka tonic," I said, clearing my throat. Two minutes earlier it would have been a club soda. As a rule I never drank during a working lunch. Suddenly the rule didn't seem all that important.

"Well, before we get down to the details of my unfortunate accident last weekend, I'm going to insist that you tell me a little about yourself," said Sally. "After all, I can't imagine anything more ridiculous than being represented by a total stranger. Can you?"

I couldn't, I told her.

The questions came one after the other, though for the most part they remained innocuous. Then, without any hesitation, Sally asked me whether or not I came from money, assuring me in the same breath that she certainly didn't care if my family was dirt poor or filthy rich.

"Do you know why I don't care, Philip?" she said. "Because either way—dirt poor, filthy rich—you're never clean."

She sat back and waited for my response to her clever wordplay.

"I never thought of it that way," I said, feigning enlightenment. From there I had little choice but to go ahead and share with Sally Devine some of the details of my upbringing.

There were no trailer parks in my past, I let her know. Nor for that matter were there any nannies. The Randalls were strictly a middle-class family from the suburbs of Chicago, with my father, Jay Randall, primarily responsible for the strict part. He had worked as an electrical engineer with the same company for most of his life and the need for precision on the job had managed to spill over into his family life. For the most part, however, I respected him. He rode my ass from time to time when I was a kid, but he worked his own ass off not only to put me through four years of college, but prep school as well before that (Dartmouth South: Deerfield).

My mother, Ellen Randall, had been an elementary school teacher in addition to a doting wife, never quite sure what all the fuss was about feminism. She was from Kennebunk, Maine, originally and loved to tell me stories when I was a kid about how my great-grandfather, *god rest his soul*, would swim in the Atlantic every morning at 6 A.M. until well past Thanksgiving. These days she volunteered at the local library. Besides returning books to their shelves, I was pretty sure my mother was the one responsible for telling people to "shhh."

Lastly, I had one sibling, a younger brother named Brad living in Portland, Oregon, who was a painter (canvasses, not houses). Having sold a piece here and there, he didn't quite qualify as a starving artist. Malnourished was more like it.

Throughout it all, Sally hung on my every word. She was either an incredible actress or truly interested in hearing about my family. When she asked me how often I saw them I wanted to lie. I wanted to tell her that we got together every holiday including Flag Day, that we were as close-knit as they come, that Ken Burns was looking into doing a documentary on us entitled *The Model Family*. As far as I was concerned, the fact that we made the Reagans look like the Waltons was none of her business.

In the end, however, I couldn't lie. The way she looked at me I knew she'd be able to tell. I suppose when you're married to a guy with the ultimate bullshit meter, some of it's bound to rub off.

"Let me see your hand," she said, grabbing my arm. Madame Devine began to trace the lines of my palm with her finger. "Do you see these two lines here going across?"

"Yeah."

"Those are your family lines. Do you see how they get wider and wider apart as you move along?" she said.

"I suppose that must mean something."

"Only that it confirms everything you've told me.

You're someone who's dealing with deep feelings of alienation, Philip, am I not right?"

At that moment I pictured Sally Devine learning to read palms at some adult spiritual-awakening class. I pictured the entire group being made up of wives of wealthy men, women who had already done the crystals thing, some having also done a weekend seminar on channeling.

"Am I not right?" Sally repeated.

"I think it's time we discuss your accident," I said.

"I understand," Sally replied, with a knowing pat on my hand.

I reached for my briefcase and retrieved a yellow legal pad and a pen. My sincere hope was that a reincarnated Allen Funt would take this opportunity to come out from around the corner with his trademark *Candid Camera* laugh. No such luck. This was all really happening.

"Let's talk about some of the proceedings we'll have to deal with in the next couple of weeks, starting with court," I said. "First off, you'll be required to go before a judge, who will hear the charge against you. Am I correct in assuming that you've never been arrested for drinking and driving before?"

"Oh, for heaven's sake, no!" she gasped.

"Good. The reason I ask is that your county has recently taken a page from Connecticut and put in place an initiative whereby first-time offenders can request to enter what's called an alcohol education program."

"Is that like AA?"

"No, it's more like Responsible Drinking One-oh-one. I think you meet once a week for like ten weeks or something. Complete the program and after a year, without any further incident, the DUI charge is erased from your record."

"Permanently?"

"Permanently."

Sally smiled. "It's kind of like a get-out-of-jail-free card, huh?"

"Kind of. Though for your offense, jail really isn't a possibility. Unless, that is, you get arrested for DUI again. Then you go to jail, no two ways about it."

Sally's smile disappeared. "So this program you're talking about, is that what you think I should do?"

"Odds are yes, except before we go that route for sure, I want to check out the police report and look at the tape."

"What tape?" she asked.

"Most police stations videotape their processing rooms. It protects them from people who make bogus brutality claims against them. Of course, the door swings both ways. It also could vindicate you. If they stated in the police report that you were stumbling drunk and on the video you come across as stone sober, we'd have a pretty good chance of winning the case, if not getting the whole thing dismissed."

"We're allowed to see that tape?"

"I am; you're not. It's kept at the prosecutor's office."

"What about my license? Jack was telling me that's a whole different ordeal."

"It is," I told her. "It's an entirely separate hearing with the DMV. As I'm sure Jack explained, the reason he wanted you to have the blood test and not the Breathalyzer was so you'd have that much more time to let the alcohol metabolize in your body. Unfortunately, despite the extra time you still came in at point one six."

Sally snickered. "I still don't think it was accurate."

"Could be, except as far as the state is concerned, you were legally intoxicated. That being the case, it's mandatory that your license gets suspended for three months."

"Shit!"

"I know," I said.

"Isn't there anything you can do?" she asked with a face that had surely gotten her out of a speeding ticket or two.

"The only thing I can do is to, once again, look over that police report and see that they followed procedure. If they screwed up in any way, we could try to get off on a technicality. I simply wouldn't bet on it, that's all."

Truth be told, a technicality was exactly what I was betting on. If there was one thing in this world on which a lawyer could rely, it was sloppy police work. Not that I blamed the cops. To learn all their standard operating procedures, all the rules they had to follow, was to realize that these poor guys could barely blow their noses without violating some regulation. Seriously, it was a miracle they could put anyone behind bars.

"Now here's what I'd like to do, if you don't have any objection," I said, removing the cap from my pen. "I want you to take me through the events of that Sunday from beginning to end. There's no detail too small, and to prove it let me apologize up front for all the times that I'm going to interrupt you with nit-picking questions. Remember, I'm the good guy, the one on your side, so it's important you tell me the truth as best as you can remember it."

Sally nodded. She drew a deep breath and started. "Okay, you see, I was at the club—"

"Back up," I immediately interrupted. "What time did you wake up that morning?"

She gave me a quick "how is that relevant?" look. I ignored it.

Sally shrugged. "I suppose it was around nine-thirty."

"Did you eat breakfast?"

"I never eat breakfast."

"Okay, nothing to eat. How about anything to drink?" I asked.

She appeared put off. "Do you mean alcoholic?"

"Not necessarily. You didn't have a coffee or juice or anything?"

"No," she said.

I waited. She knew why.

"No, nothing alcoholic either," she tacked on.

"Okay, so you go to the club for this brunch. What time did you arrive?"

"I don't know exactly."

"What time did it start?"

"Noon, though I wasn't on time."

Shocker.

"I suppose it was maybe around twelve-thirty," she decided.

"Was it a sit-down affair?"

"Eventually, though there was something like a cocktail hour to kick it off."

"Did you have a drink during this time?" I said.

"Yes. One."

"What was it?"

"A kir royale."

"Did you order it or were they being passed around?"

Raised eyebrows. "You're going to tell me that it makes a difference?" she asked incredulously.

Sorry, Sally. You get to read palms, I get to ask any damn question I want. "I apologized up front for the nitpicking, did I not?"

"You did," she sighed, "and the drinks were passed around."

"Now you're sitting down to eat. What did they serve?"

"It was a buffet. I had some poached salmon and a salad."

"To drink?"

"Another kir royale."

"Just one more?"

"Just one more."

All along I was taking notes, with Sally trying her not-too-obvious best to read them. That my handwriting was barely legible straight on let alone upside down must have been incredibly frustrating for her. As it was, the temptation to inscribe, *This woman is a complete wacko!* was all but irresistible.

"Okay, so what time did you leave the club?" I asked.

"The brunch ended officially at three. I left pretty much right after that."

"Did you feel fine to drive?"

"Absolutely."

"Then what happened?" I asked.

"I started to drive home."

"And?"

"And along the way I went to change the radio station. I must have taken my eyes off the road, because when I looked up again I was heading right for a telephone pole. I tried to swerve back, but it was too late."

"How fast do you think you were going?"

"I have no idea," she said.

"Did your air bag deploy?"

"Yes."

"Was the car heavily damaged?"

"Fourteen thousand six hundred and seventy-eight dollars," she said, sounding out every syllable. "The insurance company's appraiser looked at it yesterday."

"There was no other car involved, right?"

"Right."

"How about anyone who saw the accident?" I asked.

"No. But there was this woman who came out of her house afterward, saying she'd heard the crash and all."

"Was she the one who called the police?"

"Yes. She called before she came out."

"Did she wait with you?" I asked.

"Part of the time. She said she had a baby inside that she had to go back and check on."

"Did you say anything to her about having had a couple drinks?"

"Do I look that stupid?"

"You'd be surprised how often innocent people say incriminating things, Sally," I said. It was one of my pat lines for when I had to ask clients sensitive or down-right insulting questions. What I neglected to mention was that guilty people also often say incriminating things. Nonetheless, I think she bought it.

I pressed on. "So the police finally arrive. One car, two cars?"

"One."

"One officer, then?"

"Yes."

"Now this is when the details really matter," I said. "What happened next?"

"The cop gets out of his car, comes over, and asks me if I'm okay. I tell him I am, just a little shaken up."

"Did you use those exact words?"

"I think so."

"Good. What next?"

"He asked me what had happened—no, wait—he asked me for my license and registration, which I got for him. Then he asked me what happened, and I explained about reaching for the radio, you know, losing my bearings and all."

"Do you remember whether or not you actually said *bearings*?"

"I'm not sure exactly," she said. Suddenly she realized how it could've been a poor choice of words. "Oh, that wasn't too bright if I did say that, huh?"

"That depends. When did he ask you if you'd been drinking?"

Her hesitation was answer enough.

"Right after that," she confirmed, followed immediately by "Fuck!" It was loud enough to turn a couple of heads.

"Don't worry about it; it doesn't matter," I said to her. "The policeman asks you if you've been drinking, what was your exact answer?"

"I told him that I'd had one, maybe two drinks tops. After that, he has the nerve to ask me to walk a straight line."

"Tell me, what type of heels did you have on? High . . . medium . . . flats?"

"Medium."

"At least an inch, maybe?"

"Sure."

"You do the walk, how'd it go?"

"A little wobbly, to be honest, I was so nervous at this point."

"I don't blame you," I said. "Did he follow that by asking you to lean your head back and put your finger to your nose?"

"Exactly. I even thought I did that pretty well, but the next thing you know, he's telling me that he's arresting me for suspicion of drunk driving."

"Did he read you your rights?"

"Yes. Then the son of a bitch handcuffed me! Jack told me it was standard procedure, but, I mean, come on, isn't that a little much?"

"Yeah, I always thought that was a little excessive," I said. "Okay, he brings you down to the station. What happened from there?"

"More cops and paperwork, lots of it. Meanwhile, I keep asking to use the phone and they keep telling me, in a minute, in a minute. It was really ticking me off. Finally, I tell them I'm not going to cooperate any further unless I'm given my one phone call. How's that for chutzpah?"

"Not bad. Did it work?"

"You better believe it," she said. "I was on the line to Jack not a minute later. That's when he told me not to take the Breathalyzer, to have them take me for a blood test instead. You should have seen these guys' faces when I told them that. It was like who's ticking who off now? I loved it!"

I smiled. "What hospital did they take you to?"

"Westchester County."

"The emergency room?"

"Yes."

"And Jack met you there?"

"Right. He insisted on having the cops explain anything and everything to him. It was all his way of stalling. Though at that point, I was so tired of the whole thing I just wanted them to take the damn blood so I could go home."

"Speaking of that, who actually drew the blood from you?"

"Well," said Sally, "this one nurse was about to do it when all of a sudden there was this commotion out front. Apparently some kid had fallen out of a tree in his backyard and had just arrived. Head injury, internal bleeding, that's what we overheard them talking about. So we ended up waiting even longer. I asked Jack if maybe he hadn't pushed the kid out of the tree himself on the way over to the hospital to stall some more. I wouldn't put it past him. Anyway, this other nurse, a real old-timer, finally came by and drew the blood."

There were more questions though little else to be learned. Somewhere in between we ordered and ate, and it was only fitting that Sally's meal consisted entirely of three cucumber rolls. (Surely the calories expended on chewing alone outnumbered those in the food.) We were eating at Sally Devine's "favorite sushi restaurant," and it was a good bet that she in fact had never had the sushi there.

Last chance, Mr. Funt.

NINE

Click! That was the sound I heard every time I tried to call Jessica in the wake of her storming out of the hotel room on me. As silent treatments go, she was off to a pretty impressive start.

By nature I was a proud and stubborn guy, rarely given to fits of groveling. Nonetheless, I was ready to apologize to her pretty much by lunch the day after our spat, a lunch that found me having turkey on wheat instead of Philip on Jessica. That alone was reason enough to abort all standing principles and beg for forgiveness. Had Jessica been a friend, a coworker, or even Tracy, you can be sure that I wouldn't have been the one to give in first. My brother would undoubtedly back me up on that.

As kids, Brad and I used to have these phenomenal staring contests across the dinner table. While my mother would be clearing the dishes and my father heading for the television, the two of us would be engaged in complete eye-to-eye combat. The rules were simple: first one to blink lost. And the results were always the same: I won. Not that that deterred Brad. My younger brother was a stubborn little bastard and kept challenging me night in and night out. What he never caught on to, however, was that I was even more stubborn. Way more. At first our parents didn't mind the contests. Given all the potentially unhealthy ways that sibling rivalry could have played out, they must have considered this one to be pretty harmless. That is until one day they happened to notice that Brad had developed a nervous twitch in his right eye. After that, all staring contests were strictly forbidden.

Late afternoon. Returning from my fun-filled lunch with Sally Devine, I went over messages with Gwen. Nothing urgent. I went inside my office and promptly closed the door behind me. I dialed the number yet again. Two rings.

"This is Jessica," she said.

"Jessica, please don't hang—"

Click!

I slammed the receiver down and cursed. It occurred to me that perhaps I was going about this the wrong way. A new tactic was definitely in order.

———

"Red or white?" Tracy asked, greeting me at the door that evening with a bottle in each hand.

"Both," I told her.

"That bad, huh?"

"No, I'm all right, just a lot going on."

"You're working too hard," she said to me. "Go change out of your suit; dinner's ready in five minutes. You're going to be my guinea pig again; I found a new recipe today."

Tracy was always finding new recipes. It might have had something to do with the fact that she owned every cookbook and subscribed to every food magazine on the planet. She didn't have merely one *All New Joy of Cooking,* she had two. The reason, she explained, was that one was for making notes and comments in, the other for show. Although I didn't know exactly who she'd be showing the clean copy to, it all seemed to make sense in a weird Tracy-logic kind of way.

I retreated to our bedroom and undressed, opting for a pair of sweatpants and an old Dartmouth "Big Green" T-shirt. Much better. My four years in Hanover were right in the middle of the big debate over whether or not the college should cease using the Indian symbol. While generally indifferent on the issue, I did recognize that Big Green as an alternative wasn't exactly up there with the Crimson Tide or the Blue Devils when it came to the palette of color-based college nicknames. Still, that didn't prevent me from lifting the T-shirt from my sophomore-year roommate. Not that he'd care much nowadays. After graduation he founded a client-server software company and took it public. He could buy the same T-shirt, only with me in it, twenty times over.

When I joined Tracy back in the kitchen, she had chosen red for me. A '93 Castelgiocondo Brunello. (The '90s and '95s were reserved for company.) I took a sip and settled onto a bar stool.

"So how was your day?" I asked.

"Fine," she answered while slicing a cucumber for a salad. "Errands, gym, the usual. Oh, my mom called. She wanted to know if we'd like to get together with her and Daddy this Sunday out at their place for brunch."

I stopped myself. The thought of driving out to Greenwich to spend the afternoon with my in-laws usually had me trying to drum up some excuse—work-related more often than not—as to why I couldn't make it. As it was, though, the chance for a seamless segue was too good for me to pass up.

"Sure, sounds good," I said casually. "Hey, you know, speaking of getting together, it's been a while since we've done that with Connor and Jessica, hasn't it?"

"I don't know, I think so," Tracy said. "Will you get me the Gorgonzola out of the fridge?"

I got up off the stool and walked over to the Sub-Zero. I got her the Gorgonzola. "Tell you what, why don't you call them and see if they're around tomorrow night?" I said.

"Too short notice," replied Tracy. "Besides, I thought just you and me would do something."

"How about Saturday night, then?"

"We've got that party at the Wagmans."

"What about next weekend?"

"Okay, sure," Tracy said with a shrug. "I'll check with Jessica."

And like that, I had employed my new tactic. It was remarkably simple. If I couldn't resume my affair on my own, the least I could do was enlist the help of my wife, right?

Man, was I playing with fire.

Tracy's dinner turned out to be an almond-crusted pork tenderloin with dried cranberry–apple conserve, courtesy of *Cooking Light*. Surprisingly pretty good. Apparently after every recipe in the magazine they listed the calories and other pertinent data for the health conscious, such as fat, protein, and carbohydrates. As we were eating, Tracy delighted in telling me what all the corresponding grams and milligrams were. The ridiculous thing, of course, was that afterward, we proceeded to devour a pint of Häagen-Dazs butter-almond. Passing the container and an oversized spoon back and forth to each other in front of the television, we engaged in no discussion of nutritional information.

The following night found Tracy and me at Barocco down on Church Street. I liked it because of the food (Italian). Tracy liked it because it attracted a lot of artsy types. Black clothing, rimless eyeglasses, foreign accents. Between people-watching, she filled me in on her day, the bulk of which was spent looking at pictures of potential houses to rent out in the Hamptons. All I really wanted to know was whether or not she had talked to Jessica about having dinner. I didn't want to ask and appear overly anxious, so I waited patiently for her to tell me . . . and waited . . . and waited. Finally, while our plates were being cleared, she got around to it.

"Did I tell you that I spoke with Jessica today?" she asked.

"I don't think so."

Tracy started to giggle. She did that when she had good gossip, or "whisper," as she often called it.

"What's so funny?" I asked.

"Promise me first that you won't say anything back to Connor."

"I promise," I said.

"No, really, you can't say anything because Jessica would kill me."

"I won't say anything," I said slowly, trying to achieve the right measure of trustworthiness.

Feeling properly assured, she began: "It was the strangest thing. I called Jessica to see about getting together with them for dinner next weekend like you and I talked about, and there's this long silence from her; I thought maybe we got disconnected or something. She ends up telling me that they already have plans. No problem, I tell her. We'll do it another time.

"So we start talking about other stuff, her job and whatnot, and I end up asking her how things are with Connor. That's when there's this second long silence. At this point I'm thinking that maybe something's wrong, so I ask her."

"What'd she say?"

Tracy giggled some more. "Let me put it this way: I don't think there's anything *wrong*."

"Why? What do you mean?"

Tracy was about to tell me when we were interrupted by our waiter brandishing a bread-crumb remover. It was the kind that looked like a straight razor, a fitting analogy given that with his slow, precision strokes, our waiter looked to be shaving the tablecloth. As he decrumbed away, Tracy and I sat there in silence. Rare was the Manhattan couple who could continue to carry on a conversation under those circumstances. Saying nothing always seemed to be the accepted mode of behavior.

With a clean table in front of us, Tracy picked up where she had left off. "Anyway, so when I asked Jessica what was going on, it turned out that everything was more than all right. In fact, I think the phrase she used was 'awesome, mind-blowing, multiple-orgasm sex.'" Tracy paused to watch my head tilt as if to say, excuse me? "Not that Jessica was complaining before, she made it clear. The sex was always good, only now, for whatever reason, it's become something far more. She and Connor apparently have reached a 'new plateau of sexual awareness.' Again, her words, not mine. Are you going to want dessert?"

No, I told her. What little appetite I had left had promptly disappeared.

Said Tracy, "Honestly, I couldn't believe my ears. Sure, we had talked about sex before, but never like that. She was even talking about positions—this way, that way—oh, wait, what was that one she described to me called?" Tracy thought for a second. "Oh, yeah, get this . . . the butterfly."

"The butterfly?"

"I'd never heard of it either. The way she explained it, with great detail, I might add, is that she lies on her back by the edge of the bed and Connor, standing on the floor in front of her, lifts her up by the hips. She rests her ankles on his shoulders, and I guess from there they go at it. I couldn't believe she was telling me this. I mean, I'm glad Jessica felt like she could share it all with me. Still, it was pretty strange. One thing is for sure—that's a side of her that I've never seen before."

I sat there reminding myself how to react. Humored, intrigued, even titillated. Miffed, however, was out of the question. It wasn't easy.

Touché, Jessica Levine.

In Tracy she knew she had the perfect messenger, someone who couldn't keep anything the least bit salacious to herself. Their conversation was wholly intended to make it back to me. A little revenge for my telling Jessica to pay more attention to her sex life at home. No doubt about it. If it hadn't pissed me off so much, I would've congratulated her on being so clever. Silent treatment intact, Jessica had managed to tell me off anyway. It was a move I would've been proud to call my own.

So much for playing with fire. While the outcome could've been worse, I took little solace in that. My plan had failed. It was back to the drawing board. At least, that's what I thought. Until, out of the blue, came Tracy's postscript.

"Anyway, about the four of us getting together," she said. "It dawned on me while Jessica and I were talking that we've got that benefit thing at Lincoln Center coming up. You know, the one that her mom got us tickets for? We'll see them then."

Our waiter returned to the table. I changed my mind and ordered some dessert.

TEN

"So, Philip," I said, doing my best Lawrence Metcalf, "how goes things at the firm?"

"He doesn't sound like that," Tracy said, giving me the eye. "Besides, would you rather my father not give a shit about your job?" Thankfully it was a rhetorical question, because I'm not so sure she would've liked the answer.

The traffic was finally thinning a bit as we passed the entrance to the George Washington Bridge on the West Side Highway. It was a blue-skied Sunday in May, and the sun reflecting off the Hudson River gave it an almost postcardlike look, if you can believe that. Tracy put in the Freedy Johnston CD *This Perfect World*, and I began to sing along, tapping my fingers on the steering wheel. And for one brief, shining moment, I almost forgot where we were going.

Meet the Metcalfs . . .

Tracy's father, Lawrence Metcalf, was old money, which as anyone knows is the best kind because it comes with an assumed level of stature that no new money could ever buy. He was well aware of this, naturally, and with every sideways glance and slow stroke of his Princeton chin, he told you so. Last year he retired as CEO of Mid-Atlantic Oil, just months after securing an exploration license from the government of Kazakhstan for more than 5 million acres. It was his way of going out with a bang.

Lawrence Metcalf's old man had been somewhat of a real estate mogul in Manhattan, apparently earning the nickname "Mr. East Side" for all the blocks of prewars he had owned. He in turn was the son of a well-to-do banker, back when being a banker was more an ordainment than a profession. More important, especially as it concerned the Metcalfs to come, he was a wise investor and somewhat of a tightwad. By far the best recipe for inheritance.

Amanda Metcalf, Tracy's mother, was a transplanted Southern belle. Her friends called her "Mandy," which wouldn't have been so bad in a world without Barry Manilow. Prior to meeting Amanda I'd always wondered who on earth *Town & Country* magazine was intended for. In her I had my answer. She was tall, artificially still blond, and while she had lost some battles with gravity, she was still winning the war. (Can you say "standing reservation at Canyon Ranch"?) Lest you think that I've painted a rather unflattering picture of this woman, let it be said that in person Amanda Metcalf was a charming, intelligent, sophisticated individual. Better yet, she could tell a dirty joke without having to have had a drink.

Tracy, my wife, was the only child of Lawrence and

Amanda. On the one hand, I thought this to be a little odd given the lineage of Metcalf men. On the other, were there ever such a book as *How to Spoil Children*, I would've imagined rule number one to read as follows: only have one of them.

Tracy grew up on the private-school circuit in town, first at Greenwich Country Day and then Greenwich Academy. At Country Day, all the girls had to wear these little plaid skirts that came to right above the knee. Tracy showed hers to me once while cleaning out her closet, and it was without a doubt the most persuasive argument for Megan's Law that I'd ever encountered.

Tracy later went to Brown, the place that will forever put the *liberal* in liberal arts college. No matter what you majored in, you always minored in protesting. During her four years there, her primary cause was getting the school to divest from South Africa. As friends of hers recall it, Tracy was quite adamant on the subject—marching, passing out leaflets, speaking at rallies. In her coup de grâce, she and some others built a shantytown in the middle of campus her senior year and lived there for over two weeks. It made all the national papers.

———

The Metcalf home was a sprawling compound in the Belle Haven section of Greenwich with 280-degree water views. It had a dock, but they didn't sail. It had a tennis court, but they didn't play. I'm pretty sure they knew how to swim, but I'll be damned if I ever saw them prove it in their pool. If being rich meant having it all, being Greenwich rich meant having it all just sit there.

"I hope you guys are hungry, because Minnie made a feast!" Amanda Metcalf announced, greeting us in the foyer. She removed her sunglasses and gave us both air kisses. "I'm so glad you two could come out. Isn't it a glorious day?!"

We all agreed and headed out back to the patio.

"Where's my Precious?!" boomed Lawrence Metcalf, having heard our approaching footsteps.

"Daddy!"

Tracy broke into a skip and turned the corner onto the patio. By the time I did the same, sans skip, she had practically leaped into his arms. At this point, I'm trusting that any further explanation of their relationship can only be viewed as redundant.

After the obligatory small talk that accompanies hellos, we settled down to brunch. Minnie, the live-in, had indeed outdone herself. There were egg-white omelets with green, yellow, and red peppers. Spanish melon. Gravlax. Blueberry pancakes, along with a special batch of chocolate-chip ones because they'd been a favorite of Tracy's ever since she was a kid. To drink, Bloody Marys, each complete with a stalk of celery so huge that when you lifted it out of the glass you practically needed a refill.

"Say, Philip, do you know where the Bloody Mary was invented?" asked Lawrence. Such pop quizzes had become ritual between us. I never knew if he was testing my proclivity for useless information or just extremely proud of his. Regardless, I had no clue where the drink was invented.

"I must have missed that *Jeopardy!*," I said. It bordered on being a wiseass response, but Lawrence was too eager to give the answer to notice.

"Harry's New York Bar," he said.

"Oh, I think I've heard of that place," said Tracy, jumping in. "It's on the Upper West Side, isn't it?"

Lawrence chuckled. "Actually, Precious, it's in Paris."

"It is?" Tracy asked.

"Yep," said Lawrence with a nod.

"Are you sure?" asked Tracy.

"Yes. Your mother and I have even been there; remember, darling?"

Amanda nodded. "And if I recall, the Bloody Marys were mediocre at best."

"Your mother never did like Paris," Lawrence said, leaning over to Tracy.

"On the contrary, Paris was beautiful. It was the Parisians that I couldn't stand," declared Amanda. "In fact, if you could somehow arrange for them to all be on holiday at the same time, I might consider going back."

"Honey, we should go to Paris," Tracy announced, turning to me.

"Yes, especially after that ringing endorsement from your mother," I replied.

"No, I'm serious. It would be fun, don't you think?" said Tracy.

"Well, um—"

Tracy kept right on. "Of course it would be. And instead of doing all those touristy things, we could shack up scandalously in an out-of-the-way hotel somewhere and get naked."

The remark brought double takes all around, though

I knew the motivation for mine bore little resemblance to that for Lawrence's and Amanda's. Tracy delighted in conjuring up images of our sex life in front of her parents, and no matter how often she seemed to do it, it always managed to elicit a response from them. Nothing drastic, mind you, generally just stares of disbelief.

As for me, I had long since overcome the potential for embarrassment in these situations. No, my double take owed itself to nothing more than pure paranoia. For it was at times like these, in this case Tracy's referring to *sex in an out-of-the-way hotel*, that I would find myself wondering if she didn't already know about Jessica and me. Somehow, I would instantly conclude, she'd found out about us, the perverse thing being that instead of going instantly ballistic, Tracy had decided first to have a little fun with it. Good old-fashioned mind games. A subtle innuendo here, an off-the-cuff coincidence there. I believe the correct vernacular was "fuck with," and given the circumstances, it seemed very eye-for-an-eye.

The first TIP (Tracy-Induced Paranoia) had happened a couple of months earlier, when out of the blue she asked me if I thought Jessica was pretty. I don't know if she saw me flinch, though I suppose if she had and had called me on it, I simply would've attributed it to the uncomfortable nature of being asked to size up another woman, any woman, in front of your wife. I can't remember my answer verbatim, though I'm pretty sure it went something like . . . Yeah, I guess so. It seemed like the path of least resistance, particularly when delivered with all the apathy I could muster.

Of course, since I was a guy with purportedly nothing to hide, a natural question for me in return to Tracy's query about Jessica would've been, Why do you ask? Ultimately, though, the lawyer in me kept me silent: never ask a question that you don't know the answer to.

ME: Why do you ask, honey?
TRACY: Why do I ask? Why do I ask?! I'll tell you why I ask. . . . I wanted to know if that was why you've been fucking her behind my back all this time, you soon-to-be-served-with-divorce-papers prick!

Ouch.

Meanwhile, back on the patio, I snapped out of it with Tracy's comment about shacking up in a Paris hotel apparently still hanging over the table. Amanda Metcalf seized the moment.

"Well, if you ask me, I always did think the Eiffel Tower was nothing more than one big phallic symbol," she said.

Sometime later, the ladies excused themselves from the table to go see if there were any travel books on France in the upstairs library (not to be confused with the downstairs library or, for that matter, the third-floor study). This left Lawrence, me, and an uncomfortable silence.

"So, Philip, how goes things at the firm?" Lawrence finally asked.

How I suddenly longed for the silence.

"Things are pretty good," I said.

Normally I would've been reluctant to divulge anything more to someone asking me about my job. Beyond anything silly like client-attorney privilege, the last thing I needed was a person getting engrossed in a case of mine and wanting to follow the box score day in and day out. That said, I also knew that leaving it at "Things are pretty good" was never going to cut it with my father-in-law. There was one simple reason. In addition to the cavernous loft that I called home, there was another gift that Lawrence Metcalf had bestowed upon me when I married his daughter. He had made me a rainmaker for Campbell & Devine. Besides his own company, Lawrence and his old-boy network had paved the way for no fewer than three major corporations to put the firm on retainer. Bigger-than-big money, we're talking about. Though not exactly tax free. While it did wonders for my standing at work with Jack Devine, it was never lost on me that it gave Lawrence considerable leverage. Not only did it guarantee him all the updating on Campbell & Devine that he could possibly want from me, it also went a long, long way to making sure that I would always stay happily married to his Precious. Call it a father-of-the-bride insurance policy.

So, how goes things at the firm?

I continued: "Let's see, I recently wrapped up that medical malpractice suit I last told you about. Settled out of court, as they say."

Lawrence nodded. "What's next?" he asked.

I hesitated. Should I have cared if he knew Jack's wife had gotten rung up on a drunk-driving charge? Probably. Then two words popped into my head: police blotter. If her arrest was going to be fodder for the papers, it certainly wasn't too much of a crime for me to talk about it here. Besides, something told me that Lawrence would enjoy my entrusting him with it.

"What's next is kind of interesting," I said, "though you'll understand why it's not for circulation. In what's destined for the brownnosing hall of fame, I'm representing my boss's wife on a DUI charge."

Lawrence sat up in his chair a bit. Clearly he was intrigued by this.

"Jack Devine's wife?" he inquired.

I nodded.

"Did you volunteer for the job?"

"No, he asked me," I told him.

"Then that's not really brownnosing, is it?" he said, rubbing his chin.

"I guess not," I replied with a hint of modesty.

"In fact, I would say that's quite a compliment, a real comment on your position in the firm."

"So long as I don't screw it up."

"I suppose. Though something tells me you'll handle it fine."

This last remark from Lawrence came dangerously close to being a real compliment. It would have made a grand total of one since Tracy first introduced me to him. Could it be that I was witnessing a tectonic shift in our relationship? It certainly seemed that way the remainder of the afternoon. As our conversation continued, Lawrence Metcalf was talking to me—not at me, around me, or down to me, but *to* me—and if there was any doubt as to this development, it was put to rest the minute Tracy and her mother returned to the patio with a stack of travel books.

"Precious, I had no idea that Philip had assumed such a prominent role in his law firm," Lawrence said.

I had no idea either, was what I'm sure Tracy must

have been thinking. You wouldn't have known it from her response, though.

"I only marry the best, Daddy," she said.

The ride home from a visit to Lawrence and Amanda Metcalf was usually defined by one emotion. Relief. This visit, however, had been different. In fact, when Tracy simultaneously yawned and announced that it was time for the two of us to go, I felt a twinge of disappointment.

"What was that with my father?" asked Tracy back in the car.

I played dumb. "What was what?"

She laughed. "Don't give me that; what the hell did you tell him?"

"Nothing much. I was filling him in on what was going on at work, and I guess it finally dawned on him that I'm a little more than just a law firm lackey with a well-connected father-in-law."

"You know he never thought that," she said.

"Maybe."

Tracy reached over and started to run her hand through my hair. "For the record, I'd like to say that I think it's wonderful, him feeling that way about you . . . whatever the reason."

I looked over at my wife and saw a smile on her brighter than any I'd ever seen, wedding day included. It was a little weird, like uncharted territory, not that I was complaining. Especially when she told me to pull over.

"Huh?"

"Pull over," she said again.

"What, do you have to go to the bathroom or something?" I asked.

She laughed. "Trust me, just do it."

I pulled over onto the shoulder of the road. It was the sound I heard first. The electric hum of her automatic seat reclining. I turned and watched as she slowly went back, and back, and back. With her seat belt still on, she kicked off her sandals, planted her feet on the dash of our Range Rover, and reached up beneath her sundress and removed her panties.

"Well?" Tracy smiled.

"Oh."

And right there, on the side of the highway, I turned off the car, turned on the hazards, and proceeded to steam up the windows with Tracy for a very good ten minutes (give or take eight). When we finished, Tracy had but one thing to say: "What do you want to do for dinner?"

You know, I once read an article that talked about how most men who were having an affair found sex with their wives to be almost chorelike.

I pitied those men.

ELEVEN

Gwen eyed me suspiciously as I approached my office. "You look happy for a Monday morning," she said.

"I am happy for a Monday morning," I replied. "How was your weekend?"

"It sucked."

I had to hand it to her; she was at least consistent.

I *was* happy, though, and while I generally made a point of showing little emotion around the office, I didn't really care if anyone saw. Can you blame me? The chance to reconcile with Jessica swiftly approaching, and the adoring wife who, all paranoia aside, didn't suspect a thing about the affair. The kicker? My father-in-law, the one and only Lawrence Metcalf, suddenly thought I was a player. It was a good feeling.

Too bad it wasn't going to last.

Later that morning, Gwen buzzed me. "Philip, I've got a Tyler Mills on the line, says he's a friend of yours."

This should be interesting, I thought. "Put it through," I told her.

I got up and closed the door to my office. I did that

with all my personal calls, regardless of whether or not I actually expected them to be personal. On my way back behind my desk, I hit the speakerphone button.

"Talk about your blast from the past," I said. There was no response. "Tyler, you there?"

Finally, a voice on the other end. However, had Gwen not told me who it was, I'm not sure I would've recognized it as being Tyler's. There was something different about it, I wasn't exactly sure what, just something different.

"I hate fucking speakerphone, Philip, could you pick up the phone?"

I picked up the receiver. "Nice to hear from you too," I remarked.

"Sorry," he said, and like that, his voice was back to how I remembered it.

"No problem," I assured him. "Man, it's been a while, hasn't it?"

"Four years."

"Sounds about right. Tracy told me about bumping into you outside of Saks."

"Yeah, that was weird," he said.

"I bet. So how've you been?"

Tyler let go with a sarcastic laugh. "I've been worse, I suppose. Even got the scars to prove it."

That didn't take long. I'd been wondering if the subject of his attempted suicide was going to come up, and now I had my answer. For sure, I wasn't about to mention it. My rule of thumb? If Hallmark didn't make a card for it, you were never obligated to say something. As for his scars, rumor had it that they were of the hor-

izontal variety. Strictly amateur hour. Even I knew that
slitting your wrists vertically was far more effective.

"I assume you heard about it?" Tyler said.

"Yeah, I did."

"How did it make you feel?" he asked.

I repeated back, *"How did it make me feel?!"*

"Like, did it make you sad, depressed, ambivalent,
happy?"

"Oh, yeah, I was real ecstatic to hear that you tried
to kill yourself, Tyler. How do you think it made me
feel?"

"I wasn't sure. That's why I was asking," he said. "It
was only a question."

A very strange one at that.

"So listen," he said, "I was thinking that the two of
us would have some lunch this afternoon."

"Today? Wow, that's a little short notice for me. I've
got some things going on here at the office," I said.

"No doubt you must be busy. You and I need to talk,
though."

"Well, yeah, I'd love to catch up, it's—"

Tyler interrupted me. "You don't understand. You and
I *need* to talk."

His voice had changed again. I was starting to peg it
as somewhere between deeply earnest and menacing. Either way, I didn't much like it. Then again, odds were
he was simply a troubled guy who needed an ear to
bend. As I'm sure someone once had the presence of
mind to point out, you never really want to disappoint
a guy too much who's predisposed to killing himself.

"In that case, you name the time and the place and
I'll be there," I said.

"The Oyster Bar, one o'clock," he answered quickly. "See you there."

Before I could say yes, no, or you know, the blue-points and Wellfleets really aren't all that tasty this time of year, he hung up.

I leaned back in my chair and tried to sort this guy out. Tyler Mills and the concept of reality had always had what you might call an on-again, off-again relationship. Given his uneven demeanor over the phone, it seemed that the two were not necessarily on speaking terms these days.

We had first met years ago as sophomores at Deerfield. He was a nice enough kid, just really didn't know how to fit in. He'd always be making some comment or telling a story that came out of left field—check that, deep left field. In other words, Tyler was full of shit. Soon the mere sight of him on campus brought about a collective rolling of the eyes from everyone else. He must have caught on, though, because come junior year he had figured out a way to be tolerated, if not entirely accepted. Free pot. Let's just say if I had a nickel for every nickel bag he unloaded on us, I wouldn't need the Metcalf money.

Of course, being the school stoner wasn't exactly conducive to a stellar academic career. It was awfully time-consuming, especially when you consider having to keep track of all those bootleg Grateful Dead tapes in your dorm room. That Tyler had to blow off the occasional midterm was merely an occupational hazard. So while all of us moved on to our respective Ivy League schools, Tyler went off to the University of Colorado at Boulder. From there I basically lost track of him.

Until one Saturday night about four years back. Tracy and I were at a party somewhere uptown. We'd been dating for no more than a couple of months. A few drinks into the evening, I hear this whisper of a voice behind me.

"Anybody want to get stoned?"

I turned around to see Tyler staring back at me with a real Manson Family grin. He was wearing a down jacket and a wool hat. The fact that it was August at the time seemed to matter very little to him.

He still looked like a stoner, though now perhaps a professional one, if you know what I mean. He had caught up to me in height (six feet) and surpassed me in weight; not fat by any stretch, just a little plump. He had a scraggly Vandyke growing on his face and what little hair I could see sticking out from beneath his hat appeared to have been bleached blond from its natural black. I remember thinking at the time that he looked one plaid shirt short of being a poster boy for Seattle.

Anyway, to say I was surprised to see him was an understatement. As I was still in the "Must Impress Tracy" courtship phase of our relationship, I stood there dreading the idea of introducing him to her as a friend of mine. Sure enough, he did it for me. "Hi, I'm Tyler Mills; Philip and I were like this back at Deerfield." It would've been bad enough if he'd simply put his two fingers together side by side as he said *like this*. That he overlapped them in some pseudo–latent homosexual connotation was almost more than I could bear. Nonetheless, whatever thoughts Tracy may have been harboring on the inside, on the outside she didn't seem to mind. In fact, she seemed downright engaged by Tyler. The next thing I knew, the two were chatting it up like they were the old chums.

At some point he mentioned the novel he was writing. He was reluctant to share any details with us, except that we could think of it as a cross between *Madame Bovary* and *Fear and Loathing in Las Vegas*. Naturally. He claimed that he was nearly halfway done with his first draft and already had a couple of agents wanting to sign him.

And I was the pope, I remember thinking.

Later, when even Tracy began to steal glances at her watch, I announced to Tyler that she and I had to get up early the next morning. We exchanged phone numbers, gave lip service to the idea of getting together for dinner, and shook hands good-bye. From there, I basically lost track of him again.

Then a couple of years later, not long after Tracy and I were married, we were at another party, this one heavy with past Deerfielders, and the news broke that Tyler had tried to kill himself. A chorus of *Omigods!* ensued, along with claims from various would-be psychics that they had known something like this was going to happen. As for me, I felt a small measure of guilt. Perhaps if I'd made more of an attempt to be his friend over the years he wouldn't have been so screwed up. Where I got off thinking that my involvement could have made his life more worth living I didn't know.

I did know, however, that as I took the steps down to the lower level of Grand Central Station that afternoon to meet Tyler for lunch, I felt like I was doing a decent thing. My good deed for the day, if you will. No small accomplishment for a practicing attorney.

The Oyster Bar.

I've always thought the Oyster Bar to be a microcosm of New York City: bustling, loud, and expensive. You essentially have two choices when you walk in. To the right you can eat counter style, to the left is a cavernlike room with at least a hundred tables.*

Guessing left, I spotted Tyler at a table for two in the rear. He had the Mafia seat (back to the wall), and as I approached he stood and gave me a weak handshake. We sat down and studied each other for a moment.

"You look the same," he said, breaking the silence.

"You lost some weight," I said in return. Too much, actually. His face looked gaunt, and his clothes—a blue-striped Oxford and old chinos—gave new meaning to the term "loose-fitting." He'd already been served a coffee, and given the way his fingers were tapping feverishly against the table, it was a good bet that it wasn't his first cup of the day.

"So how've you been?" Tyler asked.

"Pretty good. Yourself?" I replied.

"Pretty fucked up, at least that's what I was. You probably know all about that, or at least the juicy parts. I'm doing better, much better now, though. Things are finally interesting for me again."

"That's great," I said. "Hey, I've got to ask: Whatever happened to that novel you were working on?"

Tyler squinted. "The what?"

---

*There is, in fact, a third choice: the "Saloon," located through a set of swinging shutter doors to the very far right. But with its wood paneling and cozy table layout, you might as well be eating at another restaurant.

"You know, the novel you told Tracy and me about when we last saw you at that party years back."

"Oh, that?" he said, rubbing his temples. "I burned it."

"As in *burned it* burned it?" I asked.

"Yeah—poof!—up in smoke, just like that."

I thought maybe he was kidding at first; that was, until I stared into his eyes. He wasn't kidding. "You mind if I ask why?" I said.

"Not at all. It's simple, really; what happened was this: I was busting my hump, pouring everything I had into what I thought would be a great work of literature, right, when one night I had this horrifying vision, quite demoralizing, really, that after all the work, all the sweat and all the sacrifice, my book would simply wind up in *The New Yorker* under the heading 'Briefly Noted.' *Briefly Noted!* Can you imagine anything more trivializing? And that was if I was lucky. I mean, think of all those books that must end up under the heading 'Totally Ignored.' So like I said, I burned it, my manuscript, right in the garbage pail. But that's my point, really."

Already my ears were tired. Nonetheless, "Your point?" I asked.

"Yeah, why I got so fucked up," Tyler said. "That book thing was the final straw, the thing that pushed me over the edge. I became so convinced that I was a complete failure that the only option left for me, I thought, was to take my own life. Crazy, right? Except let me tell you, it didn't seem so crazy at the time. Of course, that's when the real irony kicked in. Turned out I was such a complete failure that I couldn't even succeed in killing myself! Go figure. Hey, where the fuck is that waitress?!"

I sat in amazement as Tyler, who'd been speed-talking at a *Guinness Book* clip, reached into his pocket and pulled out a half-crumpled pack of Marlboros.

"Smoke?" he offered me.

"No, thanks," I told him. As he lit the cigarette and took a long drag, my sense of humor couldn't help it. "You know, those things will kill you."

He smirked and proceeded to exhale in my face. Our waitress arrived and placed two menus on the table.

"There's no smoking in the restaurant, sir," she announced.

"Eat me," said Tyler without skipping a beat.

Unsure exactly how to handle that response, the woman picked up the menus and stormed off. I figured we had a good two, maybe three minutes before we got our asses kicked out of the place. At the very least, she was sure to spit in our oysters.

"Where was I?" asked Tyler.

"Failure to commit suicide," I informed him.

"Right, well, that's when the epiphany hit me— pow!—like, crystal clear. I realized that if I was going to be sentenced to life, as it were, I might as well try to make the most of it. You know, enjoy it and stuff."

At last, an encouraging sign; something coming out of his mouth that made sense.

Tyler continued: "So guess what I did first? On second thought, don't guess; I mean, you can guess, but you'd never be able to guess right, you know what I mean?"

"I think so," I replied. It didn't matter.

"The first thing I did was start to ride the commuter trains back and forth out of Grand Central here. Every day I would do this, and every day I would wait for the inevitable asshole who would take out his cell phone and start making calls. He'd call his office, he'd call his friends, and he'd be sitting there talking as if the entire train car was his fucking phone booth. It was as if he had total disregard for the people trying to read, trying to sleep; total disregard for me. And what would almost always happen is that at some point during these calls the asshole would give out his cell phone number so someone could call him back . . . and like every other part of his fucking conversation, I could hear every digit. So here's what I would do. I would write down the number; then, to make sure there was no connection made to me, I would wait a week. Then? Then I would go to town. I would call this asshole. I would call him and tell him I was watching him, that there was no escaping me. That it was only a matter of time before I would sneak up on him, when he would meet his ultimate demise.

"Sometimes, you know, a guy would call bullshit, and that's when I would refer to some physical feature of his, or maybe the tie he was wearing that morning on the train. This would spook them, spook them real good." Tyler stopped for a moment to gauge my reaction. "So now you're probably asking yourself why I was doing this, and I'll be the first to admit it's a fair question. The answer is this: it was my way of getting even with all these pompous assholes, that's what it was."

I finally spoke up. "Let me get this straight," I said. "Because they talked loudly, that you could overhear them on a train, that's why you had to get even with them?"

Tyler shook his head at me. "Philly, you're missing the whole point here. Anyway, after a while the novelty kind of wore off. It got old. The guys would all change their numbers, you know. Well, all of them except this one guy. I didn't know if he was stubborn or just plain stupid at first. Turns out what he really was was scared. I mean, really scared. Like at one point he demanded to know what I wanted from him. Was it money, he asked, because if that's what it was he could make an arrangement. Can you believe that?! He could make an *arrangement*. It dawned on me, this guy must have a guilty conscience or something, you know, to want to pay off someone so easily. Hell, someone who he didn't know, who simply had his cell phone number. Bonkers, I tell you. But it did give me an idea.

"You see, all of us to some degree are guilty, Philly, guilty of something. I got to wondering, what are my so-called friends guilty of? That's when I decided." Tyler stubbed out his cigarette on the table, flicked it onto the ground, and looked at me expressionless, trying to milk the moment. Moment passed, he leaned in and whispered, "That's when I decided to follow them."

Our waitress arrived again, this time with some official-looking guy wearing a suit.

"Excuse me, sir," said the suit to Tyler. "There's no smoking in the restaurant here."

"I should certainly hope not; I'm asthmatic," said Tyler.

The suit looked at the waitress.

"But he was smo—"

Tyler interrupted her. "You know, the two of you do seem like nice people and all, however, I'm trying to have a lunch here with my attorney." That last word there lingered in the air for a bit as the suit looked at me in my suit . . . a far better one, I might add.

"Never mind," the guy said, and the two of them walked away. A few minutes later a different waitress arrived and placed two menus on the table again.

"I'm sorry, Tyler, what were you saying?" I asked.

"I was saying how I decided to follow around some of the people I knew, or maybe I should say, people I thought I knew, because it turns out you never really know someone. If you don't believe it, try following someone for yourself. It can be a real eye-opener."

I was starting to get the creeps. "You're serious?" I said.

"Absolutely. Hell, not everyone has deep, dark secrets. The worst Kevin Marshall does is go to a tanning salon. You remember him from Deerfield, don't you? Still, I did notice that he looks around a bit before going into the salon, like, not to be seen or anything. Funny when you think about it. So maybe he's guilty of vanity. No great crime. But still guilty.

"Tom Atkinson? You know what he does twice a week? He goes to this prostitute in the East Village. I wasn't sure that's what she was at first, until I staked her place out. You should have seen the traffic! A revolving fucking door she had there. But I'm thinking, Tom is a bachelor, after all, so there's really not a lot of damage being done. Yeah, he wouldn't want anyone to know, but the embarrassment, the potential for embarrassment, could only be so motivating a factor. Ultimately, I didn't bother."

Tyler folded his arms on the table and leaned in.

"Then there's you. You know, I was almost starting to lose faith in my little endeavor. For all intents and purposes, I was oh for two; behind in the count, as they say. Though I'm happy to report, Philly, you didn't disappoint. Not that it was immediately apparent. You were pretty crafty, staggering your entrances and exits. I mean, I knew what you were doing. I just couldn't pinpoint *who* you were doing. In fact, I was thinking about giving up, when all of a sudden you come flying out of that hotel last week—bang! bang!—with that girl.

"My guess is that you got a little cocky, a little too confident. I mean, what are the odds that there's a guy like me tailing you, huh? Wait, what was that you called me this morning? A *blast from the past?* How ironic. Because ain't this just one big fucking ka-boom! for you right now."

Tyler eased back in his chair, mighty impressed with himself. I wasn't about to hit the panic button, though.

"Let's see if I can make some sense of this," I said. "You asked me to lunch so you can break the news that you saw me walk out of a hotel with another woman." For effect, I paused a second. "This is supposed to mean what?"

"I thought you'd say something like that. That's why I brought these." He reached down and removed a manila envelope from a small black duffel bag sitting by his chair. He placed the envelope in front of me. "Go on, take a look," he said.

In that instant, the image flashed before me. A picture of Tyler in the credits section of the Deerfield year-book our senior year. He had a camera hanging around his neck and this stupid grin on his face. Underneath, the caption read: "Man on the scene—Tyler Mills, Photo Editor." I knew what was coming.

I picked up the envelope and pulled them out. A batch of eight-by-ten black-and-white photographs. Slowly, I started to flip through them. The initial ones were of me—alone—coming and going from the Doral Court hotel. They must have spanned a few weeks, if not a month. Either way, they dated back well before Tyler *just happened* to bump into Tracy outside of Saks. He hoped to be talking to me soon, he had said to Tracy that day. Indeed, just as soon as I gave him his smoking gun.

And there it was. I had flipped to the picture of me and Jessica leaving the hotel together. Our minor breach in security from the week before. The two of us, in a rush, and yet, perfectly in focus. Crisp and clear.

As were Tyler's last few shots. For good measure, he had us both individually coming and going at the Doral Court the very next day. Yes, Tyler Mills was very thorough.

I quickly flipped through the entire set of pictures again, laying them down on the table when I was done. "I still don't know what this is supposed to prove," I said, stone-faced.

Tyler laughed. "Probably nothing in a courtroom. I mean, any dumb lawyer could explain these pictures away as nothing more than a weird coincidence. What were you doing at the hotel? Oh, I don't know, I'm sure you'd think of something. Something just believable enough to create those two magical words that you scumbags live by. *Reasonable doubt*.

"Fortunately for me, this isn't about what would play out in a courtroom. No, this is different. This plays out in that most delicate of relationships that exist between a man and a woman, otherwise known as a marriage." He reached over and tapped his forefinger on the pictures. "What might not hold up in a courtroom would sure stand a much better chance back at your home, don't you think? How is Tracy, by the way?"

I tried to remain calm, but it was too late. I could feel my face getting red, the veins bulging around my temples, my fists balling up, and my fingernails digging deep into my palms. Tyler picked up one of the pictures with Jessica in it.

"She's cute," he said. "I can only hope that she was worth it." He grinned. "So tell me, was she?"

"Fuck you."

Tyler shrugged. "I'm sorry, was that a yes or a no, Philly? I couldn't quite tell."

"Fuck you," I said again, forcing the words through my clenched teeth. "And the name, you son of a bitch, is Philip."

"The way I see it, so long as I've got these pictures, your name's whatever I goddamn want it to be."

With that, I casually put my hands on the table, resting them on top of the photos. It was worth a try, I figured.

Tyler looked at me the way people look at a dog chasing its tail. He shook his head. "C'mon, Philly, you don't honestly think these are the only copies to be had, do you?"

Our second waitress returned. "You guys ready to order?"

"Not yet, darling," Tyler told her.

I waited for her to walk away. "Pretending for a minute that you actually have something on me," I said, "what is it that you want?"

"Now we're talking," he said, his eyes lighting up. "What I want is what anybody ever wants. Money, baby."

"Money?"

"That's right. Cash, cabbage, moola! What the fuck did you expect?"

"You know, if you just needed some dough, Tyler, you could've simply asked me."

"For a hundred thousand dollars?"

I gagged. "You've got to be kidding me!"

"Yeah, I didn't think so. Hence, the blackmail. So, what's it going to be, Philly? I've got an account set up and everything."

I started to laugh. I couldn't help it. Right in his face I started to laugh uncontrollably. I'd spent the past five minutes like a boxer reeling from a punch. Finally, I was starting to come around, the brain starting to kick back in. No doubt I was spurred on by the absurd amount Tyler thought he could bilk me for. It somehow made his whole scheme seem instantly less credible.

Now it was my turn.

"What's it going to be?!" I said. "This is what it's going to be, you piece of shit. First, if you call me Philly one more time, I'm going to lodge my heel into your nuts so hard you're going to piss out your asshole, pictures or no pictures. Second, if you so much as think of bothering me again about this, I promise you, you'll be wishing that razor blade of yours had actually done its job."

I stood up, turned, and began to walk out of the restaurant, leaving Tyler alone at the table. I wanted to look back, to see his reaction. I wanted to see what, if anything, he was going to do. But I knew better. In a split second, I had made the decision to call his bluff. Risk Factor 7. It was a risky gambit, for sure, especially given that Tyler Mills seemed very much the guy with little or nothing to lose. Would this be the end of him?

At the time, I could only hope so.

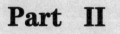

Part II

TWELVE

Sally Devine showed up drunk for her DUI court appearance.

At first I wasn't sure. Then she reached for my crotch in the hallway of the courthouse and asked me if I really had the balls for the job. Dead giveaway. Thankfully, there was so much commotion and so many people milling about that no one seemed to notice.

"For Christ's sake, Sally, you're loaded!" I whispered at the top of my lungs, all the while imagining the spectacle of standing with her before a judge.

"I am not. I just had a couple drinks to take the edge off," she slurred.

Suddenly her telling me that she'd had only a couple of drinks the day of her accident was put into an entirely new perspective. I had to act fast. Sally had been late, of course. It was nine-fifty-five, five minutes before court was in session.

"Come with me," I said, taking her hand and pulling her through the slalom of delinquents in the hallway.

"Where are we going?"

"Maxwell House," I told her.

We headed up to the second floor and found a small coffee room, probably intended for administrative personnel. I immediately poured a cup for Sally.

She protested, "I don't like coffee."

"You do now," I said. I held the cup in front of her until she finally grabbed it from my hands. She took a sip and made a face.

"Blech! This is horrible!"

I had little sympathy for her. It was already officially a bad day and it wasn't even . . . I looked at my watch—*shit!*—two minutes past ten. Court was in session. I grabbed the cup back out of Sally's hands and put it down. "C'mon," I said.

We rushed back downstairs, stopping momentarily before the doors to the courtroom so I could compose myself. Two deep breaths and I was ready. In we went.

Westchester County Court was a far cry from your favorite TV law drama. First off, the attorneys were not all attractive. Some bordered on downright ugly, almost as ugly as the room itself, a four-sided homage to the banal. Drama? There was more drama in a ham sandwich. Here, the vast majority of cases called were petty crimes and misdemeanors that, one after the other, tended to become painfully monotonous. Perhaps the only true entertainment to be had stemmed from the tired old man in a robe who sat up on the bench and looked out with a hemorrhoid-induced grimace and spoke in a dyspeptic tone that let everyone know that above all else, this was *his* courtroom. Quite an act.

Sally and I quickly found seats in one of the back rows. As we settled in, I looked over at her. Her normally alert eyes were glassy and distant. Her clothes were disheveled. I leaned over in her direction and silently sniffed. Eau de Tanqueray. This was not shaping up well at all.

I had left my briefcase back at the office, opting, instead, for my litigation bag. Though the morning's proceedings hardly called for anything so oversized, I was the type who felt naked in a courtroom without it. Any courtroom. Lifting the bulky thing up to my lap, I opened it and pulled out Sally's file. Various forms, my notes, the police report . . . Ah, the police report. True to form, it contained its share of discrepancies and procedural missteps. If it had been my intent to take this case to trial, we would've had more than a fighting chance. But that wasn't my intent. Rather, in the words of Jack Devine, I was there to make things as easy and painless as possible. And a trial, no matter how good your chances, was anything but. Sally's admittance into the alcohol education program. That's what we were there to get.

I tapped Sally on the shoulder. "Listen, when we get called and go before the judge, here's the deal. You don't say anything. I do all the talking. If by chance, and it would be a slim chance at that, the judge asks you a question directly, don't get nervous. Simply answer him as concisely and directly as possible, and whatever you say, make sure you end it by calling him sir. Okay?"

"Yes, *sir*," she replied. She was mocking me, but I didn't care. Her delivery was perfect.

What to do next? "Defending Your Inebriated Client at a DUI Hearing" wasn't exactly part of my core curriculum back in law school. Still, I felt the need to do something. So I reached into my pocket and pulled out some Tic Tacs. Technically that was something. Telling Sally to stick out one of those heavily bejeweled hands of hers, I shook a few of them into her palm.

"Are these pills?" she asked me, a little too loudly.

I pursed my lips and made a "shhh" face while raising my index finger to my mouth. Back home at the library, Mom would've been proud. "No. They're breath mints," I whispered.

Sally whispered back, "Because if they're pills, I'm telling you right now that I'm not taking them."

"Sally, they're breath mints, trust me."

She cupped her other hand over her mouth and did a quick exhale. The universal breath-check maneuver. With a sheepish grin she turned back to me. "Better make it a double," she said.

Shake, shake. I shook the box of Tic Tacs another time and a few more came tumbling out. Sally popped what was by then a handful of them into her mouth. Shake, shake. For good measure, I shook the box a couple more times and took some for myself.

As we both chomped away on Tic Tacs, I checked Sally's file yet again. Nope, no document had decided to up and disappear in the past two minutes. Though given everything else going on in my life at the time, I wouldn't have been surprised. Three days and counting. That's how long it had been since my lunch with Tyler. So far, so good. Nonetheless, it was way too early to be claiming victory. As far as I understood, blackmail threats didn't really have any statute of limitations.

Where were you, Tyler Mills? Admittedly, not knowing the answer had me feeling a little anxious. There were moments when I'd be out walking on the street and I'd quickly look over my shoulder expecting to see him—and each time I didn't see him was all the more reason for me to look the next time. It made me think of that crazy old man in the hospital gown that night when Jessica and I first got together. At the time, the old guy's world and mine couldn't have been further apart. How strange then to suddenly have a sense of his fear, be it real or imagined. Perhaps he wasn't so crazy after all.

Almost immediately after walking out on Tyler at the Oyster Bar, I had begun playing our conversation over and over again in my mind. I was mainly trying to figure out if there was some other thing I could have said, some other action I could have taken . . . something besides what I did. One troubling revelation was that I hadn't really tried to talk Tyler out of it. I negotiated and plea-bargained for a living, yet it seemed that in the heat of the moment I had forced the issue. Jumped the gun, even. Maybe with the right words I could've gotten Tyler to realize what a terrible mistake he was making. Or maybe, deep down, he had never really intended to go through with it at all. Therein lay my fear. Because maybe, just maybe, in walking out on him as I had, I'd managed to give him no other choice. Now he had to go through with it.

"Sally Devine!" came the voice of the court clerk from the front of the room.

I turned to my summoned client. "Here we go," I said. We both stood up and sidestepped out to the aisle.

That Sally tripped and nearly fell in the process wasn't what you would call a confidence builder.

"Damn heel!" she muttered while straightening herself out. I looked down, if only to play along. That's when I saw them. One black, the other blue. Sally Devine was wearing two different shoes.

———

Earlier that morning, I had paid a visit to the assistant district attorney's office. I had three objectives in mind. The first was perfunctory—to watch the videotape of Sally at the police station after her DUI arrest. I pretty much knew what I would see. Though the quality wasn't what you would call high-definition, it was clear that she'd been drinking. It wasn't falling-down drunk or anything, more like tipsy. Amid the time code, gray tones, and a faulty horizontal hold, she had what could best be described as a slightly out-of-step look to her. Happy hour with under a minute to go.

The second objective was a sacrificial lamb—to ask that Sally's charges not be read aloud out of sensitivity to her standing within the community. I may as well have been asking for a Ferrari. But that was the point, really. That in the true legal tradition of give-and-take, having shut me down already on one request, the assistant D.A. would be slightly more inclined to give me what I really wanted, my third objective—to have the case called as early as possible in the session so as to not have to waste the entire goddamn day there. Naturally, I'd need to give him a reason why he should grant me, a guy he owed nothing to, such a favor. The fact that I didn't really have one wasn't about to get in my way.

ME: May I ask out of respect for Ms. Devine's privacy and her good standing within the community that her charges not be read aloud?
A.D.A.:   Perhaps your client should have thought about
           that before getting loaded and getting behind
           the wheel of a car.
ME: Fair enough. Oh, one other thing. Before giving blood later this afternoon, I need to visit
           the homeless shelter where I volunteer in order
           to meet the man I'm donating a kidney to, so
           I was wondering if maybe you could have our
           case called as early on as possible.
A.D.A.:   (amused) I'll see what I can do.

It's an often-heard expression. "Be careful what you ask for. . . ." Sure enough, Sally's was the third case called. Favor granted. Only it was no longer such a favor. In fact, given her condition, I would've begged to have been called last.

———————

Judge Harold Bainwright didn't bother to look up. As Sally and I walked down to the front of the courtroom and took our places before him, he remained focused on whatever it was he was writing. From my angle I could see only the very top of his ballpoint pen and I watched as it moved from left to right, bobbing and seesawing in a hurried, jerky fashion. Even as the assistant D.A. began to read Sally's charges aloud to him, Judge Bainwright continued to look down. I figured as long as that pen of his was moving, we were in good shape. Go, pen, go.

Then it happened. Sally laughed.

Not any demure, fleeting moment of a giggle was this, but a true salt-of-the-earth, uproarious guffaw. It stopped everything in the room, including a particular ballpoint pen. Judge Bainwright looked up with his hemorrhoid-induced grimace to cast a wary eye on Sally Devine.

"Sorry," she announced, cowering at her sudden lime-light status. There remained a part of her, though, that found something to be very funny. God knows what it was, but she could barely suppress her smile.

Not as easily amused, Judge Bainwright swung his arm out into the air. The assistant D.A. obliged and handed him Sally's file. He pored over its contents for what was maybe a half minute, although it seemed like an eternity. Slowly, he looked up again and resumed that wary-eye thing on Sally. I was about to speak when he beat me to it.

"Good morning, Ms. Devine, how are you today?" he said, a little too pleasantly to be sincere.

I quickly tried to intervene. "Your Honor, I—"

He interrupted me. "I'm not talking to you, Mr. . . ." He glanced down at the file to learn my surname. ". . . Mr. Randall."

I looked at Sally. Sally looked at me. With a nod I let her know that it was okay to go ahead and answer him.

"I'm fine," she said. She immediately remembered my earlier instructions. "I mean, I'm fine, *sir.*"

"You do understand why you're here today, don't you?" he asked.

"Yes, sir, I do."

"And you do understand that this is a very serious thing that you're charged with, do you not?"

"Oh, by all means, yes, sir."

As she answered his questions, I placed my litigation bag down on the floor and stood there a picture of helplessness. What Sally was saying was fine. The way she was saying it, however, was a little suspect. Something was amiss.

Judge Bainwright leaned forward in his chair and looked Sally over from head to toe. I watched him, waiting for the inevitable. When I saw the double take I knew he had reached her two different shoes. What were the odds that he'd think it was a hip new fashion trend? Not very good, I concluded.

"Ms. Devine, I see your home address in Bedford listed here in your file. What I don't see is your home telephone number. Would you mind telling me what it is?"

Sally seemed momentarily stumped by the question. I looked at her as she began rubbing her forehead. *For crying out loud, Sally, he asked for your telephone number, not the square root of pi!*

Finally, she spoke up. "One . . . zero . . . five . . . [very long pause] . . . zero . . . six." Like an unsure contestant on a quiz show, she proceeded to look up at Bainwright.

"Actually, Ms. Devine, that's your zip code," he said.

Again, I tried to intervene. "Your Honor, I—"

Again, I was shut down. "Still not talking to you, Mr. Randall."

Bainwright folded his arms in front of him. "Ms. Devine, I can't believe I'm about to ask you what I'm about to ask you," he said deliberately. "Nonetheless, have you been drinking this morning?"

I turned and practically slapped my hand over Sally's mouth before she could respond. "Don't answer that!" I shouted at her. I swiveled on my heels to face the judge. "Your Honor, I know you're not talking to me, however, as I've instructed my client not to respond to your question and she's well within her rights not to do so, I respectfully request permission to approach."

Bainwright thought about it for a second and waved me forward. Why not? He had to be wondering what lame excuse I was about to cook up on behalf of Ms. Devine. For sure, I certainly was.

I began my walk up to the bench. It felt like walking the plank. After my first step, I could feel a few beads of sweat forming along my hairline. At the third step, I could feel eyes—the eyes of everyone in the courtroom watching me. So much for no drama. With two steps to go, a Philip Randall first: trembling hands. Quickly, I dug them into my pockets. With no steps to go, the harsh reality set in. I desperately needed a miracle.

Shake, shake.

There it was. Right there within my grasp. The box of Tic Tacs at the bottom of my left pocket. The same one-and-a-half-calorie breath mints that Sally had first thought were pills. That was it . . . *pills!* It made perfect sense. Hallelujah! You're a genius, Sally Devine.

"Mr. Randall, do you plan on saying something, or

is it your intention to simply stand there and waste my time?"

I looked up at Judge Bainwright, who with that last comment was single-handedly raising crotchety to an art form. This guy was old. I mean really old. Picture a linen suit after it's been through the Maytag a couple of times. That's how many wrinkles this guy had. And as he spoke, I looked at his mouth, a mouth that was surely the "before" picture for every tooth-whitening ad I'd ever seen.

"Earth to Mr. Randall," said Bainwright.

"I read you loud and clear, Your Honor," I said. I dropped to a hushed tone and began. "Sir, I realize it may appear that Ms. Devine has been drinking, but there's really a simple, albeit unfortunate, explanation. What's more, I'm afraid that I'm somewhat to blame."

I got a blank stare from Bainwright. The assistant D.A. had joined us and he too simply waited for me to continue. I did.

"When Ms. Devine met me here at the courthouse this morning she was, to put it mildly, a nervous wreck. As you can imagine, she's not what you would call a regular at these proceedings. She had no idea what to expect and despite my reassurances, was letting her imagination get the best of her. It was quite the scene. Anyway, she eventually asked me if it would be all right if she took a Valium to calm herself down. Naturally, I asked if the medication had been prescribed for her, and she was quick to produce the container to show me that it had.

"Still, I was not entirely comfortable with the idea. In fact, I was about to advise her against it when I no-

ticed that she was on the verge of tears. Her eyes had
swelled up and she was visibly shaking. Not knowing
exactly what to do at that point, I used what I thought
was my best judgment. I told her to take half of a Valium. I even watched as she broke it in two. That way,
I figured, she could relax somewhat while remaining
lucid for when her case was called.

"Except, gentlemen, I'm afraid I was had a bit. After
Ms. Devine split the pill she told me that she was getting some water at the fountain to wash it down. That's
when, as the saying goes, I let her out of my sight. If
I had to bet, she ended up taking the entire Valium. If
not more, god forbid."

I paused again and turned back to look at Sally. Judge
Bainwright and the assistant D.A. did the same. As if
taking her cue, she appeared to be swaying back and
forth a little. Her deer-in-the-headlights gaze added
nicely to the effect. Time for my summation.

"Yes, if I had to bet, that's what happened," I said
with a contemplative nod. "I apologize, Your Honor.
The compromise with half a Valium seemed like a good
idea at the time, her nerves being so frazzled and all.
Who knows, maybe if that's all she had taken she
would've been fine. The only thing I can tell you for
sure is that she's not acting like that because of any
alcohol."

Thus concluded the Valium Defense. To look at the
assistant D.A. was to look at a man who believed. Hook,
line, and sinker. To look at Judge Bainwright, however,
was to see a man not as readily convinced. He would
not be so quick with his verdict on my excuse, nor was

his expression about to reveal which way he was leaning. What seemed like a minute passed.

"Earth to Judge Bainwright," I wanted to say, only to think better of it. Instead, I took advantage of the time to mentally prepare my rebuttal should I need one. Good thing. Because the next thing I knew, the silence was broken by the sound of laughter again. Except it wasn't Sally this time. It was Bainwright. He was laughing hysterically to himself. Sally's guffaw may have been louder, but in terms of sheer creepiness, the judge won hands down. Then, as out of the blue as it had started, the laughing stopped.

Said Bainwright, "In all my years sitting up here, that was by far the biggest bunch of crap I've ever heard come out of the mouth of an attorney. You are indeed an attorney, Mr. Randall, or is that a fabrication as well? I will say this, though. As far as quick thinking and imagination under duress are concerned, you have come through with a most impressive effort. So much so that I won't spoil it by asking Ms. Devine to produce that container of Valium you profess her to have. Or, for that matter, climb down from this bench and go take a whiff of her breath. It doesn't matter how many of those Tic Tacs you gave her, young man, as you were waiting to come before me. If she's been drinking, I'll be able to smell it."

Mouth agape, I stared at him. *How the hell did he know I had given her Tic Tacs?*

The answer came almost immediately. "This is my courtroom, Mr. Randall, and you can be damn sure I know everything that goes on in it."

The assistant D.A. couldn't help but smirk. The innocent bystander, he had a front-row seat to what had become nothing short of my complete humiliation. The floor had turned to quicksand. If I couldn't save myself, I had to at least save Sally.

"I'm sorry you see it that way, Your Honor," I said. "Out of respect for your opinion, I won't press you on the matter. What I would like to do, therefore, is to move on and request that my client, as a first-time offender, be admitted into the state's alcohol education program."

Judge Bainwright slowly began to shake his head. "Like I said, Mr. Randall, I won't spoil your imaginative efforts. However, I won't reward them either. I'm inclined to deny your request for the AE program and send this case to trial."

"*What?*" exclaimed Sally, at that point able to hear the proceedings. It not being easy to speak in hushed tones for a prolonged period of time, what had started as a private sidebar conversation had become increasingly more public. I turned to her with two palms raised in the air and motioned for her to calm down. All was not lost. Humiliated as I surely was, my synapses were still firing.

"That is entirely your prerogative, sir," I said. "However, while it was certainly never my intent to argue the facts of this case before you today, given the circumstances, I believe there is some exculpatory evidence that should be brought to your attention at this time." I paused quickly only to take a breath. Any longer and Bainwright could have interceded and prevented me from continuing. I shifted into speed mode.

"To begin with," I said, "the arresting officer neglected to note the actual time of the accident, choosing instead to indicate the time when my client arrived at the police station. Consequently, the total elapsed time between the accident and the blood test procedure far exceeded the maximum allotted amount of two hours as spelled out by the state. While that alone is sufficient cause for a mistrial, I should also point out that when, in fact, that blood test was administered, it was done by a nurse who applied rubbing alcohol to the arm of my client. As the test itself is to establish the level of alcohol in the body, I would contend that the nurse's action jeopardized the validity of the results."

The rubbing alcohol bit was a definite trick up the sleeve, and it was evident in watching Judge Bainwright that it was certainly a "new one" as far as he was concerned.

"I could go on, Your Honor," I said, my voice gaining in confidence with each word. "The rest, while certainly arguable, is boilerplate. I think I've made my point. Sending this case to trial would not only be disadvantageous for the state, it would be a waste of time for all involved. Of course, that's simply my humble opinion.

"As I said, it was not my intention to argue the facts of this case before you today. I made it clear that enrollment in the alcohol education program was what we wanted, and that remains unchanged. Perhaps, in light of everything discussed so far, you could see clear to reconsider your position."

I exhaled. There were probably two or three times when Bainwright wanted to stop me, and each time I saw him about to do so I began to speak that much faster. By my last sentence, the sheer spectacle of the speed at which I was talking was easily more engaging than what I was actually saying.

Decision time.

As I stood there waiting, the image of Jack Devine ripping me a new asshole flashed through my mind. It was followed by that of Lawrence Metcalf shaking his head and muttering to himself that he always knew I was never really a player, let alone good enough for his daughter. The bottom line as I saw it was that Bainwright could have thrown every word I said right back in my face without batting an eyelash. I could practically hear him. *Being that you're so proud of that evidence of yours, hotshot, why don't we go ahead and see how it holds up in trial!*

But it was a surprise move that followed. Bainwright, of all things, seemed to defer to the assistant D.A. Nothing was said. It was rather a simple "What do you think?" look. And though I was never entirely fluent in body language, with one subtle shrug of his shoulder the assistant D.A. seemed to respond as follows: It's your call, Judge, but if it was up to me I'd let the kid have this one and put the rich bitch in the alcohol program. She may actually learn something, and in the meantime we can move on to the next case so we can finish this fucking session before Christmas, which, come to think of it, happens to be the time of year when I get to hear from all my law school buddies who went on to become defense attorneys like this slickster named Randall standing next to me and receive those big holiday bonuses that on top of their regular salaries make my compensation look like the pathetic, paltry sum that it is. *Comprende?*

Like I said, though, I was never entirely fluent in body language. The shrug from the assistant D.A. may simply have meant, "Beats me." Regardless, it was immediately after this shrug that Bainwright said to no one in particular, "Request for the AE program granted. . . . Next case." It was swift and it was decisive. It was also a lucky break.

I snatched up my litigation bag, grabbed Sally, and bolted from the courtroom before Bainwright could change his mind. Once out in the hallway I immediately headed over to a garbage bin. Shake, shake. Out went the Tic Tacs. From that day forward it was strictly Certs.

"What were you whispering to the judge about for so long?" Sally wanted to know.

"I was merely trying to get him to see things our way," I told her.

"He didn't seem to like you very much."

"He wasn't exactly a big fan of yours, either," I reminded her. "What the hell were you laughing about, anyway?"

That stumped look of hers again. "I can't remember," she said, gazing up at the ceiling. "Weird, huh?"

That was one word for it.

Before we could leave there was paperwork to be done. We went to the requisite office and filled out a bunch of forms. Enrollment in the alcohol education program cost four hundred fifty dollars. That was news to Sally. The notion of having to pay for your punishment didn't sit well with her. "It's not the amount, of course," she was quick to point out. "It's the principle of the thing. I mean, you don't pay money to go to jail, do you?" I shook my head no. After she wrote out the check and signed her name, she couldn't help one more observation. "Four hundred and fifty bucks. That's an entire day at Georgette Klinger, you know."

We left the courthouse and continued to talk. Actually, Sally did most of the talking. I listened. In doing so I determined that while sobriety was slowly starting to reclaim Sally, it had a ways to go. We entered the parking lot. As much as I needed to proceed with my day, I wasn't about to let her get behind the wheel of a car. I told her I would drive her home in her car and have a cab bring me back to the courthouse for mine. Much to my surprise, she didn't protest. In fact, her only concern was my having to take the cab.

"Don't be silly, Hector will take you back," she said.

Hector, huh? At that moment, never had a name been more synonymous with manual labor.

The ride to Bedford took twenty minutes. (Jaguar Vanden Plas, in case you were wondering. Nice car when it's not in the shop.) Between instructions to turn left or right, Sally was busy telling me what various homes had recently sold for. Eventually, she said, "Ours is the one up on the right." I pulled into the driveway. Belgian block. No mere apron followed by pavement. This was the whole shebang. I eased down on the brakes and looked around.

Crime may or may not pay. Unless, of course, you're a defense attorney. Then it pays for everything. In the case of Jack Devine, that meant a glorious old Victorian perched magnificently on a slight upward slope. It was huge, sprawling, and surrounded by what was undoubtedly a cash cow for one very lucky landscape architect. Towering trees, sculpted shrubs, blooming flowers, and everywhere in between, a spectacular putting green of a lawn. No wonder Jack had such an excellent short game.

I shifted the car into park and turned off the engine. Sally undid her seat belt. She turned and looked at me with a weird smile. I was immediately uncomfortable.

"You wouldn't want to come in and screw your boss's wife by any chance, would you?" she asked.

She was serious. At least, I thought she was serious. No, she was definitely serious.

"I'm flattered, Sally," I replied. "I'm also pretty sure it would be right up there on the list of all-time bad career moves."

She flipped down the visor and checked her lipstick in the vanity mirror. "So you're saying no to me?"

"In a sense . . . yes."

She continued to look into the mirror. "Aren't you afraid that I could get mean, irrational, dare I say spiteful, and tell Jack that you did something horrible today?"

"But I didn't."

"That's beside the point!" she snapped. "Aren't you afraid that I could jeopardize your precious career?"

"Of course I am."

She flipped the visor back up, looked at me, and frowned. I'm sure she was expecting a more combative answer, or if not that, one delivered with a discernible quiver in my voice. She had gotten neither. Sally shook her head and reached for the door, though not without leaving me with a parting thought.

"You pussy."

Minutes later, I remained sitting alone in the car, unsure of my next move. I was about to get out, when a short Hispanic man in overalls came from around the side of the garage. He opened the passenger-side door and got in without uttering a word. He smelled of soil and sweat.

"You must be Hector," I said.

"Sí," he told me.

THIRTEEN

The very next morning, a Friday, I sat in my office with Peter Sheppard discussing the Brevin Industries case. We were defending them against a shareholder's derivative suit alleging that the company intentionally misled investors with an overly optimistic securities prospectus. It was exciting stuff like that that filled the small remaining portion of my brain that wasn't already consumed by Sally Devine or Tyler Mills.

Sheppard, or Shep, as everyone called him, was another attorney at the firm, a couple years my senior. He specialized in civil law. As there was an SEC investigation under way, I was helping him out with the criminal implications involved in the case. We got along famously. The summer before his freshman year in high school he had been paralyzed from the waist down in a freak water-skiing accident. "I ventured a little too close to shore," is how he described it. At the time, doctors had told him he'd never walk again, and so far they were right. That didn't mean he was ever going to stop trying, he was fond of saying.

Without question, Jack Devine wouldn't have hired

Shep out of Stanford Law if he hadn't thought he was
a damn good lawyer in the making. He was. That he
was also in a wheelchair, however, didn't hurt his
chances. According to Shep, Jack had referred to his
handicap only once when they first met. It was when he
asked point blank if it would bother Shep if juries were
swayed in their judgment merely out of sympathy for
his condition.

"Fuck, no," Shep claimed to have answered. I'm
pretty sure it was the response Jack was hoping for. Not
because he was looking to exploit Shep, but because he
couldn't afford to hire someone unable to accept a situation for what it was. In a dreamworld, no one would
think differently of Shep because he couldn't walk. In
the awake world—the only world where lawyers lived—
most people could never get past it. Often giving in to
it. That was the situation. You didn't have to like it, you
just had to accept it. Or in Shep's case, embrace it, which
was all the better. Because in the final tally, you'd like
to think the world owed him a little bit more than a
great parking spot at the mall.

We were interrupted by a single, loud knock. "Good
morning, gentlemen," said a familiar voice.

I looked up to see Jack standing in my doorway. He
wasn't smiling.

"Morning, Jack," said Shep.

I uttered something in kind.

"Shep, will you excuse us for a second?" Jack said.

"Certainly," said Shep. He looked at me with a quick
raise of his eyebrows and proceeded to joystick his
wheelchair into a two-point turn. "We'll catch up on the
Brevin case later," he said to me before motoring out

of my office. Jack stepped aside to let Shep through the doorway. He closed the door behind him.

"I had a long conversation with my wife last night," said Jack.

I swallowed hard. "Oh?" was all I could ultimately get out of my mouth.

Jack started to walk toward me. I immediately tried to calculate the odds of surviving a thirty-one-story rapid descent should I need to escape out the window. Or worse, should I be thrown out.

Jack sat down in one of the chairs facing my desk and continued, "I think you have some explaining to do."

She had fucked me over. That's all there was to it. Because I had spurned her advances, Sally Devine had followed through with her threat. I was finished. I stared at Jack and prepared for his wrath.

"What you need to explain," he said, stone-faced, "is how much you paid my wife to make her tell me how brilliant you were yesterday." With that, he broke into a grin. His huge, bellowing laugh followed. "You did a nice job, so I was told. Quick and painless. Thanks."

"You're welcome," I said, remembering to breathe again. I had nearly pissed in my pants. I reminded him that "We still have the DMV hearing to deal with, though."

"Do you know when it is?" he asked.

"No, not yet."

"Let me know when you do, okay?"

"Sure, no problem."

Jack reached into the pocket of his suit jacket and pulled out an envelope. He tossed it onto my desk.

"What's this?" I asked.

"Open it," he said.

I picked it up and slid my finger underneath the flap. I looked inside. It was filled with hundred-dollar bills.

"I guess I still have the same question," I said, somewhat taken aback. "What is this?"

"My poker game . . . I think you've heard about it. So happens we have an opening next time out. Consider the envelope your invitation, not to mention a little ante money. We play the last Wednesday of every month, Keens Steakhouse. T-bones at seven, dealer's choice at eight. Tell anyone around these hallways that you're going and I'll shove a deck of cards down your throat. That is, of course, if you're interested in playing. It's kind of high stakes."

I pretended to mull it over for a second. "You won't get pissed when I take all your money, will you?" I asked.

"Nothing would make me angrier."

"Then by all means, I'll be there."

Jack got up and opened the door to my office, turning back to me before leaving. "Sucker!" he declared.

I laughed. Then I counted. Thirty in all, for a total of three thousand. How he had arrived at that dollar amount, I didn't know. It seemed kind of random. Not that I was complaining. But as good as the money was, it wasn't the best part. For I had been invited to go where no man—and certainly no woman—at Campbell & Devine had ever gone. The much-rumored, ultra-sacred, and storied poker game hosted by none other than Jack Devine. The value of that? Let's just say it was enough to make Tracy's father come to mind. If you thought I was a player before, Lawrence Metcalf, get a load of me now.

With a broad smile I sealed the envelope and opened my briefcase to put it away. The smile was short-lived. My poker invitation euphoria was about to be seriously tempered. There, sitting in my briefcase, was one of the photos that Tyler had shown me at the Oyster Bar. One thing was for sure, it hadn't crawled in there by itself. I picked it up. Right there in black-and-white were Jessica and I leaving the hotel together.

"Philip?"

I nearly jumped out of my chair. Gwen had stepped into my doorway.

"Oh, I'm sorry, I didn't mean to scare you," she said.

"That's all right," I told her, trying to be discreet about putting the picture back and closing my briefcase.

"I wanted to let you know that I'm going to lunch now."

"Oh, yeah . . . um . . . sure."

She remained in my doorway. "Is everything all right?"

"Everything's fine," I assured her. She was about to walk away. "Actually, do you remember anyone coming by my office recently when I wasn't here?"

She thought for a second. "No, I don't—wait, there was some guy from the building who came by yesterday morning while you were out. He said he needed to check on the air-conditioning."

"Was he skinny, about my height?"

"I think so. Wait, should I not have let him in?" she said.

"No, it's okay. If he comes by again, though, it might be a good idea to ask to see his ID."

"You don't think he was really with the building?"

"Probably not."

Gwen did a minor panic. "You're kidding me; is anything missing? Did he take anything?"

Added was more like it.

"No, nothing's missing, Gwen. It's okay."

"Are you sure?"

"Yeah, I'm sure."

"If he comes by a second time and doesn't have any ID, can I kick him in the balls?" she asked.

"Be my guest."

Gwen left, and I opened up my briefcase again and took out the picture. I held it in my hands, staring at it. So this was how it was going to be. Tyler Mills was not about to disappear from my life so easily. Don't overreact, I told myself, he's merely screwing with you, the same way he screwed with all those people and their cell phones. What did he tell you eventually happened? That's right, the novelty wore off. He got bored and moved on to his next little caper. The next scheme.

I had gotten myself into another type of staring contest. Feeling the strain as I may have been, I still wasn't about to blink.

FOURTEEN

Let the games begin.

That Monday at the office saw a barrage of none-too-subtle missives via e-mail and fax. Josephine, sitting at her post in the reception area, had been gracious enough to supply Tyler with all the contact information he needed. As far as she knew, the polite guy claiming to be updating his files on the other end of the line was a representative from the very official sounding MFA. Otherwise known as "the Manhattan Following of Attorneys," she was told.

Clever, Tyler. Very clever.

The faxes came every hour on the hour. Never from the same location. The Wall Street Officenter. The Kinko's by Astor Place and later the one up on West Fifty-fourth. The Copy Quest on First Avenue. After Gwen handed me the first one with a curious look, I made sure to get all the rest on my own. It was sort of Pavlovian. I'd hear the distant ring of the office's main fax machine and off I would go—doing my nonchalant best to get to the machine before anyone else.

Sometimes the faxes were as simple as a single page

with a huge dollar sign on it. Other times they were more involved, like the one with the complete lyrics to the song "Every Breath You Take" by the Police written out in longhand, with the line "... *I'll be watching you*" in all caps. And still other times they were copies of the actual photographs of me and Jessica, too blurry and distorted by the fax machine to be comprehended by anyone else around the office besides myself. Precisely what Tyler wanted, I was convinced. This was about giving me the proper scare, you see, not giving me up.

Yet.

As for the e-mails, he sent them in bunches, one right after the other. The messages themselves were blank. Instead, he used the subject heading of each message to string together little warnings for me in my inbox. For example:

Sender	Subject
randall_shadow@yahoo.com	YOU
randall_shadow@yahoo.com	CAN RUN
randall_shadow@yahoo.com	BUT
randall_shadow@yahoo.com	YOU CAN'T
randall_shadow@yahoo.com	HIDE,
randall_shadow@yahoo.com	PHILLY. . . .

Granted, as intimidating messages go, what Tyler had to say lacked a certain originality. The Hemingway of harassment he was not. However, the way in which he delivered them had enough of a Big-Brother-cum-modern-day spin element to render me more than a little uncomfortable. Especially after I would block his address from Yahoo and a short time later there would be more e-mails from him through a different Web directory. If it wasn't Excite, it was Lycos. If it wasn't Hot-Bot, it was AltaVista. And so on.

The whole thing was silly. The whole thing was surreal. The whole thing was also something else entirely . . . getting to me. Tyler was proving himself to be quite relentless.

Then, come midweek, he branched out from my office.

"Someone's been calling and hanging up all day" was Tracy's greeting for me when I walked through the door at home that Wednesday night.

Splendid.

"Do they say anything?" I asked, trying to quell my sudden surge of anxiety.

"No, they just hang up after I say hello."

"You should've taken the phone off the hook."

"I would have except I was supposed to hear back on a freelance job today," she said. "Thankfully, the calls stopped a while back, though it was pretty annoying at the time."

"I'll bet."

She walked over and gave me a quick kiss. "How was your day?"

"Uneventful," I told her. Unless, that is, you would consider *eventful* my being held hostage by a fax machine while at the same time scrambling to delete hordes and hordes of e-mail messages off the system as fast as possible. "How was your day?"

"Fine," said Tracy. "I thought we'd order in tonight."

"Okay by me."

Half sausage and pepperoni, the other half broccoli and capers. The usual. You get one guess as to which half was mine and which half was hers. I was deciding whether or not to have one more slice when the doorbell rang.

"I'll get it," said Tracy.

I jumped up. "No, I'll get it."

He had slipped in behind another tenant, I told myself. Probably Mr. Hullen from the third floor. As we had no doorman, most everyone in the building was conscious about letting strangers in. Mr. Hullen, on the other hand, was barely conscious. He was a sixties holdover with the tie-dyed shirts to prove it. I was pretty sure he once had an acid flashback while riding with me in the elevator. Not only would he let Tyler in, he'd probably hold the door for him.

I looked through the peephole.

The distorted face I saw was not Tyler's. It belonged to our neighbor Sarah Prescott, queen of affectation. Her loft occupied the other half of the floor. The year before, *Architectural Digest* had done a spread on her minimalist approach to interior design and how it had become all the rage among New York–based Hollywood. She had been pretty much unbearable ever since.

"Hello, Sarah," I said, opening the door.

"Philip, Philip, Philip," she began, "I am *soooooo*, so sorry to intrude upon you like this; I trust you and your lovely wife have been well. I'm doing wonderfully, thank you."

"Would you like to come in?" I asked her.

"Oh, no, *noooooo*, that won't be necessary. You see, I simply came by to drop this off for you."

I looked down to see what "this" was. In Sarah's hand was a plastic bag, and I watched as she pulled out its rectangular contents.

"I hope you don't mind terribly that I took a look-see," she said, "but when the delivery boy said you weren't home and tried to leave it with me, I had to make sure what on earth it was."

What it was was a videotape. She handed it to me.

"I don't know about you," Sarah blabbed on, "but I just think Cary Grant was the epitome of style. Did you ever see that delicious home he lived in?"

I didn't hear her. I was too busy flipping over what I realized to be a movie cassette rental. The movie? *An Affair to Remember.*

Clever, Tyler. Very clever.

"What is it, honey?" I heard from the kitchen.

"A mix-up, I'm afraid," I said.

"Oh, hello, Sarah," said Tracy, appearing from around the corner.

"Why, don't you look smashing as ever, darling," said Sarah.

"And you as well," lied Tracy.

Tracy grabbed the tape out of my hand. "Oh, I love this movie!" she announced.

"I know, isn't it the best?" said Sarah.

"Let's watch it tonight, Philip," Tracy said.

"We're not even supposed to have it," I said. I looked on the box to see where it came from. "A-1 Movie on the Run," I read, "has made some kind of mistake."

"In our favor," said Tracy. "Would you like to stay and watch it with us, Sarah?"

"That is so, *soooooo* generous of you, but I can't, I truly can't." She lowered her voice and glanced to either side. "I'm supposed to meet with Bobby De Niro in the morning to discuss his new apartment, and there remains a great deal of work to be done by me in preparation."

The scary thing was, she was probably telling the truth.

And that's how it came to be. My spending the next two hours of my life, a life that I was slowly losing control over, watching *An Affair to Remember* with Tracy. Talk about a night to forget.

After the credits rolled, Tracy got ready for bed while I read *Robb Report* in the living room. The phone rang. Telling Tracy I would get it, I walked over to the portable sitting on an end table.

"Hello?"

"Did you enjoy the movie?" came his voice.

I hit the off button on the phone so hard and fast I nearly broke my thumb.

"Was it another hang-up?" Tracy called out from the bedroom.

"Yep," I called back. I was about to turn the phone back on to leave it off the hook when it rang again.

"Listen to me, you *motherfucker*," I said into the receiver. There was more where that intro came from, and I was about to deliver it all when a voice interrupted me. It was a guy's and it was familiar. The problem being that it wasn't Tyler's.

"Fucking hello to you too, Philip!" said Menzi.

Whoops.

I apologized to Menzi and explained that we'd been getting some crank calls. He recommended caller ID, and I told him that it was a really good idea. Which it was.

"Hope I'm not calling too late," Menzi said.

"Not at all," I assured him.

"Good. Listen, tomorrow night, you free?"

"Why, what's up?"

"Standard revelry. Lewd and lascivious behavior, public drunkenness, your basic misdemeanors. I've already lined up Connor and Dwight. You in?"

I didn't need to think about it. "Absolutely," I told him.

Absolutely anything to free my mind of Tyler.

FIFTEEN

Dwight showed up sporting this moussed-up coif that was perhaps only an inch short of being a pompadour. Menzi let him have it right away.

"Hey, Dwight?" he said.

"Hey, what?"

"Wayne Newton called; he wants his hair back."

Big laughs from Connor and me. Dwight, meanwhile, didn't see the humor. Besides, he was too busy preparing a retaliatory strike. It started with looking up at Menzi's receding hairline. Said Dwight, "Least I'm gonna have hair in a couple of years, you putz."

Tough crowd. Surviving the taunts and ribbing of your guy friends wasn't that different from political campaigning. If you didn't respond quickly and decisively against anything negative, you were dead in the water.

Another guy's night out had begun, and I was concentrating my hardest on having some worry-free fun. The scene was the Temple Bar, down on Lafayette Street. And I do mean scene.

"Christ! Check out the venetian on her," said Dwight,

causing the rest of us to look at a blonde walking by our stakeout at the bar. "Venetian," of course, referred to the horizontal blind–like ripple caused by the tug of a tight T-shirt between a woman's ample breasts. That Dwight could not only take notice of such a phenomenon but also have a term for it was what made him a truly unique specimen of a male. If he had any sense of duty to country, he would leave his brain to science.

As a group, particularly in the presence of alcohol and pretty women, the four of us weren't much into discussing earnest matters. Though with a few drinks under our belts, we got as close as we were capable of getting. In all seriousness, or so he claimed, Menzi wanted to know how Connor felt about Jessica's not taking his last name when they married. The question took Connor by surprise.

"What do you mean, like, was I upset?" he asked.

Menzi nodded. "Yeah, does it ever bother you?"

Connor started to fidget with a cocktail napkin. He was either thinking or stalling.

"You could always plead the Fifth, Connor," I said to fill the void.

"God, I hate lawyers," Dwight muttered under his breath.

"No, I was merely trying to decide how best to explain it," said Connor to me. He turned to Menzi. "Let me ask you a question. You've met Jessica, right?"

"Sure, a few times," Menzi said.

"You've talked to her, gotten to know her a little bit?" said Connor.

"Pretty much."

"So you'd say you have a fairly good sense of what type of person she is?"

"I guess so."

"Okay, then let me ask you a question. Does it surprise you that Jessica didn't take my last name?"

Menzi's brow furrowed. "When you put it that way, no."

"Me either," said Connor. He took a sip of his drink.

"Wait, you didn't answer *my* question," Menzi said.

"You mean whether it bothered me that Jessica didn't take my last name? The answer is no, it didn't. The reason is this: if something doesn't surprise me, it very rarely manages to bother me."

We all fell silent for a moment.

"Shit, that was kind of deep," remarked Dwight.

"Very deep," I concurred.

"Fuckin' Grand Canyon," said Menzi. "That settles it right there; the next two rounds are definitely on me."

As we continued to drink ourselves drunk, I found myself thinking about Connor . . . how his mind seemed to work, and his background. While I didn't know a lot about his childhood spent up in Providence, I knew that, like me, his upbringing was decidedly middle-class. Unlike me, though, he never felt he was really deserving of anything more. At least that was the sense I got. Connor was thankful for his lot in life. He said he had "fallen into" being a software programmer and never thought he'd ever be making the good money that he was. When I asked him once if he dreamed about starting his own company one day, he looked at me as if I had three heads. "I just like writing code," he said.

His was a passive presence. There was nothing outwardly aggressive or confrontational about Connor's personality. Which is not to say he wouldn't openly disagree with you, or find a back door through which to provoke you, only that he rarely, if ever, seemed to get emotional about things. The one exception, of course, was when he had confided in me about Jessica and how distant she was being with him. That wasn't cool, calm logic speaking that evening. No, that was something else altogether. That was his love for her.

Yet, as much as knowing that weighed on my conscience, I couldn't wait to get back together with Jessica. I couldn't help it. I missed her smell and the feel of her hair, cool to the touch. I missed the way she came, her back arching slowly like a drawbridge going up. I missed her keeping me clued in on her twelve-month plan to usurp that "bitch of a boss" of hers and head up the ad sales department at *Glamour*. Most of all, I missed the way I felt when I walked out of that hotel room after being with her. Utterly and completely saturated with life.

I stood to go to the bathroom. With one step I knew I was loaded.

Leaning against the wall at the urinal, I started to get that prickly feeling from head to toe. It was my bloodstream's way of telling me that the party was over. Shuffling to the sink, I stared into the mirror that hung above it. I pretty much looked the way I felt.

Cold water time.

After three handfuls to the face, I turned off the faucet and began to wipe my eyes. I opened them and my pupils flared.

Tyler was standing against the wall behind me.

I turned and he was gone—or had never been there—it didn't make a difference. I knew what was happening. Knew all too well. Tyler Mills had gotten inside my head.

SIXTEEN

In my bachelor days before Tracy, I met this young, pretty thing named Melissa late one Saturday night at the Bubble Lounge. Within the first few minutes of our conversation she made a point of telling me that she was once almost "Miss November" in *Playboy*, having ultimately lost out to, quote, *this bitch from Texas*. With that, I was treated to a dissertation on the whole gestalt of posing nude.

"The Southern girls always get the centerfold," Melissa insisted. "Especially if you're from that lonely star state."

"Lone star," I corrected her.

"What?"

"Never mind." At that point I was pretty sure the Alamo to her was a rental car company.

Melissa went on. "It's the same with beauty pageants. Did you ever notice how many times Miss Texas goes on to win Miss America?"

I hadn't, I told her.

"It's like a conspiracy or something. Men seem to have this thing in their pants for girls from Texas. Why is that?" Melissa asked.

"Probably because they've never had the privilege of getting to know you better," I answered.

She blushed. I was in.

After taking Melissa back to my place for the night, however, I made an error in judgment the following morning. Lying next to me was this beautiful girl who, most likely because of her minimum-wage background, lacked any real measure of refinement. As if conducting some kind of sociological experiment, I decided on the spot to see how much impact a mass infusion of culture could have on her. It was very *My Fair Lady* of me, minus the wager.

In the weeks that followed, we MoMAed and Guggenheimed, truffled and foie gras-ed, and collected more Playbills than I would care to own up to. The "Appreciation of the Finer Things in Life Tour," I dubbed it. All of it on me. Mind you, I didn't really have the deepest of pockets back then. Anything for science, though, right? Besides, I was getting laid on a nightly basis.

Anyway, after about a month, I took Melissa to the symphony at Avery Fisher Hall. Beethoven and Wagner. Very heavy. To that point my little experiment had shown mixed results. For example: while she had learned that her bread plate was always to her left, she was still pronouncing the *g* in gnocchi. (*Ga-no-key*, she would say.) Like Rome, Melissa would not be built in a day.

That evening, I discovered that she would not be built at all. It happened during the intermission. Amid an elbow-to-elbow crowd of well-heeled ladies and gents, she asked me, after looking up from her program, if Wagner was any relation to the actor Robert Wagner. ("Because I just loved him in that *Hart to Hart* TV series," she added.) I, for one, was perfectly willing to dispense with any discussion of German pronunciation and simply answer that there was no relation between the two men. Unfortunately, there were these two women to our left who had overheard Melissa and felt the need to laugh and whisper in each other's ear. That really got Melissa's Bronx up. Without hesitation she turned to them and asked, "What the fuck is so funny?!" She then turned back to me and waited for her boyfriend to step in and stick up for her. I didn't. Not that I was embarrassed. It was more like I was having an out-of-body experience, paralyzed and capable only of watching, not acting. That's when Melissa let me have it. Profanity, tears, finger-pointing. All of it pretty much bouncing off of me except for one part, the moment when she screamed at the top of her lungs, "YOU MAKE ME FEEL LIKE A FUCKING PROSTITUTE, YOU ASSHOLE!" Finally, before storming off and never being heard from again, she threw her drink in my face. Apparently word had failed to reach her that such a stunt was only performed in the movies.

When you're dripping wet it's tough to maintain an out-of-body experience. Embarrassment set in. After looking around to see the entire symphony audience, not to mention every bartender and usher, staring at me, I accepted the handkerchief of a bearded man standing nearby. "Keep it," he said with a hand on my shoulder. "You strike me as a guy who may need it again."

That was the last time I was at Lincoln Center.

———

Encore. It had been more than four years, but Philip Randall was finally setting foot back in Philip Johnson's Lincoln Center Plaza. It was my fervent hope that the turnover rate among the staff was such that no one would have cause to remember me. Worst-case scenario: *Hey, look, there's the guy who made that poor girl feel like a prostitute!*

The evening was to be a benefit concert followed by a three-hundred-dollar-a-plate reception with all proceeds going to breast cancer research. It didn't get any more PC than that. When Tracy had first told me that Jessica's mother was providing the tickets for the four of us, I assumed that the whole shindig would be gratis. Not until I was putting on my tuxedo did Tracy clarify that the tickets were merely for the concert. The reception was our financial responsibility. The way she said it, I could tell she was thinking that I'd be mad. Not about the money. Rather, Tracy knew that nothing got my goat more than the notion of a "gift" that required you to reach into your own wallet. If it wasn't for the fact that I was finally having my chance to reconcile with Jessica (albeit with our spouses in tow), I probably would've been a jerk about it. Instead, I simply smiled and made a lame joke. Something about how we shouldn't think of it as six hundred dollars for the two of us, but more like three hundred bucks a breast. Though I wasn't exactly sure why that was funny, Tracy managed to get a chuckle out of it. She was in a good mood.

I wasn't so bad off myself.

For as quickly as it had all started, it had all stopped.

There were no more pictures in my briefcase. No more e-mails, no more faxes, no more hanging up on Tracy. No more free movie rentals showing up on our doorstep. In short, there was no more Tyler.

I tried not to kid myself. Maybe all he was doing was taking a breather. His kind of vexation, when you thought about it, wasn't easy. It was hard work. A few days off and he'd be right back at it again. Good as new. This was simply the calm before the next storm.

But a big part of me couldn't help thinking that there would be no next storm, that Tyler had given it his best shot and I had weathered it. He had now grown bored of me, as I'd initially thought he might, perhaps moving on to his next victim. For his sake, someone without the same backbone construction as Philip Randall. Yes, that's what a big part of me couldn't help thinking.

The part of me otherwise known as my ego.

The concert began at seven. The arrangement was to meet Connor and Jessica out front by the fountain at six-forty-five. Tracy and I were a few minutes early. As we stood there waiting, I couldn't get over the fact that I was a bit nervous. I took a nickel out of my pants pocket and tossed it into the water. Some inconspicuous time alone with Jessica that evening. That's what I wished for.

"Do we clean up nice or what?" came Connor's voice from about twenty feet away. I turned to see him and Jessica heading toward us.

"Shit, you almost border on handsome," I called out to him in response.

The girls kissed, the guys shook, and we switched. Like I always did in these situations, I gave Jessica a peck on the cheek. As my lips touched her flesh, I was afforded a brief glimpse into the world of necrophilia. She couldn't have been any further removed from me.

Tracy and Jessica immediately paired off and told each other how great they looked. Neither one was lying. Meanwhile, Connor and I talked guy stuff. Our jobs, the market, when the Knicks would be eliminated from the play-offs. Before we knew it, it was a minute before the concert was to start. We rushed inside.

Whisking through the lobby and hurriedly walking down the aisle, I jockeyed for position. A seat next to Jessica. It was like being back in gym class when you had to line up and count off by fours to make teams. All you'd be trying to do was rig it so you could end up together with your best buddy. Sometimes it worked, sometimes it didn't.

Reaching our row first, I stepped back for Tracy as if politely to say, after you. She was about to take me up on it when she stopped. Wait, I want to sit next to Jessica, she informed me. *That makes two of us, darling.* I nodded indifferently and went in before her. Damn. It didn't work.

The concert featured a collection of renowned musicians and vocalists, with Kiri Te Kanawa making a special appearance near the end. Although she'd always had a loyal and enthusiastic following among the opera set, it was interesting to me that Ms. Te Kanawa hadn't gained any real mass notoriety until her rendition of Puccini's "O Mio Babbino Caro" was used in a sparkling-wine commercial some years back. Given that it was for Ernest & Julio, I could only assume, as well as hope, that she got paid a boatload.

After about an hour and a half, we all stood and applauded. The lights came up, and the four of us agreed that we'd definitely been entertained. Shuffling out to the reception area, the girls went to find a bathroom. Connor and I went to find the bar.

I ordered and was handed my vodka tonic, after which Connor ordered a Newbury martini. By the time he had explained to the blank face of the rented bartender that it consisted of "a lot of gin, a little vermouth, and a splash of triple sec," I was ready for a refill. I kidded Connor. There's a place to do simple and a place to do complex, I told him. Here's a hint: any bar that has wheels on it is a sure sign to keep it simple. He laughed and took a sip of what was supposed to be a Newbury martini. Not even close, he said.

I decided that with the girls taking their time in the bathroom I would casually bring up the topic of him and Jessica. Curiosity had gotten the better of me. "How are things going?" I asked.

"I think you were right," he said, sounding a bit relieved. "Whatever was going on with her, I think it blew over. She seems fine . . . we're fine."

"Happy to hear it," I said.

We both took sips of our drinks, glancing around at the crowd in the process. It was amazing to see that there remained a few grown men in the world unaware that strictly circus clowns should wear red bow ties.

Said Connor a moment later, tacking on a word of thanks, "I appreciated the help, by the way . . . your advice and everything that night."

"Don't mention it—it was nothing."

"No, I'm serious, there aren't many friends I could've had that conversation with."

Ugh. That there was actually one fewer friend than he thought made my stomach turn. Guilt and nausea, it seemed, were starting to emanate from the same part of my brain.

I was spared having to respond as Tracy and Jessica returned from the bathroom. With them were Jessica's mother and brother, whom they had bumped into. While it made total sense, it hadn't occurred to me that they'd be there.

Jessica's mother, Mrs. Emily Levine, suffered from what was commonly referred to as Widow's Surrender, meaning that after the death of her husband, she had lost any real interest in maintaining her personal appearance. It wasn't as if she'd let herself go completely. In fact, with a box of Clairol, a month of SlimFast, and a day at Escada, she would pretty much have been back in the ball game.

"I think you'll agree with me, gentlemen," she said right away to Connor and me, "that I've got the best-looking escort in the entire place."

Another symptom of Widow's Surrender: dragging your son to social functions as your date.

We heartily agreed with her escort assessment as Jessica's brother, Zachary, rolled his eyes. He was twenty-eight, unmarried, and essentially unmotivated when it came to anything that remotely resembled a job. Jessica called it laziness. Her mother feared that it was a by-product of the boy's not having had a father figure while growing up. Certainly she didn't blame herself for it, though as she made clear to Jessica when they would discuss and often argue about it, she didn't want to blame Zachary either. Consequently, the boy was given more slack by his mother than he knew what to do with. The fact that he still lived at home with her at his age pretty much said it all.

"How did you enjoy the music?" Mrs. Levine asked the group of us.

"It was wonderful," I quickly answered, allowing me to segue into thanking her for the tickets. Her so-called gift. "It was awfully kind of you to think of us," I told her. "We must figure out a way to return the favor." Only Tracy could detect the hint of sarcasm in my voice and in doing so she gave me a fixed glare. I simply beamed a smile back at her.

The conversation turned to politics. Then movies. Then gossip. As a member of the committee responsible for the evening's festivities, Jessica's mother was in the know on many of the more recognizable guests in attendance. As she lowered her voice a few decibels, it was clear that she possessed little if any reluctance to revealing some of their secrets. A walking, talking version of Page Six in the *Post*, she was. I listened to who was "shtupping" who and which corporate executive was about to be unceremoniously ousted while intermittently stealing fast looks at Jessica. She seemed to be as amused as she was mortified by her mother's behavior. *I can't believe I came out of this woman*, I pictured Jessica thinking. As for me, all I was thinking about was when the hell I was going to be able to talk to her alone.

The time eventually came, though not until late into the night. It was right after dessert. We were at a table for eight, six of whom had seen fit to disappear for one reason or another. The two important chair vacancies, Connor and Tracy, had gone, respectively, to wait in line at the bar and to say hello to a friend she recognized from a previous freelance job. With but the space of an empty seat between us, the time was perfect. Especially because Jessica had passed on the chance to make an excuse to leave. It was as if she knew our conversation was inevitable. It didn't make sense for her to avoid it any longer.

"I've missed you," I told her.

Her reply surprised me. "I've missed you too."

"Then why did you keep hanging up on me when I called?"

"Because whether or not I missed you doesn't make it all better."

"What would?" I asked.

"I'm not sure, to be honest with you. All I know is that when you told me about Connor's suspicions, I nearly lost it."

"Yes, I know, I was there."

"You didn't exactly help the situation."

"You're right; I apologize. The whole thing had me pretty wound up as well," I said. "If it's any consolation, Connor seems to be in a much better frame of mind."

"The two of you talked about it again?"

"Briefly. Earlier tonight, as a matter of fact. I didn't

want to dwell on it, as you might imagine. At the same time, I didn't want to pretend we never had the initial conversation."

"What'd he say?"

"That whatever was going on with you appeared to have blown over."

"I suppose that's a relief. It wasn't easy," she said.

"If you don't mind, I'd just as soon not hear about your efforts."

"I was merely taking your advice."

"That you were. Which reminds me . . . the butterfly?"

She laughed. "Read about it in *Cosmo*. Did it bother you?"

"Like you wouldn't believe."

We sat there for a bit without any words. There was a six-piece band playing, and I listened as they finished Billy Strayhorn's "Take the A Train" and immediately launched into Louis Prima's "Sing, Sing, Sing." Apparently it was big band night. That or a tribute to dead composers.

Jessica turned to me. "Have you ever had a defining moment?" she asked.

"That depends. What do you mean?"

"Something that alters your entire outlook on life."

I thought for a second. "Does being born count?"

"I'm serious," she said.

"In that case, the answer is no, I don't think so. I take it you have?"

"Yes," she said. "It was the day after my wedding."

"What happened?"

"Our limo to the airport didn't show up."

"That changed your life?"

"No. But the cab ride we had to hail instead did."

"How so?"

"It was something the driver said. He was this older guy, superfriendly, and in the middle of the ride he was asking us where we were flying to. Connor tells him about St. Bart's and explains that it's our honeymoon. The driver congratulates us and starts to gush about his own honeymoon and how much he loves his wife. It was really sweet.

"So we continue to talk, and at one point the driver asks if we'd like to hear his definition of love. Sure, we tell him, why not? He straightens up in his seat and says, *'Love is when you care about someone more than you care about yourself.'* With that, he glances back at us for our reaction. Connor looks at me and says to the guy, 'That's very well put; I think you're absolutely right.' Meanwhile, I'm looking back at Connor, and do you know what I'm saying? I'm saying to myself, 'I think I've just made one of the biggest mistakes of my life.'"

It was probably a shut-up moment, but I spoke anyway. "Okay, so you realized that you didn't love Connor," I said calmly.

"Worse," said Jessica. "It was as if Connor had nothing to do with it. What I realized was that according to this guy, I was incapable of loving *anyone.*"

I looked straight at her. "Forgive me for saying this, Jessica, but we're talking about a cab driver here. At best, one man's opinion."

"Yeah, but the problem was I didn't think he was wrong, and for sure Connor didn't either. There were the three of us in the cab, and people in cars all around us, and yet, at that moment I never felt more alone in my life."

"So let me guess—you had an affair," I said.

"No, what I had was a tremendous desire to stop feeling alone," said Jessica. "Which brings me to you, or should I say, brought me. Because on that first night when you rode back with me in, of all things, another cab, for the first time in a long time, I no longer felt alone."

"I'd be flattered if I didn't know better," I said. "What you're saying is that misery loves company. Or is it narcissism loves company?"

"I prefer the expression 'two peas in a pod,' myself. It's not as condemning."

"What makes you so sure I'm incapable of loving someone?"

"Call it a hunch." She shrugged. "You're the lawyer, though. Feel free to prove me wrong if you want."

"The thing is, you never would've told me all this if you thought for one minute that I could."

"Funny how that works, huh?"

"Hilarious," I said. "Anything else you want to get out into the open?"

"No, that's it," she answered. "You can only hold a mirror up to a relationship for so long."

"So now what?"

"Haven't thought that far ahead. I'll need a little more time to think things over. Maybe you should do the same."

"Don't need to," I told her.

"Then I'll try not to keep you waiting too long."

Soon thereafter, Tracy returned to the table. Connor wasn't far behind. He had long since given up on his Newbury martini, opting instead for gin and tonics. The four of us sat for a few minutes and chatted. The band began to play "April in Paris," and we all got up to dance. Midsong, Tracy reminded me of her idea of the two of us going there.

"This is fate," she said. "We should go next April. We can send my mother a postcard telling her about all our PMFs."

I didn't get it right away.

"Paris-Made Friends, silly," she explained.

"Of course," I told her. "Though they'll definitely have to live within the Paris city limits. None of those poseurs from Versailles."

"Definitely not," she said, playing along. "We do have our reputations to think of, you know."

We both laughed and, going with the moment, I stepped back and twirled Tracy around. In doing so I happened to catch Jessica peering at me over Connor's shoulder. She was too smart, too collected, to be jealous, and had there been any question about that before the evening started, our conversation had certainly put it to rest.

Nonetheless, it couldn't have hurt my cause.

SEVENTEEN

That Wednesday in my office, four days later. It was a couple of minutes past noon. My direct phone line rang and I picked up the receiver. "Hello?"

"Room three-eleven."

"Okay," I said. I was about to say more when I heard an all-too-familiar *click* on the other end. This one, however, I didn't mind.

The moratorium on Philip had ended.

I dusted off my gym bag, had Gwen reschedule a conflicting appointment, and within minutes I was on my way back to the Doral Court hotel, a measurable spring in my step. I walked into the lobby and hopped onto a waiting elevator. Third floor. When I arrived at the room, the door was open about an inch. Walking in, I didn't say a word. I simply peeked around the corner at the bed. There, lying atop the covers, was Jessica. Completely naked.

There were no hellos. No rehashing of our last conversation. Just sex. Colossal sex. It was one of those sessions where we had to check each other for scratches and bite marks when we finished. Not that that was anytime soon. Once on the bed. Once on the chair near the bed. Once in the shower, a previously never-before-tried location for the two of us. "If I'm the one paying for the room," said Jessica, whispering in my ear at one point, "I want to be sure to take full advantage of all the amenities."

After, wrapped in towels, we settled back into the bed and traded jokes about how we'd be sore for days. Jessica nearly forgot that she had brought lunch. Salads from Pasqua. We ate and talked about everything and nothing, at one point who we'd want to be if not ourselves. Anyone in history.

Cleopatra, said Jessica.

Euripides, said I.

The following day saw an encore performance, the lone difference being that we exchanged once in the shower for twice on the bed. A thousand calories burned between us, we were lying side by side and staring up at the stucco ceiling. For whatever reason, Jessica wanted to talk about my brother. That made one of us.

"Have you heard from Brad recently?" she asked.

"No, not recently."

"How do you think his painting is coming along?"

"I guess okay."

"Does he like living in Portland?"

I shrugged. "I assume so."

"Is he dating anyone?"

"I don't know."

Jessica frowned. "You don't like to talk about him much, do you?"

I wasn't about to admit it. "I've got no problem talking about my brother," I told her.

"How about talking *to* your brother, though?"

I turned my head and looked at her. "This is a bed, not a couch, Jessica."

"I'm not trying to be a shrink, Philip. I just want to know what's up between you and your brother. You said you were really close as kids."

"We were."

"So what happened?"

"Nothing happened," I said. "You grow up, you have less in common. He wears jeans and paints all day. I wear suits and go to court. We're different, that's all."

"That's no reason not to be close," she said. "He's still your brother—your only brother, I might add."

She was pissing me off. But with how much we'd been through in the past few weeks, I was determined not to get into a fight over it. "Okay, you're right," I told her. "I should probably do a better job of keeping in touch with Brad, shouldn't I?"

"Yes, you should," said Jessica. She smiled and let it go at that, although she probably suspected there was a little bit more to the story.

She was right.

It turned out that Brad didn't like what his older brother had grown up to be. He didn't like what I did for a living or who I had married, and he didn't have any problem telling me so to my face a couple of years back while visiting over Christmas. A stubborn *and* outspoken little bastard. He claimed I was no better than the people I represented and that I had sold out for the almighty dollar.

In return, I told Brad that he was a charlatan of ideals. That if he could, he would sell his paintings for a million bucks a pop. To a pimp, to a dope dealer, to the fucking Antichrist, so long as they had the cash in hand. The desire for fame and fortune had no less of a grip on him than it did on me. He knew it, and I knew it. I told him that what he really didn't like was the fact that his older brother could buy every piece he'd ever sold to that point with one month's paycheck—and still have enough money left over to buy him some art lessons.

We nearly came to blows. Brad caught the next flight back to Portland and we rarely if ever spoke thereafter. We had argued before, plenty of times. This time was different. There was permanence to it. Things said that couldn't be taken back or easily forgotten with an apology.

And all because of one question.

I had asked Brad what he planned to do if he couldn't make it as an artist.

EIGHTEEN

Y̶ou're only as good as your next reservation. . . .
 It was another Saturday night and another dinner out for the four of us. Connor and Jessica, Tracy and me. This time at Balthazar. The topic at the table was religion, specifically the age-old question as to the existence of God. We weren't even stoned.

Jessica was making the case that there had to be some form of higher being. Otherwise, we'd have no explanation for what preceded the universe. Before there was something, she pointed out, there still had to be *something*. There couldn't have been *nothing*. It was that paradox that had her convinced there was some type of deity out there.

Connor disagreed. "Okay, let's assume you're right, that there is in fact a god out there. I have one question. Who or what created him?"

"Or *her?*" Tracy was quick to allow for.

Jessica seemed ready to answer when we were interrupted—though at the moment, I was more inclined to say spared—by a waiter brandishing a bottle of Perrier-Jouët and four champagne glasses. As he began to place a glass in front of each of us, we all looked at one another.

"Excuse me," I said to the waiter, "I think there's been a mistake. We didn't order this."

"No mistake, sir," he replied. "This is courtesy of the gentleman at the bar."

We all turned and looked over in unison. I saw him first. Probably because he was looking directly back at me. There, sitting at the bar, was Tyler, and this time he was really there.

Welcome to Risk Factor 8.

"I don't believe it; it's Tyler," Tracy announced.

"Who?" Jessica asked.

"Tyler Mills. He's a friend of ours, actually more a friend of Philip's. The two of them went to Deerfield together," she explained.

I sat there stunned, staring at Tyler, while Tracy began to wave hello to him across the restaurant. He acknowledged her with a wave back, prompting Tracy to motion for him to come over. He seemed all too happy to oblige.

I braced myself for the next storm.

Pop! went the champagne as I watched Tyler leave his bar stool and start to head our way, weaving through tables.

"Good buddy of yours?" Connor asked me as the waiter began to pour.

"Casual acquaintance at best," I said, leaning in a bit. "To be honest, kind of a loser."

"A loser, however, with great taste in champagne," said Connor.

I faked finding that amusing. Tyler arrived.

"This is so funny!" Tracy said, standing up to give him a hug. "You and I have to stop meeting like this."

"I know—first Saks, now here," he said. "What a co-incidence."

Tracy pointed at her glass. "This was so nice of you, but totally unnecessary."

"The best things in life are," was his response.

Tracy smiled.

Tyler turned to me. "How are you, Philip?"

I stood up and put out my hand to shake his. "I'm doing okay," I said. "What a surprise to see you."

"I can only imagine. Did you get my e-mail?"

"Yes, and your fax as well."

"Glad to hear it."

Tyler was dressed in a sport coat and tie, hair slicked back. The consummate "man about town" costume. It helped him appear not at all as sickly as when we had last met. I continued to stare at him. I wondered if it was only my evening that he planned on ruining.

"I want you to meet some friends of ours," Tracy said to Tyler. "This is Connor. . . ."

Connor did a half stand from his chair and shook Tyler's hand. "Tracy was wrong, by the way; this was totally necessary," he joked, raising his glass. "Thanks."

"My pleasure," Tyler said.

Tracy continued. "And this is Jessica. . . ."

I watched as Tyler extended his hand to her and the two made eye contact. He instantly appeared perplexed.

"My, you look awfully familiar. Have we met before?" he asked Jessica.

"Gee, I don't think so," she replied.

Tyler shook his head and shot me a quick glance before looking back at Jessica. "I don't know, it's strange, it's like I've seen you somewhere before," he told her.

My knees were starting to buckle.

"So what brings you here?" Tracy asked Tyler.

"The food, normally," he said. "It's so good I'm willing to overlook how disgustingly trendy this place is. Though tonight, I only stopped by to pick up a credit card that I had left behind here a couple of days ago. They were holding it for me behind the bar. That's when I looked up and saw you guys. Small world, isn't it?"

"Well, the least you can do is join us in a glass of your champagne," Tracy said.

"Yes," said Jessica, seconding the motion.

Tyler looked down at his watch. "I'm supposed to be meeting a friend uptown," he said, hedging, "though I suppose maybe I can stay for one drink."

"Oh, good!" said Tracy, immediately flagging down a waiter to ask for an extra glass.

We had one of the perimeter tables at Balthazar, which meant where Connor and Jessica were sitting was part of one long continuous booth. Connor, ever the nice guy, slid over to make room for Tyler. If he had only known. That's when I decided that in a previous life, Connor had probably been the gatekeeper in Troy.

So there we sat, all cozylike. Me, my wife, the woman I was having an affair with, the husband of the woman I was having an affair with, and the guy who knew about the affair and was trying to blackmail me for a hundred grand so he'd keep his mouth shut. More champagne, anyone?

"Tell me, what conversation did I interrupt before coming over?" Tyler asked.

"We were discussing whether or not God exists," said Jessica.

"Oh, that's an easy one," Tyler responded. "God definitely exists."

"Oh, he does, does he?" said a suspect Connor.

"Sure, only he's not a *he*," replied Tyler.

Tracy sparked to the comment. "I know, isn't it amazing how everyone assumes God has a penis?"

"You're saying God is a woman?" Connor asked Tyler.

"No, I didn't say that. What I said was that there's a simple explanation for God."

"And that is?" said Connor.

"Fear," Tyler said.

"You mean, as in the *fear of God?*" asked Connor.

"No, as in the fear *is* God," was Tyler's reply. With that, he had the floor. "You see, God is nothing more than human fear. Think about it. If there was no fear in this world, would anyone still believe in God? If there were no plane crashes, no diseases, no homicides to speak of; if we all knew for sure that there was no afterlife, no hell to be afraid of, or no heaven to be afraid of not getting into, would anyone still believe in God? Of course not." He looked at Connor. "That's why they call it the fear of God, only they don't know that's why they call it that. That omnipresent entity that we pray to doesn't exist out there in space, it exists inside us. God is merely the fear that each and every one of us harbors."

It was time for commentary around the table. Though I was fairly certain that Tyler had lost the rest of us pretty much after *Think about it*. Nonetheless, as a diatribe, it had the appearance of being profound, which was pretty much all you needed to get by in this city. Tracy, for one, was eating it up.

"So I guess we have nothing to fear but God itself," she said, being clever.

Tyler smiled. "Something like that."

Quite the impression our table guest was making. The jittery banter and manic interjections that had dominated our chat at the Oyster Bar were nowhere to be found. The Tyler that night at Balthazar was articulate and insightful. Dare I say charming. One thing was for certain: he was loving every minute of it.

"Philip, you've been awfully quiet. What do you think?" Tracy asked me.

I was in a daze. "Huh?"

"About God being the fear that's inside of us," she said. But before I could answer, her expression abruptly changed. "My god, honey, look at you, you're sweating. Are you okay?" Tracy put her hand on my forehead. "You feel hot. You must be coming down with something."

I started to wipe my face with my napkin. "No, I'm fine. It's a little warm in here, that's all."

But the more I wiped, the more I seemed to sweat. The armor was cracking. It was probably only Tyler who could tell, but that was enough. The fact that at any moment he could send my world tumbling was more than taking its toll on me. I was about to do something that I never thought I would do.

I was about to blink.

I cleared my throat. "I think we should toast," I said, with an eye on Tyler, "to all of us having a lot less to fear in the days ahead."

We all clinked and sipped. Tyler put his glass down

and looked at his watch again. "I really have to be going," he announced. Tracy protested to no avail. Tyler explained that he couldn't keep his friend waiting any longer. He stood and told Connor and Jessica how good it was to meet them. "How long have you two been married?" he asked them.

"Close to a year," Jessica said.

"Newlyweds," remarked Tyler. "Isn't that something? I wish you the very best of luck."

"Thanks," said Connor.

"It was really great to see you, Tyler," Tracy said. "Maybe next time we can actually plan something."

"Funny you should say that, because a thought did occur to me after we bumped into each other outside of Saks," he said. "I remembered how you'd once told me that you were a graphic designer. Do you still do that?"

"It's becoming more and more past tense these days, but yes," replied Tracy.

"Reason I ask is that recently I've taken up photography again. Philip can tell you how that was kind of my thing back at Deerfield. Anyway, I was wondering if you might be willing to lend your artistic eye to some of my recent pictures? That is, if you have the time."

"I'm flattered," Tracy said. "I'd love to see them."

"Great. Tell you what, let me give you my number—it's my pager number, actually. That's the best way to reach me." Tyler reached inside his sport coat and took out a pen, and with a little digging in his side pockets produced a notepad. How convenient. He wrote the number down and handed it off to Tracy, not before glancing at me one last time. "When you want to set something up," he said, "call it and I'll call you right back."

To think, everyone thought he was talking to Tracy.

"May God bless you!" said the homeless man on the corner as Tracy handed him our doggie bag from Balthazar. I didn't have the heart to tell the poor guy that his god was apparently nothing more than his inner fear. He looked like he had enough problems.

There was no going out that night after dinner. A precautionary measure, according to Tracy, due to my earlier profuse sweating. We said good-night to Connor and Jessica and walked a bit before catching a cab. "The fresh air will be good for you," claimed Tracy.

"Yes, doctor," I told her.

We walked a couple of blocks.

"You don't like Tyler much, do you?" said Tracy out of nowhere.

I looked at her strangely, the way she expected me to. "What makes you say that?"

"I can tell. You act the same way around him as you do around my cousin Richard, and I know you don't like him."

"Oh, yeah? How is it that I act?"

"Removed," she said.

"I do?"

"A little standoffish, as well."

"Gee, anything else?" I asked facetiously.

"No, that's it. Removed and a little standoffish."

"I guess all I can say is that I don't mean to."

"I'm not saying it's deliberate, necessarily."

"But you definitely sense it."

She nodded. "Absolutely."

"You're right about your cousin Richard, by the way. I do think he's an idiot."

"So do I, actually," she said. "I happen to think Tyler, though, is quite fascinating."

"Fascinating, eh?"

"Not that you have anything to be jealous about. I'm sure he's still got some issues."

Like you wouldn't believe.

Back at our loft . . .

There was only one thing on my mind at that point—copying down Tyler's pager number from an unknowing Tracy, especially after I ducked into our laundry room as she was undressing to call information. As I had suspected, Tyler Mills wasn't listed.

So I waited until Tracy went to the bathroom before going to bed. That's when I rifled through her Kate Spade and found the number. She had tucked it away in her wallet right next to our wedding picture. Oh, the irony.

NINETEEN

The following morning I told Tracy that I was going out to pick up some bagels. Within minutes of my paging him from a pay phone, Tyler called me back.

"Nice stunt," I said.

"I thought you'd like it," was his reply. "It seemed fitting. Did you know that *balthazar* is actually a term for an oversized champagne bottle?"

"Twelve liters, to be exact," I said arrogantly. It was amazing how much useless information I had picked up from hanging around the Metcalfs. I changed the subject, or rather, got back to it. "So, Tyler, you really want to blackmail me, huh?"

"Philip?"

"Yeah?"

"Take your finger off the record button," he said calmly.

Measured indignation. "I'm not recording you, Tyler."

"Yes, you are," he said. "Besides, don't you know that secretly taping someone is illegal in New York?"

He was right . . . on both counts. Nonetheless, I continued to hold my old Olympus Pearlcorder L200 up to the receiver. Not that he was about to incriminate himself over the phone.

"If you're ready to talk, we do it in person and we do it in public," Tyler told me.

"Okay, where?"

"Bryant Park. Four o'clock tomorrow afternoon. Sit on one of the benches along the Forty-second Street side. I'll be along shortly thereafter."

He hung up.

That next day, a Monday, at a few minutes before four, I entered Bryant Park and found an empty bench in the area Tyler had told me. I sat and waited. The heat of the day had begun to wane, as had much of the crowd that usually filled the lawn there. Those who remained truly had nothing else to do. There was an elderly woman sitting on the bench directly opposite mine, about fifteen feet away. She was staring off into space. With her sat a younger woman who, though dressed in street clothes, was most likely her nurse. She was reading a book. I strained to see the title, but I couldn't make it out.

"Nice to see you again, Philly."

I looked up and saw Tyler standing there before me with the same black duffel bag he originally had at the Oyster Bar. He was all smile. As he sat down, he asked me how I was doing.

"I'm here, that's how I'm doing," I told him curtly.

"That you are."

Tyler reached down into the duffel and removed a

small boxlike device. He held it in the air and gazed at it. "You know, I always used to think a gadget like this was strictly the stuff of secret agents. Lo and behold, now every Joe off the street can own one. Spy stores, I tell you, they're amazing. Veritable meccas for James Bond wanna-bes everywhere." He pushed a button and began to wave the device over my legs.

"What the fuck are you doing?!" I said, recoiling.

"Hey, you're the one with the recording fetish," he replied, moving the device up to my arms and torso.

I assured him, "I don't have a tape recorder on me."

"You'll forgive me if I don't take your word for it. To be on the safe side, this little baby vibrates if you do. Pretty nifty. It also picks up wires. You ought to look into getting one."

"I'll make a note of it."

Tyler finished up on me with his little toy. He turned it off and put it back into the duffel bag.

"Are you sure you're satisfied?" I asked him sarcastically.

"Think of it this way," he said. "The choices were making you strip down, frisking you, or this. Be glad that it was this."

What a guy.

Sitting there listening to him, I happened to look over at the nurse and the elderly woman. The nurse had been watching us. Caught in the act, she quickly dropped her eyes back into the book and resumed her reading.

"Shall we talk money?" asked Tyler, cutting to the chase. It was the setup line for which I'd been waiting. I figured it was my last chance to reason with him.

"Seriously, Tyler, how do you expect me to pay you a hundred thousand dollars?" I asked.

"I don't," came his response. "I expect you to pay me a hundred and *twenty-five* thousand."

"What the hell are you talking about?! You said—"

"I know what I said. Except that's before you decided to flex your dick and walk out on our little lunch. Yes, the original price was a hundred thousand. The thing is, if you'd stuck around, you would have known that it was a one-time-only offer. You didn't stick around, though, did you? So now the new price—cha-ching!—is a hundred and twenty-five thousand. Ain't life a bitch?!"

That crazed look in Tyler's eyes, which up until that point had been dormant, was back, as well as his love of the interjection. *Cha-ching?*

"Tyler, there's one thing I've got to know," I began, trying to invoke my most sincere tone. "Why the hell are you doing this to me?"

"Doing what?"

"*This!* The whole blackmail thing. Why are you doing this to me?"

"I tend to think you did it to yourself."

"The affair? Okay, yeah, I fucked up. As for what the hell it has to do with you, though, I have no idea. If it's only about the money, then fine, I'll pay you the stinking money. But the more I think about it, the more I think there's something else going on here . . . some other reason for you doing this."

Tyler had but one thing to say. "Care to make it one fifty?"

I wisely backed off for a moment. Silence ensued. Again, I caught the nurse watching us. I still couldn't make out the book she was reading, though whatever it was, it was obviously nowhere near as interesting as the two guys talking on the bench across from her. I couldn't begin to imagine what she thought the little box was that the thin one with the duffel bag had been waving around.

I pressed Tyler again, this time on a different front. "C'mon, Tyler, is this really what you're all about, your reason for living?"

He wasn't buying. Not for a moment. "You know what your fucking problem is?!" he snapped. "You're not asking me this bullshit out of concern for me. You're asking so you might weigh on my conscience, that I might have a change of heart—two things that I lost a long time ago. It's you and only you that you're worried about, Philly, and don't think I don't know that. Guys like you give selfish a bad name. Me? I'm just out for some money. But you? You're out for it all. Fact is, I'm doing this to you because I can, Philly, and don't even try to pretend you can't relate to that philosophy. Fuck, you *are* that philosophy."

It was time to cut my losses. I knew a losing cause when I saw one. Including when it was my own.

"Okay, I'll pay you the money. We'll split the difference on the extra twenty-five and round up," I said matter-of-factly. "Call it one fifteen."

Tyler let go with a short laugh. "This isn't a flea market, you schmuck. The amount isn't negotiable. One hundred and twenty-five thousand to the penny, and I want it tomorrow. Certified bank check."

So much for saving myself ten grand. As for the part about the certified bank check, I had expected as much. The part about the next-day delivery, however, was out of the question.

"I can't do it by tomorrow," I said.

"Why not?"

"It's not just getting the money," I explained, "it's getting the money so it's not missed. Big difference. I've got to shuffle around some accounts, three-card monte the balances. This isn't exactly an ATM withdrawal, you know?"

"When, then?"

"End of the week. I'll call you," I said.

He nodded. "The beautiful thing is I know you will. Otherwise it's show-and-tell time with Tracy and the pictures."

"Which reminds me, I'll want all of them and the negatives, of course."

"Why? You don't trust me?" He laughed.

"Can't imagine why not."

"Fine. Pictures plus the negatives," he said. "Hell, I've already given you one of the shots back."

"Yeah, I saw. Nice of you to have stopped by my office like that."

"Nice of you not to have been there. You know, while you're at it, you might also want to think about a combination lock briefcase."

Better to ignore him. "As for the pictures . . . how do I know you didn't make an extra set to keep for yourself?" I asked.

"You don't, ultimately—it's not something I can prove

to you. Blame it on Kodak, not me. In lieu of that, however, I thought I'd show you this." Tyler again reached down into the black duffel. He pulled out a business envelope. "Here," he said.

"What is it?"

"A little peace of mind, perhaps."

I opened the envelope. The first thing I saw was a big Delta Airlines logo. It was a one-way ticket to Bali in the name of Tyler Mills. First class, no less.

Tyler stuck out his arms and made "whoosh!" like an airplane. "I've got places to go and things to do, Philly. When our deal is done, I'll be out of here for good."

I put the ticket back in the envelope. "You're going to have to do better than that," I told him.

"That's where you're wrong," he said. "I don't *have* to do anything. You can take my word for it or you can take your chances and walk away again. Though I think you've learned by now that I'm not the bluffing type."

He had a point. There didn't seem to be much of a choice.

"Okay," I conceded, "but one more question. What if Tracy calls you before the end of this week to get together with you?"

"I set it up for the following week, naturally. You come through with the money and I postpone. After that, I disappear like I said, never to resurface again. She'll get over it, and you can continue to fuck Jessica all you want. By the way, did I mention how wonderful it was to meet her? I mean—wow!—she's even more lovely in person. Of course, I imagine her husband, Connor, must feel the same way. Man, the set of *cojones* on you,

Philly! All of you breaking bread together like there's nothing going on. Pretty fucking amazing."

I'd had about enough. "Are we done here?" I said.

"We're done. Just don't disappoint me again."

I stood up and looked over at the elderly woman and her nurse, except they were no longer there. The bench was empty. I thought for sure that I would have seen them leave.

Before walking away I turned back to Tyler. "You know, there was a time when you and I were friends," I said to him.

Replied Tyler, "You were never my friend."

I called Gwen from the street and told her that I wouldn't be returning to the office. "Is everything all right?" she asked me. It was a question I'd been hearing a lot in the last week. I told her that I appreciated her concern although none was needed. I could tell she knew I was lying.

Twenty blocks, I must have walked. The nine-to-fivers were beginning to spill out of the office buildings and fill the sidewalks on their way home. I, on the other hand, had no destination in mind. That is, until I looked up and saw the sign for an Irish pub. I ducked in and took a seat at the bar. Never was a drink-and-think session more in order.

The place was nearly empty. Hollow was more like it. Scattered patrons, mostly male and mostly older, talking either to each other or themselves. After the bartender set me up, I tried to sort through the events that had brought me to where I was—the proverbial back against the wall.

I got to thinking. To pay or not to pay?

If not paying was going to cost me my marriage and nothing more, maybe I could cope. Tracy and I didn't exactly have a never-ending love story going on. Losing out on the loft and all the money where it came from would be a tremendous kick in the wallet, but when all was said and done, I'd still be making a good living at Campbell & Devine.

Were it only that simple.

Lawrence Metcalf could giveth and he could taketh away. My screwing over his Precious would cost Campbell & Devine dearly. Beyond the clients that Lawrence had initially helped bring to the firm, he and his old-boy network would see to it that others walked as well, or never came aboard at all. You could bet on it. It was how the game worked. It wouldn't matter that we were the Green Berets of law. When you're blackballed you're blackballed, and as much as Jack Devine could be sympathetic to my plight as a guy caught with his pants down, he'd know there'd be only one way to halt the carnage. He may have thought of me as a son, but I had little doubt that when it came to his law firm, it was billings before any perceived bloodlines. I'd be out on my ass for sure.

Then there was Connor. It was bad enough that I was sleeping with his wife. As far as being a friend to him, I had no delusions. Still, how could I add insult to injury by allowing him to find out? There was no telling how hard he would take it.

No telling at all.

So I pay, right? As much as I loathed the idea of giving one penny to Tyler and being taken advantage of in that way, I'd suck it up. A hundred twenty-five thousand dollars was a lot of money, but it was money that I had. Or at least had access to. Give it to him and be done with it.

Again, were it only that simple.

The only assurance I had that paying Tyler off would be the end of the ordeal was Tyler himself. It wasn't much of an assurance. A one-way ticket to Bali? Nice touch. It didn't mean he wasn't coming back, and if he did, who was to say he wasn't coming back for more? After all, as Tyler had pointed out to me himself, he no longer had a conscience.

I was starting to know the feeling.

Who the hell was Tyler Mills to think that he could waltz into my life and take it over? And what kind of life did I have if I simply rolled over and let him do it?

Time for a change of plans, I thought.

The beautiful thing about desperation, I mean real desperation, is how it manages to lift every self-imposed barrier from your being. It washes away every line drawn in the sand and erases every preconceived notion you may have had about yourself. In other words, it's complete freedom.

I knew I wasn't a saint, but I didn't see myself as capable of killing. Not that I didn't feel a certain justification. I was being blackmailed, after all. So after a little rationalization and a lot of Jameson whiskey, it was settled.

Before he could take away my life, I would take away his.

TWENTY

"Son of a bitch!" said Paul Valentine.

"Motherfucker!" said Danny Markelson.

"Cocksucker!" said Steve Lisker.

Yeah, it's pretty amazing what a little green felt spread out over an innocent round table will do to the vocabulary of grown men. Jack Devine had just thrown down a full boat to best a king-high flush, a Broadway straight, and trip queens with an ace kicker. It was something like his twentieth pot of the night. As Jack raked in the chips with his arms spread like he was hugging a California redwood, he couldn't resist rubbing it in. "You know, you guys should really check out my instructional video." The quip got a chuckle out of Davis Chapinski, the only other guy not in the hand other than myself. He knew to fold when Jack first raised. Then again, Davis Chapinski played so tight he could have shot golf balls out of his ass.

All in all, it was quite the cast of characters. Wealthy clients and other influentials gathered together at Keens Steakhouse in a private back room that up until that evening I had never known existed.* The dinner tab, as was apparently the custom, had been picked up by Jack. Although it was no doubt a magnanimous gesture on his part, I couldn't help thinking that it was more akin to putting bait on a hook. Feed 'em for five hundred dollars at the start of the evening. Fuck 'em for five thousand by the end of it. If not a lot more.

My playing experience was limited to the occasional game back in college, as well as a couple of sit-ins with the grinders down in Atlantic City. While that and a token could get me on the subway, I knew enough not to waste my time sizing up the competition as we were eating. There was no point. Only when we got down to dealing the cards could anything worthwhile be gleaned. That was the beauty of poker. The Great Equalizer. It didn't matter if you hailed from the mail room or the boardroom, were handsome or butt ugly, the game was the game and you either played it well or you didn't.

The seals of two brand-new decks were broken promptly at 8 P.M. Buy-in was for three grand. (Thus the envelope of thirty hundreds Jack had given me at

*Old-line New Yorkers will remember that the restaurant used to go by a slightly different name: Keens Chophouse. I never knew officially why they changed it, though I had a hunch that some marketing consultant probably sat down with the owners at one point and explained that they could capture more of the ever-lucrative, expense-account-toting, meat-eating male demographic if they dropped the "Chop" in favor of "Steak." Never mind that the place had been called Keens Chophouse for roughly a century. Such was the restaurant business on the island of Manhattan that you'd do pretty much anything if it meant even a mere .07 percent increase in gross receipts.

the office.) Were I to need more chips over the course of the evening, it was explained to me that a personal check made out to cash was the accepted procedure. Indeed, the rich were always good for it. As for the betting, antes were twenty-five dollars a pop and there was a fifty-dollar ceiling on all raises until eleven-thirty. After that, things were to get a little funky, with pot-limit stakes for the last half hour bringing the game to an agreed-upon end at midnight. It was kind of like a metaphor for life. You could spend the majority of it playing all your cards right, but one wrong move at the wrong time, and like that, you could lose everything.

As for the aforementioned players . . .

Paul Valentine was the one sitting to my immediate left, the same Paul Valentine as in Valentine & Company, one of the city's premier public relations firms. You name the government official or Fortune 500 company and odds are that Valentine at one time or another counted them among his clients. The word *access* comes to mind. (For sure it had come to Jack Devine's mind.) Valentine was tall, with a Catholic-school posture that made him seem that much taller. He wore horn-rimmed glasses and a half grin that seemed to imply he knew something good that you didn't. No doubt he did.

Moving clockwise, there was *New York* magazine cover boy Danny Markelson. Entrepreneur extraordinaire. One record label, two Soho art galleries, and a host of other right-brain-inspired ventures across the country. His latest coup had been developing a line of trendy supermarket-bought pastas intended to create—

in addition to huge profits—racial and religious harmony. The Payos Pasta (fusilli) was a big hit. But my favorite by far was the black squid ink fettuccine, or Rasta Pasta, as it was called. Pretty ingenious. Though it may not have played well in Peoria, in every bustling metropolis the folks were literally eating it up. An avid sailor, Markelson had the look down to a tee. Jeans, docksiders, Polo shirt, gold Rolex. It all matched perfectly with his curly blond, unkempt hair, two-day growth, and Revo-stenciled tan face. If the guy had looked any more relaxed, I would've felt the need to check for a pulse.

To Markelson's left was Steve Lisker, portly CEO of BioLink, the genetic-engineering company. Gruff, hardnosed, and abrasive. An SOB with a Ph.D. I liked him instantly. A year back Lisker had gotten wind that a certain well-known publication was about to run a critical exposé on him claiming that his scientists had already successfully cloned a human embryo. Lisker placed a call to Jack and Jack sprang into action, threatening to plague the parent company of the publication with everything from lawsuits to locusts. Needless to say, the article never saw the light of day. Which is not to say that it wasn't 100 percent accurate. Only that it wasn't in one of our paying clients' best interests.

Next to Lisker sat Jack in his Brioni best, and finally, to Jack's left and my immediate right, was Davis Chapinski. Bought Microsoft at eleven in the eighties, Cisco at fourteen in the nineties. Fucking Nostradamus. If it hadn't been for the fact that he had a face only a mother could love, I would've been insanely jealous.

That was the table.

"Seven-card stud, high spade in the hole splits the pot," said the PR man, Valentine. With his last shuffle he placed the deck to his right, directly in front of me. I promptly cut the cards and prepared myself yet again for his carnival routine of ascribing a catch phrase to each and every card he dealt up. Tremendously annoying. Particularly because he had this overwhelming compulsion to rhyme everything. "The eighter from Decatur, the five to stay alive, the six just for kicks . . ." I'm sure Valentine thought he was entertaining. Much as I'm sure a Vegas lounge singer thinks of himself as entertaining.

With two down and one up dealt to everyone, I peeled up the corners of a ten of spades and a three of diamonds. *Jesus.* With my six of hearts door card I was blessed with yet another intriguing combination of nothing. Ten, three, six, off-suit. It didn't get much worse than that. Though with the way my cards were running, I didn't want to speak too soon.

Not only was I unlucky, but my head wasn't exactly at the table—not a good thing when you're playing high-stakes poker. I looked down at my chips. The three grand Jack had staked me was nearly depleted.

But it's not every day you decide to kill someone. At least, it wasn't for me. It is every day immediately afterward, though, that you think about it. Every waking moment, to be exact. After stumbling out of that Irish pub and crawling into bed forty-eight hours prior, I'd woken up the following morning with a few sobriety-induced reservations. I pushed them as far out of my head as I reasonably could.

The decision to do it was one thing. How to do it

and get away with it was something else. I needed a plan and fast, but the only relevant experience from my chosen profession was backstabbing. Too messy. If I was going to pull this off, I was going to need something more clever and a little bit cleaner. As to what that would be, though, I hadn't a clue.

For two days I had racked my brain, and for two days I had come up with nothing. The end of the week was quickly approaching—deadline for when I had to get back in touch with Tyler. I considered the idea of trying to buy a few more days for myself. Trouble with a certain money transfer, I'd tell him. There was a chance he'd buy it. Unfortunately, there was a much greater chance that he wouldn't. Plain and simple, time was running out for me.

Think, Philip, think.

That's when I heard it. Jack's voice. It was a couple of hands later and his turn to deal. He took a puff of his Hoyo de Monterrey, positioned the deck in his palm, exhaled, and announced, "Five-card draw, one-eyed jacks and the suicide king are wild."

Of course! Suicide. That was it. I'd make Tyler's death look like a suicide. If done right, it would be an open-and-shut case. After all, Tyler had tried it once, so he was predisposed. He had motive. Who wouldn't believe that he was capable of trying to kill himself again? It was so logical. Perhaps the only stretch, especially for those familiar with Tyler's knack for failure, was that this time he was actually going to succeed with it. But hey, everyone gets lucky at least once in life, right?

I was still thinking of Tyler's impending suicide when

Jack finished dealing five cards to everyone. I picked
mine up and looked at them. For the first time that night
I liked what I saw. Meanwhile, Jack pulled out his silver IWC pocket watch and realized that eleven-thirty
had come and gone. "Gentlemen, I do believe we're now
playing at pot-limit stakes," he declared.

It was Chapinski's initial bet. "Check," he said.

On me. "Check, as well," I said.

To Valentine. "Open for a hundred," he said, splash-
ing the hundred and fifty already in the pot from the
antes with a lazy toss of chips.

Markelson didn't hesitate. "Make it two-fifty."

"You call that a bet?" said the CEO, Lisker. "That's
not a bet. *This* is a bet." He counted out five hundred
in chips. "I see the two-fifty, and I raise another two-
fifty."

"Uh-oh, here we go," said Markelson.

He was right. You could feel the adrenaline snow-
balling. A fast one thousand sat in the center with five
hundred owed by Jack if he wanted to call. He wanted
to. Said Jack, "You guys are gluttons for punishment."

The betting was back around to Chapinski.

"'Pinski, that'll be a half-grand to play with the band,"
rhymed Valentine.

"You gotta be fucking kidding me!" he answered,
chucking his cards into the center. Chapinski and his
sphincter were out.

My turn. For sure, they all thought I too would fold.
Hell, I didn't even have enough chips in front of me to
call the bet. I did a quick count. Exactly four hundred
on the felt. After mulling it over for a second, I reached
for my checkbook. Despite my not being the first to

have done so that evening, a certain quiet fell over the table. In that moment, I felt like I could read everyone else's mind. *Poor kid; in over his head and he doesn't even know it.*

It was beautiful.

As I was making out the check, I glanced over at Jack. He knew what he paid me as an attorney at Campbell & Devine, and he knew who I was married to. Losing the hand would sting, but it wouldn't exactly put me on food stamps. Still, he looked uncomfortable. It was his invitation that had brought me to the game, and I could see in his face that, just like at the office, he felt somewhat responsible for what happened to me.

So imagine his face, and that of every other bigwig at the table, when I finished signing my name on the check and announced that I wasn't merely calling. I was raising. The pot limit, no less. I slid my remaining four hundred in chips into the center and placed a check for eleven hundred dollars right next to it.

Pow.

Valentine, who had started the whole thing with his initial hundred-dollar bet, dropped instantly. All eyes shifted to Markelson. He was two-fifty into the pot and owed another twelve-fifty if he wanted to call. He looked at his cards again. Clearly he thought they were good. How good, however, was the question. Ten seconds later, he too was south.

Lisker. Maybe he had the makings of a great hand. Or maybe his earlier boasting, "That's not a bet. *This* is a bet," made folding out of the question. Regardless, after a slight pause, he counted out the thousand he owed and tossed the chips in.

Finally, it was Jack's turn. He was already five hundred into the pot, and though you never wanted to throw good money after bad, his decision seemed the easiest. Or at least he made it look the easiest. The thousand he owed had already been counted out by him. Into the pot it went. The grand total so far: five thousand dollars.

The hand was now Jack, Lisker, and me.

Jack put down his cigar and picked up the remainder of the deck for the draw. He looked at me.

"I'm all set," I told him, prompting a few relieved chuckles from those who had dropped.

Meanwhile, Lisker took one card and Jack exchanged two for himself. I waited and watched as both of them looked to see if their hands had improved, not that I would know either way by their expressions. Maybe someone like Jessica had a tell. No chance in the world with these guys.

It was my bet first. There would be no check and raise this time. Only a check—for the pot total of five grand. Announcing the amount, I placed it on top of what had come to look like the Ayers Rock of chips.

Joked Markelson, "Nothing like a friendly game of poker, eh, boys?"

Lisker looked me in the eyes. "I think you're trying to buy it," he said. "I think you've been tanking it all night to bluff out a big one. Pretty slick, kid."

Odds were he didn't believe a word of what he was saying. A reaction. That's all he wanted from me. A laugh. A look down. Anything that might give him a better read on my hand. Five thousand dollars told him it was worth a shot. Though by that point it was becoming more and more obvious that the money was the least of what this hand, or the whole evening for that matter, was all about. A fact that Jack was all too willing to admit after a few more seconds of waiting.

"You know, it would be a hell of a lot faster if we just grabbed a ruler and whipped our dicks out," he said.

It was classic Jack. Funny, but with a purpose. In this case, getting Lisker to put up or shut up. As it turned out, it was put up.

Lisker removed an alligator skin–covered checkbook from inside his suit jacket along with a stainless-steel Montblanc. "Call," he said.

"Wow. . . ." said Markelson, half under his breath.

Valentine, eyes wide, spared us any rhymes and remained silent.

As for Chapinski, he muttered something about it being a huge pot and resumed counting his chips.

I looked at Jack. I knew what he was thinking. If he was to call and lose, he'd be out a fair amount of money. If he was to call and win, I'd be out a fair amount of money. Assuming that he'd feel guilty if I got my clock cleaned by him and his cronies, even if he won he would in a way be losing. I sensed an exit strategy in the making.

"Hey, who the fuck invited this kid, anyway?!" said Jack, throwing his cards away into the center. As most everyone else chuckled, he looked at me as if to say, I hope you know what the hell you're doing.

I did.

"Let's see 'em, gentlemen."

I was about to show my hand when Lisker beat me to it. He was that sure he had the winner. With a huge shit-eating grin, he turned over a monster. Two aces, two sevens, and a one-eyed jack. A wild card.

"I took mercy on you, kid," Lisker said, looking at me. "I could have fucking raised you!"

I looked down at his full house. I looked up into his eyes.

"I wish you had," I said back slowly. Almost as slowly as I laid down my cards. The nine of clubs, ten of clubs, jack of clubs, and queen of clubs. My last card? The king of hearts. The one and only suicide king.

I watched his face. For a split second, Lisker thought he had me beat. But a split second later, he knew otherwise. What he thought was a straight was really a straight flush. I too had a wild card.

The tabled howled. Lisker cursed. Then he cursed some more. All of it, I was sure, heard by anyone and everyone remaining out in the restaurant. The CEO of BioLink had lost out to a young punk of a lawyer, a first-time player in the game, no less.

"Nice hand," Valentine told me. "Glad I got out when I did."

"Yeah, good one to watch," said Chapinski.

"Hey, Lisker, maybe your company ought to clone this kid," said Markelson.

Lisker was desperately trying to compose himself. "One's quite enough, thank you," he said.

As for Jack, he folded his arms and waited for me to catch his eye. When I did, he cocked his head and suppressed a smile. What more could he say?

I raked in the pot. It was fifteen thousand dollars. Not bad for a night's work, I told myself, and all of it hinging on one very fateful playing card. The one card that spelled the beginning of the end for Tyler Mills.

Yes, indeed. It was time to plan the perfect suicide.

TWENTY-ONE

No loose ends. That's what I kept telling myself. If I was going to do this, and do this right, there had to be as little left to chance as possible. Regardless of how remote, I couldn't afford the risk of involving anyone or anything that could conceivably be linked back to me. Which is why even before the suicide idea surfaced, I ruled out hiring someone—a professional—to do my dirty work. Not that I knew how to arrange something like that anyway.

No, this was going to be a one-man job, and I was the man.

Method. I thought about lethal injection. I could get close enough to Tyler to do that. Remembering a case I had studied in law school entailing a hospital mix-up, I knew that a massive amount of potassium would be both deadly and untraceable come the autopsy. Except there was one drawback as it pertained to me. There'd always be the risk of a tiny puncture mark on Tyler's skin. And wouldn't you know it, he'd have Quincy for a coroner.

I kept thinking.

I was in my office, door closed, with Gwen holding all my calls. I had put a CD on my shelf system. The Tindersticks. For some reason, the lead singer's voice always brought out the worst in me. Sure enough, after three songs I had the idea.

Tyler would hang himself.

It made perfect sense. Since he'd slit his wrists to no avail, hanging was certainly a most believable Plan B for a guy bent on taking his own life. Of course, no matter how politely I could ask him, Tyler wasn't about to willingly dangle from his rafters.

Enter: ether.

Nothing like a little rubbing alcohol mixed with sulfuric acid to make a guy more amenable to putting a noose around his neck. More important, ether happened to metabolize in the body in super-quick fashion, probably no longer than the time it took for me to call the New York Public Library reference center and find all of that out. A good lawyer always did his research.

That said, Target and Wal-Mart weren't exactly stocking a broad array of volatile anesthetics the last I checked. So where was one supposed to get ahold of this uncommon household item? The same place everyone else gets their hands on things they have no business getting their hands on: the Internet. If the average disillusioned seventh grader could use it to learn how to build a bomb, surely I could finagle 50 ml of ether.

Covering my tracks, though, took some doing.

The guy behind the counter at the mailbox rental place had obviously never seen a driver's license from the state of Iowa before. If he had, he would've known mine to be the fake that it was, bought for eight dollars and change at one of those East Village stores that, with their bogus picture IDs and eclectic collections of bongs, manage to do quite well with the underage set. When asked by the mailbox guy to produce the second piece of ID required, I intentionally fumbled around a bit with my wallet (the one I had bought earlier on the street for four dollars, not the Fendi one I usually carried). Finally, I asked if my business card would be okay. No problem, I was told with an "I'll cut you some slack" head bob. My handiwork from the do-it-yourself business-card machine at the Hallmark store near my office was promptly handed over. Hank McCallister, Certified Public Accountant, 114 Castleton Lake Road, Des Moines, Iowa, 50318, it read. Clean, simple, and believable. For the record, Hank McCallister was actually the name of my junior high school gym teacher. He hung around the boys' locker-room showers too much, if you know what I mean.

The term *cyberholics* popped into my mind. I was looking around at the geek-chic clientele hanging out at the OnLine Cafe where I logged on to the innocuous-sounding MRT Supplies Corp. for my ether. On the company's Web site, they were calling it "ethyl oxide" and passing it off as an industrial solvent. It was the equivalent of a legal end around, a loophole that I was more than happy to jump through. Well versed in the ways of anonymity, the company proudly displayed its money-wiring codes.

The rather large woman who processed my Money-Gram was eating an egg-salad sandwich. There was a little glob of it on her chin, out of tongue's reach. It distracted me momentarily from staring at the mole on her cheek. Whereas Cindy Crawford's was thought of as cute and round, this woman's was huge, kidney-bean shaped, and had a thick black hair growing out of it. Still, the woman couldn't have been nicer. The way I saw it, she was either extremely comfortable with who she was or in complete denial. I couldn't exactly tell. I filled out the form and gave her the amount in cash that I wanted to wire, and we were done. The account for MRT Supplies Corp. would be credited within minutes.

"Thank you very much," I said to the mole woman.

"You're quite welcome, Mr. McCallister," she said back with a smile. In hindsight, I probably should've told her about the glob of egg salad.

The prepping was proceeding nicely. No one could ever prove that Philip Randall had ever heard of MRT Supplies Corp., let alone purchased 50 ml of ether, or ethyl oxide, from them. No mailbox rental place would ever show any record of a Philip Randall, either. If there was any connection to be made, the only person who had anything to worry about was one Hank McCallister of Des Moines, Iowa.

Like I said, no loose ends.

The last chore of the day was a stop at Chase Manhattan to have funds from my and Tracy's brokerage account wire-transferred into our checking account. Call me nuts, but we didn't make a habit of keeping a six-figure balance in it. Once the wire went through, I could have the certified bank check that Tyler was asking for drawn up—exactly as I had told him. What I hadn't told him, though, was that the check wouldn't have his name on it. It would be made out to cash. It was my way of eliminating any paper trail between the two of us. He was never going to get the chance to cash the check, of course, but after I had it credited back to my account, the bank would still have a record of it on file. Making the check out to Tyler was a potential loose end. Making it out to cash was essentially subpoena proof. I'd simply chalk up the amount to a foolishly long-running gambling debt out on the golf course. *Damn that double or nothing!* Sorely needing lessons would be the worst anyone could ever accuse me of.

———————

By Friday midafternoon, I had everything I needed, including a three-quarter-inch nylon rope for hanging and a pair of gloves for no fingerprints. The rope was a backup in case there were no bedsheets to be found in Tyler's apartment. The makeshift nature of a bedsheet noose, I thought, would add that extra touch of authenticity to the event. It smacked of the right amount of suicidal desperation.

Time to phone Tyler. Only not from my office. I didn't want records showing any more calls between us. That there was already one was okay, to be thought of as merely two old friends catching up. A series of calls, however, would possibly be perceived as something more.

Wanted: a pay phone that listed its own number. Very hit-and-miss in Manhattan. The first two I walked up to on the street weren't even working. Hell, one was missing the receiver altogether. Time to move inside.

Looking around I saw a Chinese restaurant up the block. I walked in and found their pay phone in the back by the kitchen. Its phone number was listed above the

Touch-Tones. I paged Tyler and stood there waiting. Nearby, an elderly Chinese couple was tallying the lunchtime receipts at one table while all the waiters ate at another. After about a minute, my loitering caught their attention.

"Could I get an egg roll to go?" I asked, thinking that might stop their staring.

One of the older waiters said something in Chinese to one of the younger waiters. They both looked annoyed. The younger one put down his chopsticks, stood up, and walked over to me.

"Is that all you wanting?" he asked me in quasi English. I nodded. He turned and walked back into the kitchen, coming out a few seconds later. "It come in couple minutes," he told me before returning to his lunch. Sure enough, everyone else had stopped staring.

Within another minute the pay phone rang. At the very least, Tyler was prompt.

"Hello?"

"I thought it was you," he said. "Are we all set?"

"Certified bank check for a hundred and twenty-five thousand dollars. Is that all set enough for you?"

"I suppose I should expect you to be a little testy."

"You *think?*"

Said Tyler, "Meet me in a half hour at—"

"Whoa, whoa, whoa. . . ." I broke in on him. "How do you think I make all that money? It's called a job, and I've got a meeting in twenty minutes that I can't miss. I've done everything you've asked so far, so give me this one. We'll do it early this evening, seven o'-clock. Just tell me where I should meet you."

There was a heavy sigh followed by a prolonged silence on the other end.

"Are you still there?" I asked.

"Yeah, I'm still here. Meet me on the northeast corner of Ninth Avenue and Thirty-fifth Street. Seven o'-clock, as you wish. Lord knows I wouldn't want you to miss your big important lawyer meeting."

He hung up.

I stood there at the phone for a moment. There was no meeting I had to go to. The point of stalling with Tyler was so that the likes of Gwen, and whoever else, would leave the office for the weekend knowing that I was still there. Working late would be my alibi were I ever to need one. Again, I wasn't planning on needing one.

I left the Chinese restaurant, egg roll in hand, and returned to the office. Back behind my desk, I called Tracy, telling her that there was an emergency with a client and that I'd have to burn the midnight oil. On a Friday, no less. We previously had made plans to see a movie together. It had been my suggestion earlier in the week, knowing that I would end up having to cancel on her. All in all, there was minimal disappointment. She told me that she'd probably stay home and read. I apologized and told her that we would try to do it another night.

For the remainder of the day, I sat there in my chair and mapped out the evening as best I could. Time passed agonizingly slowly. At about five-thirty, Gwen popped her head in to let me know she was leaving. I wished her a good weekend and asked if she had any plans.

"Self-loathing on Saturday, followed by self-pity all day Sunday," she said with a straight face.

I shouldn't have asked.

Come six o'clock, I took a stroll around the corridors, being sure to be seen whenever possible. I stopped by Shep's office and engaged him in a brief bull session. He had the unique gift of having humorous things happen to him in the most mundane settings. This time it was while getting his teeth cleaned.

"I'm lying there in the chair," Shep started to explain, "and they've got this really hot new dental hygienist."

I interrupted him to comment that he was dangerously close to sounding like one of those bad letters to *Penthouse*.

"Not to be confused with those good ones," he was quick to point out. "Anyway, you know how they've always got some easy-listening music pumped into the rooms to relax the patients? Well, I'm lying there, and it turns out this hygienist likes to sing along with the songs as she works. I mentioned she was really hot, right?"

I nodded.

"So, she's scraping away at my teeth, when all of a sudden that song 'Kiss You All Over,' or whatever it's called, starts playing. She's like six inches away from my mouth going, *I want to kiss you all over . . . over and over.* In this real sultry voice too. Mind you, she had one of those protective masks over her face, so it sounded a little muffled, but still, I couldn't help it."

"Couldn't help what?" I asked.

"Popping a chubby right there in the chair."

"Get out!"

"I'm serious. I'm sitting there with a tent in my trousers and the whole time I'm going, please don't look down, please don't look down!"

"Tell me she didn't."

"No, thank god, she was too busy singing. Close one, though."

I cracked up. It was funny to picture it. It was also an answer to a question that I had never had the gumption to ask Shep: Where exactly did his paralysis from the waist down begin? I was heartened by the inference that he could still get laid.

At six-fifteen, I returned to my office and went over my billable hours for the week. It was either that or organize my paper clips.

Six-thirty. I ate one very cold egg roll.

Finally, at six-forty-five, I loaded up an old backpack of mine with everything I needed and ducked out of the office. As I rode the elevator down, I remember it getting very warm.

TWENTY-TWO

T yler cupped his hands and lit a Marlboro. He was
wearing an old pair of jeans and an even older Deerfield sweatshirt—most definitely on purpose. Waving out
the match, he asked me, "You like being a lawyer?"

I was in no mood for his bullshit. Given the circumstances, however, I indulged him. "Most of the
time," I replied.

"Ever help a guilty person go free?"

"Probably," I said without hesitation. He wasn't the
first to pose such a question and he wouldn't be the last.

Said Tyler, "You're comfortable with that, helping
guilty people go free?"

"I sleep fine, if that's what you're asking. Though if
I'm not mistaken, you were the one who told me that
we're all guilty of something."

"I did say that, didn't I?"

We were standing amid a row of run-down storefronts. A nearly empty outdoor parking facility was our
backdrop. Across the street, high above a billboard, was
one of those electronic display signs that alternated between the time and the temperature, neither of which

appeared to be correct. Clearly Tyler hadn't picked the location for its ambience. Or maybe he had. Regardless, it was a part of Manhattan that I rarely had occasion to be in. No clients, no restaurants or shopping to speak of. A block up was one of the many entrances to the Lincoln Tunnel. It was still rush hour, on a Friday to boot, and cars with New Jersey license plates were lined up bumper-to-bumper, waiting to get in. It explained the less-than-subtle aroma of exhaust in the air.

"So, I believe you have something for me," said Tyler, finally getting to the point.

"What, no gadget to wave over me first?"

"You wouldn't be that stupid."

He was right. The microcassette recorder had been left behind. I reached into my suit jacket and pulled out the bank check. I held it out to him without ceremony. Slowly he took it in his hand and gave it the once-over. I could see his lips move as he read the amount.

"What's with the made-out-to-cash bullshit?" he asked.

"So I don't have to explain who the hell you are to my accountant," I said. "What are you worried about? The money's there. That's what a bank check is for."

Tyler stared down at it again. "Looks real enough," he said.

"That's because it is."

Tyler tossed his half-smoked cigarette to the curb. He folded the check in half and stuffed it into the front right pocket of his jeans. "Thanks, Philly," he said, all happy now. "You're truly a man of your word."

"I presume you are as well."

A squint of nonrecognition, followed up by, "Oh, of

course . . . the pictures." Tyler pulled up his sweatshirt to reveal the same manila envelope he had first shown me at our lunch. Tucked lengthwise into his jeans, it sort of looked like a cummerbund.

Opening the envelope, he removed the photos plus five or six cut negative strips. "Expensive roll of film, huh?" he cracked.

I didn't give a response, though many nasty ones came to mind.

Tyler slid the pictures along with the negatives back into the envelope and handed it over to me. "Wouldn't leave it lying around the house if I were you," he said.

"Not to worry," I assured him. Then I needed him to assure me. "This is it? You only made *one* set of prints?"

"One was all that was necessary."

He had his money. I had my negatives. While not exactly quid pro quo, the transaction was complete. Yet somehow I could tell he wasn't ready for our last rendezvous to end.

Said Tyler, "Screw the accountant, what are you going to tell Tracy if she asks about the missing money?"

"She won't ask."

"How do you know?" he pressed.

"I know. Believe me."

Tyler wasn't about to. "You'd think someone would notice if that much money had disappeared," he said. "Unless, of course, you two are so stinking loaded that this was merely chump change for you, in which case I've let you off far too easy."

"Hardly."

"Perhaps I should have asked for more."

"Perhaps I've paid you too much as it is."

"No, I definitely don't think that's the case," he said, shaking his head. "I'm sure you do very well for yourself, Philly, but it's your darling wife who has *set for life* written all over her." He peered over my shoulder. "What's in the backpack, by the way?"

"What?" I asked him with my best confused look.

"I said, what's in the backpack?"

"Everything that's required to end your life," I held back from saying. Instead, "Everything that would be in the new briefcase I ordered if it had arrived yet. I ditched the old one and took your combination-lock suggestion. I guess you can never be too careful."

"Isn't that the truth."

I had prepared myself for the question knowing it might have been coming. Tyler seemed to have no misgivings about my made-up answer. There would be no further discussion of my backpack. Rather, he stood there looking at me, his eyes fixed on mine. It was as if he was trying to figure out what I was thinking.

"You want to know, don't you?" he asked.

"Know what?"

"I don't blame you, actually. If I was in your wingtips I'd feel the same way. It would bother me too," he said. "Plane ticket or no plane ticket, you want to know if this is truly the last time you're ever going to see me. I can tell. I mean, yeah, you paid me off and, yeah, I told you that I'd never bother you again, but how do you really know that I'm going to stay away, that one day you won't turn the corner and—wham—there I am?"

"I'd be lying if I said the thought hasn't been on my mind. The answer, ultimately, is that I don't know. I'm not the one calling the shots here; you are."

Tyler shook his head as if disgusted. "That's what gets me, Philly. Hearing you talk like that," he said. "Sure, you did the right thing by giving me the money; it's just that . . . ah, fuck it, never mind."

I took the bait. "What?"

"It's just that, well, with everything I thought I knew about you, I expected—how should I say—more of a struggle. No, that's not the right word. Challenge . . . yes, that's the right word. . . . I expected more of a challenge. Not that I'm complaining."

"No, it's more like gloating," I sneered, my anger beginning to show.

"Maybe," said Tyler, scratching his head. "I suppose you did play it tough at first. Though I'm telling you, you should've seen your face when I sent that bottle of champagne over at the restaurant." Tyler flashed an exaggerated look of fear, much to his own amusement. "I don't know, call me crazy, but it sure looks like you bent over and took it up the ass from there on out."

Hell, it was like he was asking for it.

Without saying a word, I stepped off the curb and out into the street to hail a cab. Tyler threw his hands up in the air.

"Aw, c'mon, Philly, I was only kidding!" he said.

"Good-bye, Tyler," was all I replied.

I waved at a vacant cab waiting at a red light the next block up. The driver spotted me. No matter what Tyler was going to say at that point, I was dead set on ignoring him. Except he didn't *say* anything. What he started to do was sing. Right there on the sidewalk, he started to sing Frank Sinatra's "My Way" at the top of his lungs. I couldn't help turning back to look.

Regrets, I've had a few;
But then again, too few to mention.
I did what I had to do
And saw it through without exemption.

I planned each charted course,
Each careful step along the byway,
But more, much more than this,
I did it my way.

Green light. The cab pulled alongside of me and I got in. Tyler kept on singing. The cab sped off almost immediately. Still, Tyler kept on singing.

"Take a left onto Thirty-fourth Street," I told the driver in response to his "Where to?" glance over the shoulder.

One block south later, the driver obliged. After he completed the turn I shouted for him to stop the cab. Before he could get pissed off, I dropped a five-dollar bill over the front seat and into his lap. "For your trouble," I said, reaching for the door handle. I grabbed my backpack, hopped out, and rushed over to the corner. Slowly, I peered around it.

Tyler was no longer singing. Not too far from where we had stood I saw the jeans and plain white back of his sweatshirt. He was walking away from me, which was what I wanted. Had he been walking toward me it would have been a mad dash for cover.

I waited until Tyler reached the next corner. I deemed that to be the safe distance. What was Tyler's safe distance, I wondered? How much ground had been between the two of us when he followed me around?

Something told me he got a lot closer, if only for the fun of it. The *challenge*. He had stalked me for god knows how long—days, weeks, a month? It seemed amazing that I had never caught on, that I had never sensed a presence behind me. I had been oblivious, absolutely oblivious. Which was precisely what I was betting Tyler would be that evening. For indeed, the tables had turned.

The stalker was about to become the stalked.

I reached into the backpack and removed a Cubs baseball cap. I put it on and pulled it down snug right above my eyes. I hastily removed my suit jacket and tie, stuffing them into an outer compartment of the backpack. I had known there would be no time for a full wardrobe change; a wardrobe modification was the best I could do. Staying as close to the storefronts as possible, I started to ease my way back up the block.

My hope was that Tyler lived somewhere in the vicinity, as the more terrain there was to cover the more likely it was that I could lose him. Our previous meeting places—the Oyster Bar and Bryant Park—were both nearby midtown locations. A good sign. Not that it really mattered. I was prepared to follow Tyler into the next time zone if that's what it took.

One block became another, then another, and one more. Tyler kept walking and staring straight ahead, seemingly suspecting nothing. That-a-boy, Tyler.

A few blocks later we were right smack in the middle of Hell's Kitchen—a part of Manhattan the brochure didn't talk about. Truth be told, it wasn't nearly as bad as the nickname suggested. Most of the streets were decent, if not actually quite nice. What ruined the curve were the remaining ones, which looked like Dresden after the Second World War. That's what always amazed me about Manhattan—how a short stroll in any given direction could take you from posh to poverty and back again.

Tyler turned.

A right turn. As soon as he disappeared around the corner I sprinted, nearly taking out a bag lady and her shopping cart in the process. Once at the corner myself, I leaned my head out just enough to give my left eye a view. What it saw was Tyler turning into an entrance a short distance away. I started to reach into the backpack for the handkerchief and ether. This is it, I thought. Tyler was home and I was about to make my move. At the same time, though, something made me look up. It was a neon sign right above where Tyler had entered. "Billy's Hideaway," it blinked. A *bar?* With a check for a hundred and twenty-five grand burning a hole in his pocket, you'd think the guy would want to go straight home and stuff it under the mattress. Not Tyler. It would seem that a celebratory drink was in order.

Make that drinks, as in plural. I planted myself across the street from Billy's Hideaway behind a double telephone kiosk. I prayed for a short wait, but after fifteen minutes it was clear that Tyler hadn't merely popped in for a quick shot. I resigned myself to being there for a while.

I stood and waited. The shadows across the street began to grow heavy and longer. Twilight gave way to darkness. There was one advantage to that, I thought. I would be a little less exposed when tailing Tyler once he left the bar. I looked at my watch. *If* he left the bar. All sorts of images went through my mind. Some were harmless, like Tyler standing atop a bar stool and declaring that drinks were on the house. Others made me worry, like Tyler blabbing away about his big score. I began to fear that he would name names—my name—in relating all the details. In the days to come, I'd be forced to hope that no person listening in was a big reader of the obituaries and capable of putting one and one together.

Over an hour passed. *So this was what it was like to be on a stakeout.* As much as I wanted to duck into a nearby deli and quickly grab some coffee, I stayed put. There was no way I was going to let Tyler slip by me. Out of boredom, I picked up the receivers on both pay phones. Neither one gave me a dial tone.

Finally, he came out. I crossed the street and fell in line behind him. It wasn't what you would call a straight line, though. Meandering was a more apt description for Tyler's walking, or as I'd often heard it called, the Inebriated Shuffle. All the better. His reaction time would be that much slower.

As predicted, the darkness allowed me to stay closer to him. It didn't hurt that the street lamps appeared to be maintained by the same city department that was in charge of pay phones. Were Tyler to look over his shoulder, all he would've seen was the very occasional pool of light cast from overhead. I was sure to be lost amid the black.

Something told me it wouldn't be much longer. That something was when Tyler didn't light up another cigarette. He had been chain-smoking the entire time, and when I didn't see the flare of another match right away, I got the sense his apartment was nearby. On the other hand, he simply could've been out of cigarettes.

I found out soon enough. Not a minute later, Tyler stopped in front of an entrance midway down the street. What little light existed was enough to see him dig into his pocket for keys. He was home, Lucy. There would be no false alarm this time.

I reached into the backpack and grabbed the ether, popping the squirt top of the Poland Spring bottle that I'd poured it into. Right behind it came the handkerchief, folded in a square and ready to receive. No need to look down. I'd feel the wet against the palm of my hand through the cotton. My eyes would be needed for the charge.

Quickly, I glanced around the street. It was empty.

I knew from the adrenaline of sport and the adrenaline of sex. The heightened awareness. The blood pumping. Yet as I sprinted toward that entrance knowing what I was about to do, the pure reckless abandon of it, I discovered a certain rush that I'd never before experienced. To strike a comparison would be to imply that some other feeling came close. But nothing did. Had any drug that I'd ever tried been remotely similar, I'd undoubtedly have been the biggest junkie of them all. Perverse as it may sound, Risk Factor 9 wasn't without its reward.

The timing was perfect. There was no chance for Tyler to react. When I caught up to him, his back was to me as he was about to push his way through the second glass door of his building. He had obviously heard me behind him—or something, at least—because he was starting to turn his body. Maybe he saw me, maybe he didn't. I wasn't sure. If he did, it was merely a glimpse, a fleeting second of something white being slapped over his face. What he must have been thinking as it happened . . .

That ether stuff really works. Within a few seconds and with minimal struggle, Tyler's body went limp in my grasp. I looked behind me. No one. I looked ahead of me. No one. So far, so good—no witnesses. Though if I wanted to keep it that way I had to move fast.

On went the gloves. Mental note: wipe the first door free of any fingerprints when leaving.

Tyler's keys had fallen to the floor. I picked them up and started to check the directory. You didn't think he'd actually have his name listed next to an apartment number, did you? Neither did I. It would be too easy. Hastily, I fumbled around on his key chain and found what looked to be the mailbox key. It was trial-and-error time. Four mailboxes had apartment numbers without names. On the third try I knew where Tyler called home. Apartment 4F.

The ground floor hallway was as narrow as can be, with stairs right in front. It was dimly lit and reeked of garbage, two of the three necessary requirements for a place to be officially labeled a dump. I was convinced I'd see the third requirement crawling about at any given moment. Mind you, I wasn't expecting Trump Tower. In fact, my plan banked on the belief that Tyler was slumming it to a certain degree. Doormen and elevators would have obviously made things a bit more complicated.

The trick at that point was getting Tyler up the stairs

without being seen. That's why I had to do a little solo journey first to make sure the coast was clear. As for what to do with my unconscious cargo in the meantime, I spotted a space tucked behind the stairwell, in the shadows and out of the way. Breathing hard, I grabbed Tyler under his arms and dragged him over to it. For a skinny guy, he sure did weigh enough.

Hurry, Philip.

Having further brushed up on my pharmacology, I knew that ether, when inhaled directly, would knock someone out for approximately fifteen to twenty minutes. The clock was ticking.

I hightailed it up to the second floor. I heard plenty and saw nothing. The muffled sounds of canned laughter from a TV, along with a baby crying, but the hallway was empty.

Up the stairs to the third floor. I peeked left and right. It too was empty. Quiet, this time, as well.

Onward to the fourth floor and apartment 4F. More trial and error with the remaining keys. The second Medeco did the job. I was in. I opened the door and groped for the light switch. Short of a sign that read "Tyler's Place," it was his apartment, all right. The unbelievable mess had his name written all over it.

Leaving the door cracked open I headed back down, checking for people again at every floor. *Tick, tick.* I needed everyone to continue their hermit ways for a few minutes longer. Returning to the ground level, I found Tyler still passed out as could be, reeking of alcohol, ethyl and otherwise. I picked him up again for the long climb ahead. In what little time had elapsed, I could've sworn he had gotten heavier.

My back was aching by the fifth step. Between the backpack and Tyler, I would've been quite the sight, exactly what I couldn't afford to have happen. As gingerly as possible, I turned the corner on the second floor and started up to the third.

Shit!

Halfway up the steps to the third floor I heard the metallic *snap* of a lock down the hall. Someone was coming out. With a frantic look behind me I realized there was too much ground to cover for a retreat. I stayed still and held my breath. At the same time, I was trying to balance Tyler on my shoulder as I went up on the tips of my toes to catch a glimpse of who was coming. It was all very Ringling Brothers. The door opened and I heard footsteps. They were coming my way.

Fuzzy pink slippers, that is.

All my planning was about to go to waste thanks to someone wearing a fucking pair of fuzzy pink slippers. Or was it? Because as soon as I saw them they stopped. With the slant of the next flight of stairs obstructing my view, all I could see were the slippers and the matching set of fat female ankles that filled them. What was she doing? Why had she stopped? When I heard the next sound, I knew. It was the sound of hinges, yet it wasn't a door. It was the trash chute. Lo and behold, she was taking out the garbage. (At least someone did around there.) I listened to the clanking of bottles and cans fade away. It was music to my ears. The only thing left for her to do was turn around and go back to her apartment. *Bring it on home, fuzzy-pink-slipper lady!* Which was precisely what she did. As the door to her

apartment closed behind her, I exhaled my lungs out.
It appeared I would live to see another floor.

Maybe. The final flight of steps looked like the
Hillary Step on Everest. Little did I know that I
should've trained for the evening. As much as I wanted
to stop and rest, it would've left me exposed to other
neighbors that much longer. I kept going. I had to.

It was all clear on the fourth floor as I carried Tyler
into his apartment. With a great swell of relief I put
him down on a couch, or rather *the* couch, for that and
a folding chair made up all of the available seating. As
for the rest of the furnishings, to call them sparse would
be all too kind. A room at Motel 6 had more character. It also had the benefit of maid service, something
Tyler's place was sorely missing. Newspapers, pizza
boxes, clothes, beer cans. All of it strewn about so ran-
domly it almost seemed to form a pattern, if that makes
any sense.

The first order of business was to look up, everywhere. Tyler would need someplace from which to hang
himself, and though I was prepared to improvise, a little luck was much preferred. I found it in the bedroom.
An exposed pipe that ran across the room about a foot
below the ceiling. Thick, sturdy, and supported by a
wraparound bracket mounted to the side of the wall. It
was perfect. Nonetheless, I took no chances. Stepping
up on an old-fashioned radiator, I grabbed hold of it
and made sure it could support my body weight. It was
plenty strong.

Stepping back down, I looked at Tyler's unmade bed.
Scrunched up at the bottom was a plain white sheet,
the no-frills variety. I picked it up and gave it a good

hard tug. It too was plenty strong—the rope I had bought would stay in my backpack.

The thing from there on out was to think and act like Tyler. That meant doing everything the way he would've had to do it. I took off my gloves and started with fastening the noose with a slipknot at one end of the sheet. The other end got a double knot tied around the pipe. The measurement that mattered was from the floor up. I stood under the noose and felt a good six inches or so of space above my head. Dangle room, for lack of a better term.

The time had come.

I would get Tyler from the other room and get it over with as fast as possible. Be done with the blackmail, the threats, and the fear. Be done with it all.

So how come I wasn't moving?

Worse, why did I suddenly feel nauseous?

Feet planted, the room on a turntable. I felt dizzy. The urge to vomit. My stomach churning, with a feverish chill spreading out over my backside.

The adrenaline, I told myself. System overload. The rush of it all had been too fast, too great. I was coming down exceedingly hard. Crashing.

Give it a minute, Philip. It'll pass.

I gazed up at my handiwork, the noose hanging from the pipe, and the room spun faster. I quickly looked away. My eyes landed on an old mirror propped up over a makeshift dresser by the bed. I hadn't seen it there until I spotted my reflection staring back at me. It was cold and it was detached, and it made me wonder, really wonder, for the first time.

Up until that point I had focused so much on my

plan, the details and the precautions, that I had conveniently avoided thinking about what it was I was doing. As I stood there in that bedroom of Tyler's apartment, however, there was no more avoiding it. I knew why I was there. I knew why I wanted to do it, why I felt I *had* to do it. Yet there was one thing I was overlooking.

Actually doing it.

Without warning the thought of it had swarmed over me. Engulfed me. I realized what was happening. My wave of nausea had nothing to do with adrenaline. I was suffering from a major change of heart.

What the hell were you thinking, Philip?!

That's when I understood. It was like a moral eclipse, the whole thing. My view of right and wrong, good versus evil, had been obstructed by my desire-turned-methodical-obsession to rid myself of Tyler—and in the process rid myself of what had become an all too real reminder of my own transgressions. Some would say that my morality had always been subject to at least some form of partial eclipse. But this . . . this was a personal darkness that I had never known.

I guess my conscience was alive and kicking.

From there the decision came almost effortlessly, and as fast as you can say *psychosomatic*, the nausea and dizziness disappeared.

It would be as if I had never been here, I told myself.

I would go get Tyler off the couch and put him in his bed. He'd wake up later with a horrific hangover, but at least he would indeed be waking up. He'd have my money and I'd have to live wondering if he was ever going to tangle with me again. I figured I could deal. I had to deal. The alternative was knowing that I had murdered him. That, so I discovered, was something I couldn't live with.

I started to walk toward the other room to pick Tyler off the couch. When I came through the doorway I abruptly stopped.

The couch was empty.

What I saw next was a shiny blur out of the corner of my eye. It was the steely blade of a knife, and it was coming right at me. I recoiled, arms raised, as it missed my body and caught the top of my left hand with a cutting swipe. The blood was instant. The realization wasn't too far behind. That ether wasn't all it was cracked up to be. Tyler was conscious. A little groggy, maybe, but definitely awake. He also looked pretty pissed off, to put it mildly.

"You stupid motherfucker!" he yelled, pointing what turned out to be a very large kitchen knife at me. He was backing me into his bedroom.

I looked down at the blood dripping off my fingertips. I gathered this was what they meant by being caught red-handed.

"Wait a minute, Tyler," I pleaded. "This isn't what you think."

"Oh yeah, what is it then?"

Before I could give him an excuse, though, he saw it. The noose. The sheet hanging in the corner of his bedroom. Damn, I should have taken it down first.

Tyler looked dumbstruck. He could hardly fathom it. "Isn't that something," he said. "I suppose that was for me, huh?"

"No," I said. "I mean, *yes*, it was for you, but I couldn't go through with it. I couldn't do it."

"You're damn right you couldn't do it. Sorry to get in the way of your little execution here," he said, no longer yelling. His voice had turned calm and deep. The knife remained pointed at me in his outstretched hand.

"You have to believe me, Tyler. I know what it looks like, but I wasn't going to do it. You can have the money; it's yours. This was incredibly stupid of me."

He laughed out loud. "That's the fucking understatement of the year."

I started to look around the room for something to grab. The odds of talking Tyler out of coming at me with that knife again were decreasing by the second.

"You know what this is going to be, don't you?" he said.

"What?"

"Self-defense, that's what. You were going to kill me and I stopped you. It's that easy."

"Tyler, please . . ."

"You know what the amazing thing is? I actually thought you might consider trying something like this." He glanced at the noose. "Well, not quite this. I have to admit that was pretty ingenious—making it look like a suicide." He raised his forearms into the air, exposing the scars on his wrist. "Who wouldn't believe it?" he said with a crooked grin.

"Two hundred and fifty thousand!" I spurted out.

"Come again?" said his look.

"I'll double the hundred and twenty-five thousand. I'll give you two hundred and fifty thousand!"

Tyler pursed his lips. "Tempting, Philly, very tempting," he said. "But you know what idea I like better? The one where after I kill you, I end up fucking your wife. I'm pretty sure Tracy was starting to have a thing for me anyway. She might be a little frigid at first, it being my knife and all that did you in. Except I know she'll come around; she'll more than understand the self-defense part. Then, who knows, with a little work, maybe I can start up with Jessica on the side. Wouldn't that be a hoot? I guess I always was a little jealous of you."

Knife raised, he lunged.

My instincts took over. Before the blade could come down on me fatally, I grabbed under Tyler's wrist, stopping the motion of his arm. I glanced at the serrated edge of the knife, already stained with my blood, as it hovered over me—my body shaking, trembling from the strain. It was his strength against mine. I may have outweighed him, but he was consumed by rage and that was enough to begin pushing me back. I felt Tyler's bed behind me, and my knees began to cave with no more room to retreat. The knife was getting closer.

I fell back on the bed, desperately holding on to Tyler's arm while at the same time trying to evade the knife. He rode his momentum downward, pushing the struggle in his favor. He was right on top of me, the blade inches away from my chest.

"What a way to go, huh, Philly?" Tyler said between gasps of breath. He flashed a checkmate smile. He knew I couldn't hold him off much longer and he was right. Ever so slowly, the space between the tip of the blade and me began to disappear.

I felt it and I screamed out in pain. The knife cutting into my flesh. A quarter of an inch. A half an inch. The bull's-eye of blood growing on my shirt.

Any farther and I was dead.

What a way to go, huh, Philly?

No, I told myself. No way. Not here, not now, and certainly not at the hands of Tyler Mills. One final push, I needed. It was my last chance. Closing my eyes and gnashing my teeth, I summoned up every last bit of fight.

And then some.

Maybe he let up for a split second thinking he was about to prevail. Or maybe I was so afraid of dying that it only seemed that way. Out went the tip of the knife from my chest. Back went Tyler's arm. His expression said it all. This wasn't quite settled yet.

I rocked to my side and it caught him off guard. He momentarily lost his balance. It was all I needed to bring my legs back and plant the heels of my wingtips against his stomach. With one hip-sled thrust I sent him flying away from me. *Smack!* went Tyler's body against the wall. The knife dropped to the ground. For a second we both stood staring at it. He was closer to it, though not by much. If I dove and got it, we had a different ball game. If I dove and missed, it was game over for me.

I stayed put. I was up from the bed and ready for his next charge. Tyler scooped up the knife and came at me, arm raised and head down. He barreled toward me. With an eye on the knife, I waited until the last possible split second and sidestepped him. A matador to his bull.

He couldn't stop his momentum. Over the bed Tyler

tumbled headfirst, right into the other wall with a tremendous thud. I got up and turned around, ready for him to charge at me again.

"C'mon, you son of a bitch!" I yelled.

But Tyler lay there motionless. His slack body was hunched up against the old-fashioned radiator. The noose hung above him. At first I thought maybe it was a trick. I inched closer to him. It was no trick—Tyler was unconscious. I spotted the knife on the ground a foot from his hand and I kicked it away. Standing over him, I grasped what must have happened. That wasn't a thud I had heard after he tumbled, rather it was a hollow and resounding *clank*, and the huge swelling above his eyes confirmed it. Tyler's head had gone right into the pipes of the radiator. He was really out. I bent down and grabbed his wrist, placing my thumb over his scars. Within seconds I realized it.

Tyler wasn't unconscious.

Tyler was dead.

The feeling was panic, exhaustion, and relief all rolled into one. I could barely catch my breath as I stepped back and tried to digest what had happened. The implications and the consequences.

What do I do?

Think, Philip!

I go to the cops, that's what.

Are you crazy, Philip?

Talk about a self-incriminating story. They'd never believe it, at least not the part that I'd need them to believe. Hell, I could hardly believe it.

I unbuttoned my shirt, gently lifted up my undershirt, and looked at my chest. I saw the raw slot of pierced flesh above my nipple with blood all around. The bleeding itself, though, had stopped.

The same couldn't be said for my hand. I grabbed one of Tyler's T-shirts off the floor and tied it around tight over the gash to cut off the pressure.

Again with the question. What do I do?

Truth be told, I knew all along. By entertaining other ideas, I was merely trying not to feel so depraved about it.

I'd do exactly as I had decided earlier: *it would be as if I had never been here.*

I worked fast. Down came the noose, the sheet tossed back on the bed. I grabbed a sponge from the sink and went around wiping up all the drips of my blood. I cleaned the knife and placed it in one of the kitchen drawers. I put Tyler's keys down on a table. I even retraced all my steps to make sure I hadn't left a footprint in the dust.

But if it wasn't me who had been in the apartment, who had?

To look at Tyler lying there was to know this wasn't a household accident. He hadn't just tripped and hit his head while home by himself. Someone else had been in the apartment. Some type of altercation had occurred.

That's when I walked over to Tyler's door, took out a dime, and loosened the screws a little on his sliding chain lock. I put my gloves back on and lifted the chain into the lock—and with one quick pull on the door, the chain lock went flying. Forced entry it would be. They would say Tyler had been the victim of a robbery gone bad. Jesus, the apartment already looked like that anyway.

. . . To think I almost left without it.

Wanting to further build the robbery premise, I had decided to see if Tyler had a wallet on him that I could empty out. That's when I remembered the check. I rushed back into Tyler's bedroom and dug into his right front pocket. There it was, the bank check, all folded up. As for his wallet, I found that as well. I removed the sixty-two dollars in cash he had and spilled a couple of his credit cards around on the floor before tossing the empty wallet on the bed.

Said robbery to me.

I grabbed my backpack and took out my suit jacket, putting it on. It barely covered the bloodstain on my dress shirt. After taking one last look around the place, I was ready to get the hell out of there.

I peeked out into the hallway. All clear. It remained all clear for the rest of the trip downstairs. Reaching the ground floor, I remembered my mental note to wipe the front door clean. That done, I finally slipped back into the night. Never had the anonymity of the city been more welcome.

I looked down at my hand. The mock tourniquet wasn't really doing the job. It was a pretty deep cut that would've normally required a stitch or two. I needed to take care of it. But home, with Tracy there, was out of the question. So too was a hospital. Then I remembered—the first aid kit that we kept at the office. That was where I would go. Perfect. Especially when I realized that there'd be a clean dress shirt waiting for me in my credenza. I always kept a spare around in case of a coffee stain or some other mishap. This was some other mishap, all right.

I walked briskly to the corner and flagged down a cab.

It was a short ride back to Campbell & Devine. Passing the night watchman in the lobby, I tucked my hand wrapped in Tyler's now blood-drenched T-shirt inside my jacket. Glancing up from his small TV set for a moment, $8.50-an-hour simply nodded at me.

The elevator seemed to take forever.

Thirty-one floors later, I stepped out into quiet and darkness.

The first aid kit was in the supply room. I dressed my hand in gauze and, after removing my shirt and undershirt, put a large bandage over my chest. My backpack had become the receptacle for everything, especially everything with blood on it. I'd later toss it in a Dumpster behind some restaurant on the way home. Good as gone.

As for Tyler's pictures, they got the paper pasta treatment in the copy room. Jessica and me and the Doral Court hotel. Shot by shot through the office shredder.

Then I saw the blinking light.

Heading into my office for that clean dress shirt, there was a phone message waiting for me. I logged on. "You have one new message," I was told. "Message one ... new ... from an external number ... received today at seven-fifty-seven P.M."

I pressed 2 to play it, fully expecting to hear Tracy's voice.

Nope.

"Hello, Philip, it's me," I heard, along with music playing and people chattering in the background. I knew instantly who it was, although I couldn't really believe it. It was too weird. Tyler had called me from a pay phone inside Billy's Hideaway. I listened. . . .

Don't know exactly when you'll get this message, but I wanted you to know that I really was kidding back there on the corner. I'm a sucker for Sinatra; what can I say? I guess I didn't want you to think that you were dealing with an obnoxious winner or anything. But I did win, didn't I? Whoops, there I go again. Adios, Philly!

I erased the message and sat there in my chair. Adios indeed, Tyler.

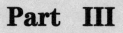

Part III

Part II

TWENTY-THREE

L ess than twenty-four hours later. Less than three blocks away from Tyler's apartment.

Tracy and I walked into FireBird on Forty-sixth Street in the Theater District and were led back to her parents, who'd already been seated. The table was located in what was called the China Room.

When I'd finally gotten home the night before, Tracy was thankfully asleep. She hardly stirred when I climbed into bed. As for bandage spin control with her, the one on my chest was a nonissue; I always wore a T-shirt to sleep and, given our respective schedules, was able to dress and undress on the sly. My hand, however, needed explaining. The next morning I told Tracy that I had carelessly tried to open a package at the office with a pair of scissors. She looked at me with general indifference and suggested that I be more careful next time.

I'll try, dear.

"Hello, Precious," said Lawrence Metcalf in his baritone voice, standing to kiss his daughter on the forehead. I forgot to mention how that was something he

always did with her. The kiss was never on the cheek,
always the forehead.

"Hello, Counselor," he next said, turning in my direction with a pat on the back. To be sure, that was definitely not something he always did with me. It was
always Philip, never *Counselor*, and for that matter, it
was always a polite handshake, never a pat on the back.
I was heartened to see that the passage of time had not
diminished my newly found status in his eyes.

Tracy and Amanda had already started talking about
their outfits when I made my way around the table to
deliver the patented mother-in-law lean-down-but-don't-
smear-the-makeup kiss hello.

"Not to put you on the spot, Philip," said Amanda as
I took my seat, "but do you think it's right that your
wife should have a better wardrobe than the woman who
brought her into this world?"

Instant minefield. "I plead the Fifth, naturally, on the
grounds that my answer could have me sleeping on the
couch later tonight," I said, trying to charm my way out
of it.

"We wouldn't want that, now would we?" said
Amanda. "It would mean one less chance of me having
a grandchild."

Zing.

She didn't do it often, but when she did it was with
the deft touch of a wrecking ball. That being the reference to the fact that Tracy and I were childless. The
subject was taboo for Lawrence, never wanting to upset
his Precious, though it was obvious that he shared with
Amanda the desire to have a new trust fund to establish. Personally, I found the remarks to be harmless and

paid them little mind. Tracy was less understanding. She construed them as a condemnation of our marriage and the choices that the two of us had made together—at least I think that was how she once phrased it. Clearly, it was one of those mother-daughter things.

The fact was that beyond looks and money, another component of Tracy's appeal for me had been her ambivalence toward raising a family. It wasn't that she absolutely didn't want one. She simply wasn't champing at the bit, that's all. In light of my trust fund reference, it was as if the whole idea of our having kids was in escrow, to be decided upon at a later date. Which was perfect, as far as I was concerned. Tracy's ambivalence was mine as well.

Vodka, caviar, and blinis to start. Lawrence and I partook of all three, while the ladies said *nyet* on the vodka, and opted for champagne. Taittinger. The restaurant was buzzing with the pretheater crowd, and the waiters, mostly Russian, were scampering about trying their best to speed things along. Few things in life created a greater sense of purpose than an eight o'clock curtain. Lawrence and Amanda were in the city that night to see a play, something about a prominent English family in the early 1900s that was immersed in politics and scandal, or so Amanda described.

"Politics and scandal . . . a little redundant, if you ask me," said Lawrence. "Though perhaps with enough Stoli here, I might enjoy it."

"Fall asleep is more like it," Amanda came back.

The question about my bandaged hand was asked and answered. The topic became the annual trip that

Lawrence and Amanda took to Bermuda, which was fast approaching. A week at Cambridge Beaches.

"We're going to be Tenners," said Amanda to me.

I looked at her, puzzled. "Ten-what?"

"*Tenners,*" she repeated. "It's what the resort calls people who have been coming for ten years. They actually post your name on a big red board outside the main dining room."

"It's the least they could do for all the money we've pumped through there," said Lawrence.

Retired oil executives, it should be noted, didn't spend money, they pumped it.

"You're the one who always wants to go back," said Amanda to her husband.

"Because you can't find a better meal on the island, that's why," he said. He turned to me. "Did you know that their chef is the only one in Bermuda to have the Meilleur Ouvrier de France designation?"

More than not knowing that, I didn't know what the hell he was talking about. On the other hand, Tracy, ever the foodie, not only knew but was dutifully impressed.

More Bermuda talk ensued. The brightly painted homes, shopping in Hamilton . . .

"Maybe this is the year I finally get your father on a moped," Amanda said to Tracy.

Somehow I didn't picture it.

As we were talking vacations, Tracy segued into a description of the cottage in the Hamptons that "we" were renting for the month of August. East Hampton, to be exact. It was Tracy's gig, really. She stayed out there for the entire month. I showed up on the weekends. This was the year she was going to take up painting, she excitedly explained. Sitting behind an easel, brush in hand, looking out onto the ocean and capturing the moment.

Again, somehow I didn't picture it.

A short time later we ordered our entrées and various *zakuski* for appetizers. We had begun to carry on with our conversation when out of the corner of my eye I saw it coming. At first I thought maybe Lawrence had asked for it while I was still immersed in the menu. His expression, however, said otherwise.

It was another bottle of champagne.

With a heavy Russian accent, our waiter announced, "You have friend at other table."

No fucking way.

I spun my head around so quickly I nearly gave myself whiplash. It was impossible. It couldn't be. Tyler Mills, back from the dead. Maybe I only thought that he was dead, thought that he had no pulse before I left him in his apartment. Or maybe, through some weird scientific phenomenon, his heart's stopping had been temporary. My mind raced with the possibilities, logical or not. In that moment, anything was possible, anything. My eyes jumped from table to table. Show yourself, Tyler Mills. Show me that goddamn face that I thought I'd never have to see again.

There was a tug on my sport coat. I didn't react to it right away, as I was consumed by looking for Tyler. The tug grew stronger, becoming a yank, and I turned around impatiently.

It was Tracy and she was saying something to me. I was looking at her and I could see her lips moving. I could hear her, but the words weren't getting through. They weren't making any sense. It was all just noise.

"I said . . . Philip, look what you did!"

With that, I heard her. It was like tuning in to a radio station. From static to clarity in an instant. She let go of my sport coat and pointed to her knocked-over champagne glass on the table. My doing, apparently, in my haste to turn and search for Tyler. I looked at Tracy and I looked at her parents. Another waiter had rushed over to lay a napkin over the spill, and I looked at him too. Of everybody, he was the lone person not staring at me wholly perplexed. Amid my acute horror and hysteria, I realized what a minor event I had caused.

"You can dress him up, but you can't take him out," I said, trying to take the self-deprecating route back to composure.

"At least you could've made it my water glass instead of the champagne," said Tracy, half kidding at best.

"I think we have plenty to go around at this point, Precious," Lawrence declared, pointing to the new bottle and attempting to defuse any possible tension between his daughter and son-in-law. There wasn't any. Had the champagne spilled on Tracy's outfit, however, it would've been a completely different scenario, I assure you.

"I can't believe we didn't see them. It was such a nice thing for them to do, wasn't it?" said Amanda, glancing over her shoulder and returning a wave. "Now exactly what is the protocol here, honey? Do they come to us, or are we supposed to go over to their table and thank them?"

"You're asking the wrong guy," said Lawrence.

Alas, there would be no life after death for Tyler Mills. The champagne and the coincidence were courtesy of Ted and Allison Halpert, friends of the Metcalfs' from Greenwich who were in the city themselves for a show. They happened to be sitting on the opposite end of the China Room. To be on the safe side etiquette-wise, Lawrence and Amanda both got up and went over to their table. Tracy and I stayed behind.

"Are you okay?" Tracy asked me. "Because you certainly don't look okay."

"I'm fine," I told her.

"Are you sure? You've been acting kind of strange lately."

"Yes, I'm sure. I'm okay."

Our waiter had given Tracy a new glass as well as bringing two for Lawrence and me. The remainder of the first bottle was poured and the second bottle, a matching Taittinger, was opened.

"How bizarre is this?" said Tracy. "Everywhere we go, someone sends us a bottle of champagne."

"It's bizarre, all right," I said.

"You know, this reminds me, I never did call Tyler after that night we saw him at Balthazar. I should really do that."

I was afraid she'd say that.

I considered trying to talk her out of it, choosing ultimately to let it be. I would allow nature to run its course. There would be a natural evolution of events. Tracy would page Tyler. She wouldn't hear from him. She would page him again, and for the second time, she wouldn't hear from him. That would tick her off and she would resent Tyler. *How dare he not return her call?*

Then one day, in the not too distant future, word would make its way through the grapevine that Tyler had been killed. The news would send Tracy reeling. She would be shocked. She would resent herself for ever resenting Tyler. There would be crying.

Ever the Good Husband, I would be there to console her. Ultimately, after her tears began to dry up, she would decide that she needed to take her mind off of everything. She would go shopping or get a pedicure, or perhaps both, and within a rather short period of time, all would be right in the world again. At least her world.

Yes, that was definitely how it would evolve. It was as sure as Darwin.

Lawrence and Amanda returned to the table after thanking our champagne benefactors, the Halperts. Their youngest daughter, Mindy, had become engaged the night before, so they were "bubbling over with excitement." Thus, the champagne. Lawrence went on to reveal that some years back he had tipped off Ted Halpert about a certain oil company trading on the NASDAQ Small Cap that was about to be bought. (By Lawrence's company, of course.) Halpert had made a killing. In return, Lawrence made sure that the guy would forever be in his debt. Some men collected cars, others rare stamps or coins. Lawrence Metcalf, I had come to learn, collected friends. He was awfully good at it.

By the time our dinners arrived, Tracy and Amanda had already professed to being stuffed. Even Lawrence, a man who prided himself on having a hearty appetite, was looking down at his giant tureen of borscht with less than excited eyes. As for me, I was still starving. My grilled, marinated lamb loin was devoured within minutes, and I was only too pleased to help Tracy with her plate of salmon. Dessert, anyone? Had the Metcalfs not been pressed for time to make their play, the charlotte russe would've had my name all over it.

"What shall we do now?" Tracy asked me.

We had said good-bye to Lawrence and Amanda and were standing outside the restaurant, not quite eight o'-clock on a Saturday night. All dressed up and nowhere to go. Which was kind of weird for Tracy. Always one to make plans, for whatever reason she hadn't thought past our dinner with her parents. We started to talk about calling some friends, maybe catching another couple in the same "nothing to do" predicament. As Tracy took out her Star Tac, though, I had a different idea. A movie. I called it the makeup movie, for my having canceled on her the night before. Moreover, I told her, she could pick the film. That all but guaranteed that I would soon be subjecting myself to some type of chick flick.

Thirteen blocks south later . . .

In the darkness of a theater at the Cineplex Odeon in Chelsea, I paid little attention to what was on the screen. While I had fully recovered from my earlier episode about Tyler, I couldn't get him completely out of my head. Mostly, I wondered about how and when his body would be discovered. Who would be the one to find him? A friend, a neighbor, the superintendent? Whoever the person was, it was sure to give him or her a nightmare or two. I, for one, knew it wasn't the easiest of images to shake from memory. In fact, by that point I had given up trying. The stillness of his apartment. His body lying there limp, up against the radiator. It didn't

take long to realize that I'd be carrying it around with
me for some time, if not forever. It wasn't quite on par
with guilt. That was reserved for had I actually gone
through with my original plan. No, this was more like
a scar. A little unsightly blemish on the psyche.

Okay, maybe it was a rather large unsightly blemish.

TWENTY-FOUR

There's an old saying in the legal profession: "The only thing that matters more than what you know as an attorney is *who* you know." I'd like to offer up a slightly revised version: "The only thing that matters more than what you know as an attorney is what you know about another attorney." How else could you explain what happened with Sally Devine's DMV hearing?

It started back when Jack came by my office the day after the poker game.

JACK: You lucky little shit. A straight flush?!

ME: All skill, baby. Besides, you dealt it.

JACK: I did, didn't I? You being my guest, I'm surprised no one accused me of rigging the deck.

ME: You mean you didn't?

JACK: (laughs) Tell me, have we heard from our friends at the DMV?

ME: Earlier this morning, in fact. They scheduled Sally's hearing a week from tomorrow, eleven A.M.

JACK: No good. No good at all. Call and say you've
             got a conflict, make it medical, and tell them
             that Tuesday next week at any time in the af-
             ternoon would be good for you.

Huh?

I didn't understand, and the look on my face said as much.

"I'll explain later," Jack told me. "Let me know if you have any problem making the switch."

I nodded and watched as he turned and walked out of my office. He had been oblique with me before. Never to that extent.

———————————

A little DUI-DMV primer.

Get nailed for DUI and, in addition to having to answer to the courts, you have the Department of Motor Vehicles with which to contend. They wield a mighty big stick, most would agree, as they are the ones who ultimately decide the fate of your driver's license, a little laminated rectangle that you never realize how much you love and cherish until there's a chance it might be taken away from you.

If at the time of your DUI arrest you agree to perform the Breathalyzer test and fail it, your license gets suspended for three months. If you refuse the Breathalyzer test altogether, your license gets suspended for six months. In both cases, however, you have the right to request a DMV hearing in which to dispute the circumstances. If you have the slightest of arguments, as any lawyer will tell you, it's definitely a right you should exercise. You have nothing to lose . . . except your license, of course, which you would've lost anyway if you were to forgo the hearing.

That's the upshot. A little simplified, a lot abridged, and still probably more than you'd ever want or need to know. Oh, and one more thing: it so happens that the DMV arranges for practicing attorneys to reside over the hearings.

———————

I told the lady on the other end of the line that she sounded exactly like Lauren Bacall. It was something I always did. Whenever I needed cooperation, if not an outright favor from a stranger over the phone, I was sure to comment early in the conversation how much he or she sounded like a certain beloved celebrity. High-pitched women were told Goldie Hawn. Younger guys, David Duchovny. Guys a few years senior, Michael Douglas. And in the case of the older, slightly husky-voiced woman named Priscilla whom I got transferred to at the Department of Motor Vehicles in Westchester . . . Lauren Bacall. Priscilla really liked that. They always do. They never come right out and say that they're flattered; you can just tell. A generally reliable way to butter someone up without appearing overly fawning or kiss-ass.

After listening to Priscilla tell me that *The Big Sleep* with Bogart and Bacall was one of her favorite movies, I proceeded to explain that I had an important doctor's appointment on the morning for which Sally's hearing had been scheduled.

"Well, we don't want you to miss that, do we?" said Priscilla, sounding most accommodating.

Ever so casually I suggested as an alternative hearing date the Tuesday afternoon that Jack had specified. Through the phone I could hear the pages of Priscilla's desk calendar being turned.

"How's three o'clock?" she asked.

"Perfect," I told her.

"Tuesday at three it is. Hearing room number two," she said.

"Thanks, *shveetheart*," I said back, doing what was admittedly a really bad Humphrey Bogart. It was good enough for Priscilla, though. She howled in her not-even-close-to-Lauren-Bacall voice and told me to have a wonderful day.

There, I had done as Jack had asked. The problem was, Jack hadn't done what I'd asked: tell me why he wanted me to switch the hearing date. Twice I approached him about it and twice he made some excuse as to why he couldn't explain it to me at that particular moment. It was an odd kind of brush-off. Apparently, I would be told when he was good and ready.

The morning of the hearing arrived. A gray, rainy storm front morning, the Tuesday after Tyler's death. That's when Jack was good and ready. He stepped into my office and closed the door behind him. With the low smattering of thunder rumbling intermittently outside, there was an almost dramatic feeling to the moment. Jack was finally about to explain. Looking me straight in the eyes, he began, "His name is Jonathan Clemments and he has an almost flawless record as an attorney out in Westchester. The *almost* is on account of him having too much to drink one night at a bar association party a couple of years back here in the city. Clemments and a woman other than his adoring wife, Cathy, took it upon themselves to screw each other's brains out behind the closed door of a copier room. How he wishes it had been a locked door. As for me, I thought it was a bathroom."

Jack paused.

"Shit, you walked in on them?" I said.

Jack nodded slowly.

"What'd you do?" I asked him.

"Nothing. I waited until Clemments and I made eye contact and then I closed the door to the copier room and walked away."

"You didn't say anything to him?"

"Nope."

"Not even to him afterward?"

"Nope," Jack said again, shaking his head. "I just tucked it all away for a rainy day."

With that, the corners of Jack's mouth curled up in one very wicked-looking semismile. We both turned and gazed out the window. Boy, was it ever pouring that day.

By that point I had already pieced it together. Jack saw it in my face . . . there was no need to say it out loud. He knew Jonathan Clemments was one of the attorneys who resided over DMV hearings in Westchester, and somehow, some way, Jack had been able to find out what his schedule was—that very Tuesday afternoon, it turned out. Not exactly the kind of information the DMV readily hands out, you might imagine.

"So here's what I'd like you to do," said Jack. "First, you and Sally should intentionally arrive ten minutes late to the hearing. Of course, Sally was probably going to do that anyway, but if she happens to be on time, you still wait. When you do go in, introduce yourself to Clemments and hand him your business card. See that he looks at it and sees what firm you're with. If he doesn't, be sure to introduce Sally to him, and say her full name. One way or another I want the name Devine to be kicking around in his head when you apologize for being late. And as for that apology, this is what you should say, word for word: *Sorry to keep you waiting. I was making some copies and, well, you know how screwed up those copy machines can get.*"

I sat there and stared back at Jack, taking everything in. The absurdity, the cruelty, the brilliance of it all.

"Do you think you'll have any problem doing this?" Jack asked.

I knew he wasn't referring to my memorizing the apology line. He wanted to know if I would have any moral objections to carrying out his game plan. *Moral objections?* Shit, Jack, after Tyler, this was child's play.

I shook my head no.

"Good. Oh, and if you can," he added, "when delivering that line to Clemments, you might want to punch the word *screwed*."

"Naturally," I said.

"By the way, what's with the hand?" Jack asked, looking at my bandage.

"A little accident with some scissors, no big deal."

Jack agreed. "Listen, at the hearing, don't worry if things don't go well. I told Sally that if she ends up losing her license, you'd be more than happy to chauffeur her around. How's that for motivation?" he said with a chuckle.

"You're a regular Knute Rockne."

Onward to the hearing.

I had called Sally prior to the drive out to Westchester so she would be sure to meet me inside the front entrance of the DMV. In addition, I told her what to expect during the hearing. She had sounded sober. I kept my fingers crossed.

Sure enough, she was late. Thankfully, though, that's all she was. There was no smell of alcohol, only perfume—something I could tell for sure when she walked right up to me upon arriving and gave me a kiss on the cheek. Apparently, all had been forgiven, or maybe the right word was *forgotten*, since she last left me sitting there in her driveway.

"Am I late? . . . I'm sorry," Sally said, closing her umbrella and removing a scarf from around her head.

"It's okay; don't worry about it," I said.

"How do I look?"

I took a step back and eyed her up and down. It was the House of Chanel goes to the Department of Motor Vehicles. With her still perfectly set hair, movie-star makeup, and French-tipped nails, she made for quite the impression. Personally, I was just happy that her shoes matched.

"You look like a million," I told her.

"Is that all?"

Obviously I had forgotten what tax bracket I was talking to. "Make that five million," I said.

"That's more like it," she said with a nod. "Ooh, what happened to your hand?"

I explained.

"I know, I hate scissors," she said.

"So, are you ready?"

"I hope so. Do I have to call this guy *sir* as well?"

"If he asks you anything, yes, though he probably won't."

"That's what you said the last time," she reminded me.

I refrained from pointing out the extenuating circumstances surrounding "the last time." There was no need to revisit it. Instead, I glanced down at my watch to see that it was about ten after three. We were sufficiently late as per Jack. Sally and I walked into the DMV building and made our way up some stairs, finding hearing room 2 at the end of a hallway.

Jonathan Clemments was skinny, medium height, with black stringy hair that hung on an angle like a guillotine blade across his forehead. He was also annoyed. He had good reason. Here was a guy who was about to decide the driving fate of Sally Devine. The last thing he probably expected was that she and her attorney would have the audacity, the stupidity, to keep him waiting.

Jack, I hope you know what I'm doing.

The room was one long folding table, some chairs, and a reel-to-reel tape recorder for a future transcript of the proceedings. I walked over to Clemments and introduced myself. We shook hands and I pulled out my business card. "Here," I said, handing it to him. "I saw some Japanese businessmen do this once." He didn't find the line funny. Nonetheless, he did look down and read the card. Fact was, seeing the name Sally Devine in the file for his next case would hardly give him pause. It wasn't that uncommon a last name. Seeing it on my business card, however, and putting one and one together would be a different story. His slightly bewildered expression was all I needed to continue.

"I want to apologize for being late; it's all my fault," I said. "I was making some copies back at the office and, well, you know how *screwed* up those copy machines can get."

As fast as you can say "Casper," his already pasty-white complexion turned all the more pale, and I watched as his Adam's apple immediately went south in a none-too-subtle gulp. He looked to be somewhat of a nervous man to begin with. This certainly could not have helped.

"Copy machine?" he repeated, his voice on the verge of cracking.

"That's right, it really screwed me over," I said.

(Jack would love the fact that I got to say the magic word twice.)

For a few seconds, attorney Jonathan Clemments did nothing except stare at me. Eventually, he seemed to come around.

"Uh, should we, ah, get started then?" he stammered, finding his way back to his chair on one side of the table. Sally and I took our seats opposite him. It was only the three of us in the room. From that point, I didn't know exactly what to expect. My experience with the threat of blackmail had been limited to the receiving end. I was pretty sure, though, that it was his move. As for Sally, she was sitting there picking a piece of lint off her suit.

Clemments turned on the recorder and slated the names of everyone in the room, as well as the date and the case number. He opened up his DMV file on Sally and began to sort through some of the papers. I took the opportunity to remove my own file on Sally from my briefcase, laying it on the table across from his. "Mine's bigger," I thought about joking. Looking at the reels of tape spinning on the recorder, however, made me think otherwise. Besides, Clemments probably wouldn't have seen the humor in that line either.

As he picked up and turned over each sheet of paper, Clemments said aloud what it was. The police report . . . the arresting officer's statement . . . suspension notice . . . notice of rights . . . He went on and on, and as he did he began to regain his poise, sounding very official. I was starting to wonder if maybe Jack's plan wasn't going to work after all.

"Hmmm," said Clemments.

Hmmm?

He had made his way through all the documents, and while scratching his head, picked up the entire pile and started to go through them again. This time, he refrained from announcing their contents. After the second run-through, he delivered the same response.

"Hmmm."

"Anything wrong?" I asked him.

"I don't seem to see the hospital report on the blood alcohol results," he said. "Do you have a copy?"

Amazing.

It was one of the biggest softball lobs that I'd ever had thrown my way. Clemments was claiming not to have the main piece of evidence that would have made all of my possible arguments and excuses on behalf of Sally crash and burn. Was there a chance that the report really wasn't there in his file? Sure. Kind of like there was a chance he had gone home that night a couple years back and confessed to his adoring wife, Cathy, that he had been banging another woman.

"I have a copy of it, Jonathan," I told him. "You do realize, though, that for verification purposes, only the original is admissible in this hearing?"

Absolutely, he did. This was his song and dance, after all. His squirming body left little doubt about it. But all that reel-to-reel recording machine heard was the following: "I'm afraid you're right, Philip."

Sally, while paying attention, had remained clueless to what was happening. Clemments turned to her.

"Ms. Devine, it looks like this is your lucky day," he said. "Due to a clerical error, the Department of Motor Vehicles has no choice but to reinstate your driver's license effective immediately. I do hope that you don't interpret this oversight as lessening the seriousness of the crime that you committed. With that, I strongly urge you to reevaluate your driving habits, if you haven't already done so by now."

"Yes, sir," said Sally.

Clemments turned off the recorder. Sally looked at me as if to ask, *That's it?*

I nodded. That was it.

Clemments had immediately started to fill in some paperwork, and I interrupted him to say good-bye. He stood and shook Sally's hand first. She said something about taking his words to heart and headed straight for the door.

My turn. "Nice to have met you, Jonathan," I said, careful not to sound too aware of what had happened.

"Likewise, Philip," he said. His nose wrinkled. "Oh, and be sure to say hello to Jack for me."

*   *   *

Fittingly, the rain had stopped. As we walked out to the parking lot, Sally announced that she wanted to celebrate. I raised an eyebrow.

"No, not drinks," she said.

I was beginning to tell her that I had to get back into the city when she interrupted me. "Cake!" she practically shouted.

"What?"

"Cake. I think we should go have cake. What's your favorite?"

"Uh—"

"Mine's simple," she said. "Flourless chocolate with raspberry ganache. Is that okay with you? You're not on a diet or anything . . . ? Because I think that would be the perfect way to celebrate."

"Sally, I . . ."

"I won't take no for an answer, Philip," she said. "At least not this time," she added, catching herself. "Which reminds me, I owe you an apology." She looked around. "Though a parking lot is no place for an apology, certainly not a Sally Devine apology. So what do you say, shall we go find a pastry shop somewhere?"

I sighed. "Let 'em eat cake," I said.

I followed Sally in my car as she led the way to some French patisserie place in town. I wasn't surprised to see that they had the exact flourless chocolate cake with raspberry ganache that Sally had talked about, especially after it became clear that everyone working in the place knew Sally by name, and vice versa.

I polished off two pieces and I could've had a third. In the wake of Tyler, I continued to have this insatiable appetite. What fodder for a shrink I would've been. Meanwhile, for a woman who was so determined to have cake, Sally took maybe four bites. She seemed more enamored of her peppermint herbal tea. Her right pinkie, the only finger besides the thumb on that heavily bejeweled hand of hers that was without either a diamond or a sapphire, pointed demurely into the air each time she raised the cup to her lips.

"Would it make you uncomfortable if I spoke openly about myself and perhaps my marriage?" she said. "The reason I ask is because for me to apologize to you, I need to do that . . . speak openly, that is. I realize you work for Jack, and I know you probably look up to him, which is okay. My intention isn't to ruin that."

"Sally, if you're worrying that I would say or repeat anything back to—"

"No, it's not that. I mean, I don't want you to say anything to Jack; it's just that I know what it's like sometimes when someone you don't truly know very well starts confiding in you. It can be a little unsettling."

"It's fine," I said. "Confide away."

Sally took another sip of her tea and followed it with a long look up. "It goes something like this," she said. "I'm a forty-eight-year-old woman who never had a career, was unable to have children, and who drinks to get attention. My husband cheats on me and the scary thing is, I'm not sure that I blame him. Even if I could blame him, what are my options—leaving him? Where would I go, what would I do? This is all I know, Philip: living in that house, getting dressed up, and going places to be with people who simply know me as one more wife of a powerful man they have to be nice to. If I disappeared tomorrow, it wouldn't make a difference to them. It wouldn't make a difference to anyone, which is basically what I'm trying to tell you."

"What are you saying?"

"What I'm saying, Philip, is that my car accident was no accident."

"Jesus, Sally. . . ."

"I know, and like I said, you can't say anything to Jack."

"I won't, but what you just told me doesn't get much more serious. I think you need to get some help."

"I would think so too if it wasn't for one thing."

"That being?"

"I hit the brakes. I had steered right for that telephone pole and gunned it, but at the last possible second I tried to stop. I guess that's what it took to realize that I didn't really want to die."

I gave her a skeptical look. "That doesn't mean for sure the feeling won't come back," I said.

"It does with me."

"Sally, you were still drinking in the days after it, though."

"I didn't say I solved *all* my problems," she said. "But now that you mention it, I haven't had a drink for two weeks, and you know what? I've lost three pounds because of it. If I'd known sobriety was such a great diet I would've stopped drinking years ago!"

She laughed and I looked at her. It was a genuine laugh, I could tell, not one performed for my benefit. Hell, maybe she was going to be all right after all.

"Will you do me a favor, though, Sally?"

"What's that?"

"I'll honor your request not to say anything on one condition. If you find that things start to go bad for you again, you call me. I want you to feel like you can do that."

"I already do," she said.

"Good."

"Will you forgive me for making that pass at you?"

"I already have."

"Good." She smiled.

Later, as I drove back into Manhattan, there was only one thing I was asking myself: What was it with me and suicidal people?

TWENTY-FIVE

Tracy was crying.

I walked into our loft, turned the corner of our foyer, and saw her sitting there alone on the couch, her head in her hands. I took a seat beside her, saying nothing.

"He's dead," was all she could get out.

"Who?" I asked, as if I didn't know.

Tracy sniffed repeatedly and tried to catch her breath. "Tyler."

"You're kidding me!"

"They think someone broke into his apartment when he was asleep."

"Oh, my god, I don't believe it."

Tracy started to cry louder. If grief was an engine, disbelief was its pistons. "I know," she wailed. "I don't believe it either!"

I put my arm around Tracy and tried to console her. The Good Husband. I had fully anticipated having to endure this moment. What I hadn't anticipated was that it would be happening so soon after the fact. The grapevine was fast but not that fast, not even in the age of the grapevine.com. There was no way the word could have spread so quickly. Sit tight, Philip, the answer is sure to come.

A half a box of tissues later . . .

"She sounded so sad," Tracy said.

Thus began the story. Tracy and her artistic eye had finally gotten around to paging Tyler. However, from there the evolution of events hadn't progressed as I'd expected. Tracy's page had not fallen on deaf ears.

"Who sounded so sad?" I asked.

"Tyler's mother."

"His mother?"

"Yes. She's the one who called me back when I paged Tyler. She's the one who told me."

"Wow," I said. There was no need to pretend with that reaction. Tyler's mother? In the years that I had known him, dating back to Deerfield, I'd never heard Tyler say as much as one word about his parents. On the other hand, no one, including myself, had ever thought much to ask.

Said Tracy, "His mother told me that they found out two days ago. Tyler was discovered dead in his apartment. He lived by himself, so they don't know yet how long . . . I mean . . . when it actually happened. The landlord found him. Tyler was late on his rent, so the landlord had gone to see him. Anyway, Tyler's parents went to the apartment after the police notified them. His mother found his pager. I guess she held on to it."

"I can't believe she would call you back like that," I said. "She doesn't even know you. Hell, she doesn't even know me."

"That's the thing. After I told her who I was and how

you went to school with Tyler, she just started talking, telling me how both she and her husband were so blown away by the whole thing and how the police don't seem to have any leads. She was thinking that maybe by keeping Tyler's pager on she'd get a chance to talk to one of his friends, you know, find out if maybe Tyler was in some kind of trouble."

"Is that what they're thinking?"

"I don't know. I guess with his history anything's possible."

"I still can't believe it," I said. "We saw him, what, like a couple of weeks ago?"

Tracy nodded and reached for another tissue.

"I guess that's the thing with life . . . why you can't take it for granted," I said, looking to initiate some closure on the conversation, or at least move beyond the initial shock. It was too late for Tracy to go shopping, so I knew there'd be more of the ordeal with which to contend. Though I didn't realize how much more until Tracy broke some more news to me.

"The funeral is tomorrow morning," she said. "I told Tyler's mother that you and I would both be there."

What?

I nearly choked on my own tongue. She couldn't be serious. Quick, Philip, make up an excuse. "Oh, no, did you say tomorrow morning?" I said, sounding my somber best.

"Yes, ten o'clock. Why?"

"I'm meeting with the Brevin Industries people all morning. You remember how I mentioned that case to you." I looked at my watch. "There's no way I can cancel it at this hour."

Tracy's eyes said it all: disgust. "Perhaps you weren't paying attention before," she said, accenting every syllable while gradually raising her voice. "Somebody killed Tyler—he's dead!—and all you can think about is your stupid fucking meeting tomorrow?! Jesus Christ, Philip, could you be any more of a self-absorbed *asshole?*"

No, I suppose I couldn't.

"You're right, I'm sorry," I said sheepishly. I wanted to be careful not to push it. I sank back on the couch and resigned myself to the unthinkable. There was no way around it. Like it or not, I was going to Tyler's funeral.

"Where's it being held?" I asked.

"It's in Westfield, New Jersey. Tyler's mother gave me directions. She said it's about half an hour out of the city."

I got up, and Tracy wanted to know where I was going.

"To call Gwen . . . reschedule the meeting in the morning," I explained.

"Thanks," she said, easing up on me a little. "I know you weren't exactly the best of friends with Tyler, but his mother assumed we'd be there. I couldn't say no."

"I understand. You did the right thing."

I went into the den, closed the French doors behind me, and plopped myself down on an ottoman.

Fuck.

TWENTY-SIX

Tracy was in her bra and panties, holding up two black suits against her body. "Which one says *I'm grieving* the most," she asked me, "the Donna Karan or the Armani?"

From where I stood across the room, they both looked like the same outfit. Nonetheless, I told her, "Definitely the Armani." Never mind that I didn't know which was which. As any intelligent married man will tell you, the more inane the question from your wife, the more important it is to give a quick and decisive answer.

Tracy nodded in agreement. "You're right, the Armani; simple, elegant . . . it says mourning but not in a depressing way."

I turned to phone the garage so they could have our car ready, and all along I couldn't help thinking one thing. Please, lord, let this day go by as fast as possible.

We got on the road, and it didn't take long to realize. The only way Westfield, New Jersey, could've been a half hour out of the city, as Tyler's mother had claimed, was if we had been the lone car on the road. No such luck. I hated traffic. Tracy hated to be late. The two of us were a dangerous combination in the front seat of the Range Rover. By the time we ultimately did arrive, we were barely speaking to each other.

We hadn't missed much. In fact, we hadn't missed anything. It made any lingering friction from the car ride between us seem kind of pointless. As we walked toward the entrance of Saint Catherine's Church, we saw that everyone there for the service was still milling about out front and in the vestibule. *Saint Catherine's*, huh? In light of Tyler's interesting take on God, it was safe to assume that he had been a lapsed Catholic at best.

Almost immediately, I wondered if maybe we didn't have the right funeral. Tracy and I were the only ones who could possibly have been viewed as contemporaries of Tyler's. A few small children notwithstanding, the vast majority of those in attendance were easily twenty years our senior. Acquaintances of his parents, I assumed.

"Didn't he have any friends?" Tracy asked me, looking around surprised.

"Not many that I knew of," I replied.

"Maybe they couldn't make it on such short notice," she said, as if to give Tyler the benefit of the doubt.

"Could be."

Tracy pointed. "Do you think those are his parents?"

I followed Tracy's finger and saw an older man and woman facing what looked to be an ad hoc receiving line. "I'd have to believe so," I told her.

"There's just the two of them there—Tyler must have been an only child."

"I think he may have mentioned that to me once," I made up.

She grabbed my arm and began to walk toward them. "C'mon," she said.

"Whoa, what are you doing?" I said, not budging.

"What do you mean, *what am I doing?* We're going over there so we can introduce ourselves and say our condolences. What'd you think I was doing?"

"Do we really have to?" I tried. "We're here, isn't that enough?"

"No, it's not enough," she said, almost amused by my lame reasoning.

I started to grasp for anything. "Look at how long the line is."

"It's just going to get longer," she said. "They're obviously greeting people first. Now, c'mon. It's the right thing to do."

My wife—wise in the ways of funeral protocol, and at that moment not about to take no for an answer. All that was missing was the leash around my neck. Begrudgingly, I started to walk with her toward Tyler's parents.

Traffic I may have hated. Funerals I loathed. Not because they were sad, or reminded me of my own mortality, but because of the simple fact that I never knew what to say at them. I could wax eloquent in the courtroom and be as hail-fellow-well-met as the rest of them most anywhere else, and yet, for some reason I could never bring myself to deliver lines like "He'll be deeply missed," or "I am so very sorry" to a grieving member of someone's family. And that was at funerals where I hadn't actually been a participant in the person's death. You can imagine my additional reluctance.

We made it to the front of the line, Tracy first.

"Mrs. Mills, I'm Tracy Randall; we spoke yesterday on the phone."

"Yes, of course, Tracy, thank you so much for coming," said Tyler's mother, slowly and deliberately. She looked to be on a few Tic Tacs herself, if you know what I'm saying. Early sixties, mostly gray, tall, and relatively thin. A New Jersey society type, if there was such a thing. In addition to her black outfit and black hat, she had black circles around her eyes. Safe to say she hadn't slept for a few days. She turned her head and looked at me. "You must be Philip," she said.

I nodded and was about to say something trite and expected from the funeral lexicon when she continued: ". . . Tyler told me so much about you."

I froze.

"Of course, that was a long time ago, back when you were classmates at Deerfield."

I unfroze. "Those were good times," I said.

"I often wonder," she responded. "You know, Tyler never seemed to be the same after that place."

Awkward silence. There was little I could say to that. "Hey, you're the one who sent him there" probably wouldn't have gone over too well.

Tracy saved me. She had moved on to introduce herself to Tyler's father and, not wanting to hold up the line, started to pull me over.

"I hope we can talk more after the service," I told Mrs. Mills.

The conversation with Mr. Mills was short and sweet. There was no "Tyler told me so much about you." Actually, there was no Tyler anything. When I explained that I knew his son from Deerfield, the man, also in his early sixties, mostly gray, tall, and relatively thin, simply shook my hand again and told me that it was good of me to come.

Translation: Next!

That was fine by me. Tracy and I moved it along and over to a flower bed, where we stood and waited for Tyler's parents to greet the remainder of the line behind us. That morning, on the walk to the garage for the car, I had negotiated with Tracy that our obligation ended after the service. The burial and any possible reception to follow we were planning to skip. Which was why, having endured the encounter with Mr. and Mrs. Mills, I figured the worst was over.

Ha!

As everyone eventually began to proceed into the church, Mrs. Mills, in all her pharmaceutically induced calmness, walked up to Tracy and me.

"Philip, I was wondering if I could ask you something?" she said.

"Sure, anything," I answered.

"I was wondering if maybe you could get up and say a few words on Tyler's behalf during the service?"

Again, I froze.

". . . It would mean a great deal to me, and I know it's something Tyler would've wanted," she added.

Don't be so sure, Mrs. Mills.

I was starting to hem and haw about not having prepared anything when out of the corner of my eye I caught Tracy's glare. Said the glare, "You can't say no to a grieving mother, you stupid idiot, don't you know anything?!"

Fucking Tracy and her funeral protocol.

"I'd be honored to, Mrs. Mills," came out of my mouth. I wasn't exactly sure how it did.

"Thank you," she said. "I'll mention it to Father Whelan so he can have you come forward at the appropriate time."

Mrs. Mills walked off.

I looked at Tracy. "What the hell am I going to say?"

"Something nice, I would hope. Think of it as your ultimate closing statement. If that doesn't help, lie your ass off."

"Thanks," I told her. "You're a big help."

We headed inside the church. I tried my best not to look at the coffin as we took our seats.

The pew felt especially hard. I sat there fidgeting, trying my damnedest to think of something that I could stand up and pass off as part of my fond remembrances of Tyler. I flashed through our years at Deerfield. After eliminating every anecdote that involved either smoking pot or making fun of him, I was essentially left with nothing. The hymns were flying by, and Father Whelan had already used the phrase "senseless tragedy" a dozen times in his eulogy. I was definitely in the on-deck circle.

Which was precisely when I thought of my grandfather.

During my second year of law school he had passed away. My father's father. It was a stroke. He and my grandmother had been living in Florida for about six years after spending most of their lives in Philadelphia. Despite its being doctor's orders (arthritis), my grandfather had moved away reluctantly. "Death's Triple A Club," he called Florida, always quick to tack on that he was "just waiting to get called up." He too liked his baseball.

Anyway, at his funeral, the usual suspects among my relatives stood up and read poems or gave speeches. My uncle Timothy played his guitar. All in the good name of my grandfather. It was nice, though none of it was particularly moving. Then, right as everyone thought there was no one left who wanted to speak, an elderly man sitting in the back row rose to his feet. He slowly walked up to the lectern. You could see my relatives looking at one another as if to ask, "Who is this man?" At the time, nobody knew. They simply watched as he cleared his throat and started to talk. What he shared with us was one of the most heartfelt stories that I had ever heard.

I mention all of this because on that day of Tyler's funeral, it also became one of the most heartfelt stories that I had ever stolen. All I had to do was change the names and places. That, and have the guts to actually tell it.

"Now," said Father Whelan, giving me a nod, "I'd like to ask Philip Randall, a very good friend of Tyler's from their days at Deerfield together, to come forward."

Tracy squeezed my hand—the nonbandaged one—for good luck as I made my way out into the aisle and up to the front of the congregation. I stood there for a second and looked out at everyone waiting for me to begin. Here goes nothing, I thought.

I've been thinking this morning about whether or not you can ever truly know someone. You may think you can, you may hope you can, and yet, often it seems, you can never really know for sure. But one thing I do know is that the story I'm about to tell you is very much real. And I think it says a great deal about who Tyler Mills really was.

It begins back at Deerfield. Tyler and I were walking in the woods around campus one afternoon during the fall of our sophomore year when we came across a brass compass lying there on the ground. It was old and its glass casing was scratched. Nonetheless, there was no denying the fact that it was beautiful. Its shine may have been gone, but somehow it still managed to sparkle.

As we had both seen the compass at the same time, my immediate concern became which one of us would be able to keep it. To be honest with you, I wanted it to be me. However, I also knew that I had no more claim to it than Tyler had. So there we stood, alone in the woods, staring at this beautiful compass that we had both found together.

That's when Tyler had an idea. To prevent either one of us from being disappointed, he said, maybe what we should do is take turns holding on to it. One of us would have it for one year, and after that we'd hand it over to the other person for the next, and so on.

I remember looking at Tyler when he finished telling me his idea. It was a great idea, and I felt awful. I had been so preoccupied with wanting this compass for myself that it never occurred to me that we both could share it. I was embarrassed at how selfish my thoughts had been.

So from that day forward, that's what we did. We took turns holding on to the compass. Tyler let me have it the first year and then I gave it to him for the next. For the first few years, the exchange happened in person, and we were always sure to make an occasion out of it. It was something that we kept private, never telling anyone else about the arrangement.

Of course, as the years went by and our lives took us to different places, it became harder and harder to meet up in person to exchange the compass. That didn't mean we didn't do it. It just meant that every other year a small package would arrive in my mail, just like it had the previous year in Tyler's. And inside this package the compass would always be there, and in my case, there'd also always be a little note from Tyler. It said the same thing every time.

May this compass remain as true as our friendship.

Last night I went to my drawer and took out that old, scuffed-up compass and looked at it. You see, it's been my year to hold on to it. Come this fall, though, if you happen to see it on the ground by Tyler's grave, I respectfully ask that you let it be. Because that's when it will be his turn to watch over it.

It's funny; to this day that compass still knows how to point north. But I'll tell you this much: it will never be quite as true as my good friend Tyler Mills.

I stopped and I stood there for a second looking out at everyone. There wasn't a dry eye in the church. Even Father Whelan was choked up. One lady in the fourth row was sobbing so loudly her husband had to escort her out. Damn, I was good. I left the lectern and returned to my seat. The pew no longer felt so hard.

Tracy, tissue in hand, leaned over to me and whispered, "Why didn't you ever tell me about that?"

"Because it never happened," I whispered back, leaving off the *you idiot*.

We stood for the final hymn.

After the service you practically had to peel Mrs. Mills off of me. She rushed up and plastered a hug so hard it nearly knocked me over.

"Tell me you brought that compass with you," she said. "You have to let me see it."

Uh-oh.

"I'm afraid I didn't," I said.

"Will you send it to me? Please, will you do that?" she begged.

"Of course," I told her.

Right after I go and find one that matches the description in a pawnshop somewhere.

Yep . . . I was going to hell, all right.

That afternoon I returned to the office to find Jack insisting on a blow-by-blow account of Sally's DMV hearing. The fact that he'd been forced to wait until I got back from "my friend's funeral" had driven him crazy.

To make it up to him I was embellishing the story whenever possible, such as claiming that attorney Jonathan Clemments could barely get Jack's name out of his mouth due to the fact that he had been stuttering so much out of fear. "De-De-De-Devine," I said, pretending to imitate the poor guy. Jack laughed so hard he was practically in tears. He joked that the finishing touch would be arranging for a copy machine repair guy to visit Clemments's office out in Westchester every day for a week straight. Jack went so far as to summon Donna into his office to make the necessary calls, though he quickly changed his mind. "On second thought," said Jack, "I hate end-zone dances."

TWENTY-SEVEN

I could've sworn he winked at me.

From the portrait of him that hung in the reception area of our office, I could've sworn that Thomas Methuen Campbell had winked at me as I walked into work the following morning. It was coming up on a week since that night at Tyler's apartment, and here was the founding father of Campbell & Devine looking down at me from his perch on the wall as if to say, "Don't sweat it, kid."

I was inclined to take his advice.

All things considered, the only downside for me at that juncture was that I had quickly put on a few pounds. Tracy noticed and said she would use more recipes from *Cooking Light* in the future. I told her not to worry. While my hunger had been relentless, I knew it was finally starting to subside. Slowly but surely, I was beginning to feel like myself again.

So was Raymond's mother, apparently.

He was checking me into a room at the Doral Court later that day and telling me that his mother had finished with her chemotherapy. The cancer in her stomach hadn't spread, and she was in remission.

"I told you the devil was no match for her," I said.

"No, but those hospital bills might be," Raymond replied.

I knew it was merely a knee-jerk comment on his part. He wasn't angling for a handout by any stretch. If I had thought he was, I never would've done what I did next—make a check out to him for a thousand bucks. I don't know what came over me; I just did it.

"Give this money to your mother," I said, sliding the check across the counter.

Raymond was genuinely shocked. "Mr. Randall, there's no way I can accept that."

"Sure there is, it's easy. You simply put it in your pocket."

"When I mentioned those hospital bills I—"

"I know . . . you weren't playing me," I said, although I regretted the choice of words almost immediately after they left my mouth. There was nothing worse than a white guy trying to talk street.

Raymond either didn't notice or didn't care. He was too busy trying to decide what to do about my offering. After glancing to see if his supervisor, or anyone else for that matter, was looking, he reached for the check with those long fingers of his.

"I promise you that I'll give this to her," he said.

"I'm sure you will."

"I don't know how to thank you."

"Don't worry about it," I said.

Raymond again glanced around the reception area, and again no one was looking.

"Wait, I know how," he said. He gave me that slight smile of his, combined with that all-too-aware tilt of his head. He handed me my room key while at the same time stuffing my registration and credit card slip inside his jacket. "This one's on me," he said.

Who was I to say no?

I didn't tell Jessica she was a freebie that afternoon. There was no way I could share the story of giving Raymond's mother money without sounding like a braggart. Besides, since Jessica and I had officially resumed our matinees, our conversations had remained at a minimum, at least *before* the sex. There were lost orgasms to be made up for and only a lunch hour at a time to do it.

However, as I hadn't seen her since Tyler's demise, she did manage to ask about my hand while I was hastily unbuttoning her blouse. It was amazing how one little bandage could trigger so many questions—all the more reason why I wasn't about to let Jessica see my second little bandage.

"Why do you still have your T-shirt on?" she asked me.

"Because I feel fat," I replied, mimicking perhaps every girl I had ever dated. Jessica laughed and let it go. Little did she know I wasn't completely joking.

If you haven't already guessed, our newest favorite position had become that so-called butterfly of hers, especially when she told me that she hadn't really tried it with Connor. True to its billing, it made Jessica come harder than ever before. Though with the way she rested her ankles on my shoulders while I lifted her up by the hips, I wasn't so quick to agree with the name. "The wheelbarrow" seemed more like it.

We were getting ready to leave.

Said Jessica, "Tracy told me about the death of your friend Tyler. I couldn't believe it."

"Neither could I," I said. "Nice city we live in, huh?"

"There were no witnesses or anything?"

"Apparently not."

"It's kind of weird, having met him that one time. I didn't realize, though, that you really weren't that crazy about him."

"Tracy said that?" I asked.

"No, actually Connor said you had mentioned that to him."

"Tyler was a little troubled, that's all. It was hard to be his friend," I said.

"What'd he do for a living?"

"I'm not sure he did anything."

"You mean he was unemployed?"

"No, I mean I don't think he ever had a job."

"Sounds familiar," she said snidely, alluding to her brother.

"Hey, you don't think Zachary is going to climb up a water tower one day with a high-powered rifle, do you?"

"No, I don't think so," said Jessica, ". . . he's afraid of heights."

I laughed about that all the way back to work.

Later that afternoon, I was in my office with the door closed when Gwen buzzed me.

"Philip, there are two gentlemen here to see you," she said.

I wasn't expecting anyone. "Do they have an appointment?" I asked.

"No, but they do have very shiny badges."

TWENTY-EIGHT

Whatever you do, Philip, don't freak.

"Tell them I'll be right with them," I said to Gwen.

I figured I had about a minute. Anything less would come across as a little too fearful; anything more and they'd think I was crawling out on the ledge to escape. Instinctively, I reached for the Drawer. Bypassing the cologne, floss, and hair gel, I took a hit of breath spray while grabbing the comb. I went over to the mirror behind my door and checked for loose hairs. I needed to look collected. I also needed to look busy. Hastily, I grabbed a Redweld file and spread some documents out on my desk and coffee table. *Gentlemen, do I look like I have the time to go out and kill somebody?* Hey, with a little luck maybe they were just collecting donations for the Police Athletic League.

That would take a shitload of luck, I realized.

It was show time. I opened the door to my office and walked out.

"Philip Randall?" said the shorter of the two.

"Yeah, that's me," I said.

Both men flashed their badges. Gwen was right; they were indeed very shiny.

Continued the shorter one, "I'm Detective Hicks and this is my partner, Detective Benoit. We were wondering if you could spare a few minutes of your time?"

I shrugged. "Sure, c'mon in," I told them. "Gwen, will you hold my calls?"

She nodded. The way she was watching everything unfold, you would've expected to see a bucket of popcorn in her lap.

I led the detectives into my office and closed the door. "Excuse the mess," I said.

"Not a problem," said the tall one, Benoit, in a friendly enough fashion.

You watch enough cop-buddy movies and you begin to think that all partners are supposed to look like direct opposites. Not these guys. Despite the height difference, they could've easily been brothers. Both looked to be in their forties, both had dark hair and mustaches, and both wore the cynical expression of having been exposed to every appalling thing you could ever imagine in New York City. As well as a few things you couldn't.

I took a seat behind my desk as Hicks and Benoit helped themselves to the two chairs in front of it. They struck relaxed postures. A positive sign, I thought.

"Do you guys want some coffee or anything?" I asked.

They shook their heads. "No, thanks, we're all set," said Hicks.

"So what can I do for you?" I said.

The two exchanged glances. It was as if they were asking each other who wanted to do the talking. Hicks volunteered. "We understand you were a good friend of Tyler Mills," he said.

"I don't know if *good* is the right word, but we were definitely friendly with each other," I replied. "I had a feeling that's why you guys were here."

"You were expecting us to be talking to you?" asked Hicks.

"Tyler's mother, Mrs. Mills, told my wife that there were no leads, at least right after it happened. I figured it was only a matter of time before you got around to all of Tyler's friends."

"Turns out he didn't have that many friends," said Hicks.

"So what took you so long?" I joked. I didn't care if they laughed. It showed I was loose. "Seriously, though, do you think Tyler was in some kind of trouble?"

"What makes you say that?" came back Hicks, clearly a proud graduate of the "try to trip 'em up" school of interrogation.

"It's been my experience that a victim often knows the perpetrator," I explained. I was a lawyer, after all.

"It's been our experience as well," said Hicks with a nod toward his partner. "When was the last time you talked to Tyler?"

I thought for a second. "I guess it was the last time I saw him. It was by accident, really. My wife and I were out to dinner with another couple about a month ago when we bumped into him."

"You didn't hear from him or see him again after that?" asked Hicks.

"No, I don't think so."

"No phone communication?" Hicks pressed.

I checked off all the calls in my mind, making sure that all of them after that night at Balthazar had been safely via pay phone. "No, I don't remember any," I said.

"Did Tyler ever mention to you that he was planning on leaving the country?" said Hicks.

The plane ticket to Bali. Although it certainly didn't implicate me, I had never thought to look for it in Tyler's apartment. The detectives had obviously found it. "No," I said, "he never said anything about going anywhere."

Next question. "How is it that you knew Tyler originally?" Hicks asked.

"We went to school together."

"College?"

"No, prep school."

Oooooh, get a load of fancy pants here, I imagined the two saying to themselves. As if I couldn't have just answered "high school." It didn't help that at about the same time, Benoit—very much the silent partner to that point—was casually looking around my office. His eyes moved off the picture on my bookshelf of Tracy and me skiing in Aspen and stopped on the knitted pillow that was lying on my couch. "It's hard to be humble when you're from Dartmouth," it read.

Great.

"Getting back to Tyler being in trouble," said Hicks. "Was there anything that you and he ever talked about that would possibly make you think that was the case?"

"To be perfectly blunt, I always used to think the biggest threat to Tyler was Tyler," I said. "You guys know he tried to kill himself once, right?"

"Yes, we know all about that," said Hicks. "By the way, what happened to your hand?"

"I cut it with a pair of scissors trying to open up a package," I replied, suddenly grateful for all the other times prior that I had had to answer the question. I was good and practiced. By this time the excuse sounded very convincing coming out of my mouth.

Hicks was about to ask another question when Benoit interrupted him.

"I think we've taken up enough of Mr. Randall's time," said Benoit, standing up. That surprised Hicks a bit, but he followed suit and rose to his feet. I had begun to notice a slight pecking order between the two of them, and from that last bit it seemed likely that Benoit had maybe a few more years on the job. He reached inside his Moe Ginsburg and took out a card. "If you can think of anything that might help, like why someone might have a beef with Tyler," he said, handing me the card, "please give us a call."

"Absolutely," I said. I shook their hands and was about to show them out when I couldn't leave well enough alone. "Out of curiosity, how did you get my name?" I asked.

"Tyler's mother," I anticipated hearing, when instead I watched as the two of them looked at each other again. Benoit volunteered this time.

"Actually, Mr. Randall," he said, "it was your number we got first. It seems that the very last phone call Tyler made was to you here at your office the night he died."

"Are you serious?"

Hicks chimed in. "Yes. He called a little before eight P.M. Were you here?"

Nice try, detective. He had fed me the time hoping once again to trip me up. If I answered yes or no directly it would've meant that I knew something only the killer or the coroner could know for sure—the actual day that Tyler died. I wasn't about to make it so easy for these guys.

"Was I here?" I repeated back. "Well, that depends, what day are we talking about?"

I detected a slight look of disappointment from Hicks. "Last Friday," he said.

I pulled the weekly calendar on my desk toward me and I flipped back a page. "As a matter of fact, I was here working late," I said. "Not always in my office, perhaps, but I was here."

"You don't recall speaking to him, do you?" said Benoit.

"No."

". . . Or getting a message from him?"

"No."

"Of course not," Benoit said, as if correcting himself. "You would've mentioned that to us before when we asked. It's not like you would've forgotten, right?" Benoit stepped and opened my office door. "Thanks again for your time, Mr. Randall."

"No problem," I said, struggling to keep the strain in check. "Wait, I'll show you the way."

"Not necessary, we'll find it," said Benoit with an easy smile. "After all, we are detectives."

The two men walked out past Gwen at her desk. As soon as her eyes were done following them they snapped back to me. For sure, she was dying to know what had happened.

Truth was, I wasn't exactly sure.

I closed my door again and sat back behind my desk, thinking. A lot of it didn't make sense, starting with the bit about Tyler's last phone call. There was no way the detectives could've known about Tyler's calling me from a pay phone inside Billy's Hideaway that night.

Wait a minute. . . .

I had only *assumed* Tyler had called me from a pay phone.

That's when it hit me. The fucking hypocrite. Tyler had gone on and on about people and their cell phones, the way he would harass them, and what does he end up having? A cell phone. It all started to make sense. How else could he have always returned my pages so quickly?

Like that, I shifted into lawyer mode. The 3 D's: deconstruct, discern, and deduce. Hicks and Benoit had obviously gotten Tyler's cell phone records. That's how they knew I was the last person Tyler had called. It immediately made me wonder how long Tyler's message to me that night had been. It was short, but how short? Under two minutes and it was plausible that he had called, gotten my voice mail, and hung up without leaving a message. Over two minutes and they would think there was a good chance they had caught me in a lie.

I got up and started to pace in my office. As I walked back and forth, so did I waver on what really had taken place. The phone call bit aside, the meeting with the detectives had been too short and their questions too crafted. It was way too cat-and-mouse. Something was up.

You're screwed, Philip.

Or was it just my paranoia kicking in? Interviewing Tyler's friends was SOP for the investigation. If the detectives truly had something on me, I wouldn't still be sitting in my office, I told myself. But there I was, and they were gone. Forget it, they didn't have anything on me. How could they? I had gone to great lengths to cover my tracks, to remove any trace of myself from the threat of suspicion. So what if I was the last person Tyler had called? Somebody had to be. That hardly suggested motive on my part.

You're far from screwed, Philip.

It continued like that for the rest of the afternoon. I paced the carpet in my office believing one thing one minute and another thing the next. My fervent hope was that I'd never see Detectives Hicks and Benoit again. My greatest fear was that they were just getting warmed up.

TWENTY-NINE

Right away, Tracy wanted to know what was wrong. So much for my trying to act normal. The more I told her that it was nothing, the more she didn't believe me. My reticence made her angry, and within ten minutes of my coming home, Tracy told me I was on my own for dinner. She had very little patience when it came to not getting her own way. She stormed off into our bedroom. I decided to get some air.

It was a comfortable night, warm and mostly calm, save the occasional breeze that filtered its way in from the Hudson. There were your dogs on leashes, your couples walking arm in arm, your delivery guys on bicycles. All the outdoor tables in front of the restaurants I passed were full of people and their conversations. Pockets of noise that would build and fade, build and fade, as I'd go walking by.

I wanted so badly to call Jessica, if only to hear her voice. But she was most likely "out of bounds," as we called it—at home with Connor. In any event, there was nothing I could tell her, nothing at all that I could share.

This was one of those things I was going to have to
wait out all on my own.

I ended up at the Old Town Bar, though no one ever
called it that. It was always the Old Town, the "Bar"
being a given. There I found a booth, a burger and fries,
and more than a few pints of Sierra Nevada. It had been
some time since I'd last eaten dinner out alone, or, for
that matter, paid for one in cash. I barely had enough
on me to cover the tip.

When I got home Tracy glared at me from her side
of the bed. I said nothing and got underneath the sheets.
I didn't have the stomach to make peace. Literally.
When not tossing and turning the remainder of the
night, I was getting up and swigging Mylanta right out
of the bottle. I wondered if ulcers could really develop
this fast.

The following day my heart skipped a beat every time
Gwen buzzed me in my office. My time sheet for that
date may have indicated five billable hours on the Brevin
Industries case, but I assure you that they got fifteen
minutes of my undivided attention at best.

Later, back at the loft, I was relieved to see that Tracy
wasn't holding a grudge. My not wanting to tell her
what was bothering me the night before seemed to have
been forgotten. It may have had something to do with
the fact that it was a Friday night and we had plans.
One of Tracy's former roommates from Brown was in
town with her new boyfriend and there was a reservation at Mesa Grill waiting for the four of us. Tracy knew
all too well that she couldn't exactly go through the entire dinner without talking to me. So she made nice. In
return, I was in better spirits. I was a full day removed

from the visit of the detectives, and for the first time
the scales were beginning to tip in favor of optimism.
Maybe the whole thing would blow over after all. No
repercussions. The money I would save on Mylanta alone
would be astounding.

In hindsight, they were probably just fucking with my
head.

———————

Gwen didn't need to buzz me this time. My office door
was open that Monday morning and I could hear them
talking to her. Detectives Hicks and Benoit were back
for a return visit. Something told me that it wasn't simply to say hi.

I got up and walked out to Gwen's desk. There they
stood. The cynical expressions remained the same. The
tone, however, was far from cordial.

"We should step inside your office," said Hicks to
start things off. There were no *hellos* or *nice to see you
agains*. Nonetheless, I had no reason to change my tone.
I shrugged as I had the previous time and turned back
into my office. They followed and closed my door behind them.

"Mr. Randall, to get right to the point, we'd like for
you to come in for some additional questioning," said
Hicks.

"What, are you arresting me?" I said.

"No," said Benoit, "your coming with us would be
strictly voluntary."

"And if I don't cooperate?"

"That's your prerogative," said Benoit. "Though some

might be inclined to view that as a curious choice on your part at this juncture."

"You'll forgive me if I appear reluctant. I'm a little familiar with the game, as you can imagine," I said.

"Then you know that the questions simply won't go away," said Benoit, "which means neither will we until we get some things cleared up. So why don't we make it simple. You grab your jacket and come with us. If you'd like, you could also grab a lawyer."

I would've been grabbing a lawyer regardless of whether or not Benoit had mentioned it. Still, his words echoed in my head. I was an attorney being told that I needed an attorney. This was not good, not good at all. I thought for a second. There was only one thing left for me to do.

Paging Jack Devine.

I told Gwen to go down to see if he was in his office. Hicks and Benoit expected as much. Their attempts at not giving a shit were a little too practiced.

She returned alone, however. Jack was at a doctor's appointment, of all things, though due back shortly. "Have him meet me there," I told her, deciding that it wasn't feasible to wait. Gwen took down the precinct and the address. Off I went with my two new friends.

Sitting there in the backseat of their unmarked Ford, I tried to think of what mistake I had made. Something that I'd forgotten to do . . . that overlooked loose end. Nothing came to mind.

"You know, I once thought I wanted to be a lawyer," said Hicks, raising his voice from the driver's seat so I'd know he was talking to me.

I indulged him. "What changed your mind?"

"The thought of helping somebody get away with a crime, that's what," he said. "How do you deal with it?"

The fact that it was an obnoxious question aside, it was a little eerie. Tyler had essentially asked me the same thing: whether I was comfortable with helping guilty people go free. Perhaps the spirit of Tyler was now inhabiting Hicks's body, I thought. That I could have such a thought was reason enough to lower the window and let some air blow on my face.

With his question unanswered, Hicks turned back to me. "Did you hear me?" he asked.

"I heard you," I said. "You know, it may seem like it because of your job, Detective, but not every lawyer is a defense attorney. You could've practiced environmental law, for instance."

"What, you mean like defend trees?" he said, amused.

Benoit, who had remained uninvolved up to that point, if not completely uninterested, let go with a brief chuckle. It was not clear whether he was laughing with, at, or simply near his partner.

The subject was dropped.

Once inside the precinct, we took an elevator up to the fifth floor and walked back to a small interviewing room complete with a one-way mirror. Here I would learn the reason behind this unfortunate turn of events for me. My mounting curiosity to know, however, was not about to overtake my good sense to sit tight for Jack. When the detectives started to play down their additional questioning so as to get started without him, I asked for a cup of coffee and a few minutes of their patience. That way, we won't have to repeat anything, I told them.

The wait was short.

Two minutes later, the cavalry of one entered the room with guns blazing. Said Jack, slamming his briefcase on the table, "You guys have got to be pretty fucking sure of yourselves to be dragging one of my lawyers down here. That, or pretty fucking stupid."

"We didn't drag him in here; he came voluntarily," said Hicks, taking offense.

Jack ignored him. "The next time you want to come to my office and speak to one of my attorneys, and I don't care if it's only about the fucking weather, you clear it with me first!"

Hicks stood up and was about to go toe to toe with Jack when Benoit motioned with his arm for Hicks to back off. Benoit looked at Jack calmly. "I'm about to get myself some more coffee; would you like some?" he asked.

Jack immediately calmed down. He was satisfied. His balls-of-fire entrance was all about the unofficial hierarchy—which of the two detectives was the one with whom he really had to deal. While Hicks was standing there wondering why in the hell his partner was offering to get coffee for some pompous asshole of a lawyer, Benoit had managed to make one thing perfectly clear. He was the man as far as Jack was concerned.

"Thank you, but I'll pass on the coffee," Jack said. "However, a few minutes alone with Mr. Randall here would be most appreciated."

"Will five be enough?" asked Benoit.

"It should be," said Jack.

"By the way," said Benoit, "it might be a good idea

to introduce ourselves. I'm Detective Benoit and this is
Detective Hicks."

"Jack Devine," said Jack.

They knew.

"We'll see you in five minutes," said Benoit.

The two were almost out of the room.

"Oh, Detective Hicks, would you mind putting the
light on in the next room, please," said Jack, looking at
the one-way mirror.

Hicks frowned. "It would be my pleasure," he said
in all insincerity, slamming the door behind him.

Before saying a word, Jack did a lap around the room
checking for a microphone or camera. The flicker of
some lights could suddenly be seen through the one-way
mirror. Jack walked over, cupped his hands around his
eyes, and leaned against the glass, peering in to make
sure we didn't have an audience in the other room. We
didn't.

Jack turned to me. "Let's go," he said.

"What do you mean?"

"I mean we're leaving; I don't like it. You should've
never agreed to come."

"Don't you even want to know what's going on?"

"I don't need to. Whatever it is, it's not something to
be settled right here in their backyard."

I didn't agree. "I'd sooner nip it in the bud," I said.

"That's what they want you to think."

"At least let me tell you what the situation is, or at
least what I think the situation is."

"Fair enough," said Jack, sitting down in one of the
metal chairs. "Except I don't want to hear *your* take on
what's happening. I want the indisputable for now. Sim-

ply tell me everything that's transpired involving you and the two detectives, starting with when they came by your office."

I nodded and spoke slowly. "The first time was last Thursday. They wanted to talk to me about the death of my friend, Tyler Mills. He was the one whose funeral I went to."

"The one killed in his apartment?" said Jack.

"Yeah."

"What questions did they ask you?"

"Basic stuff," I said. "How well I knew him, was he in any trouble, when was the last time I saw him. The only wrinkle was at the end, when they informed me that the last call Tyler made before he died was to me at my office. It was news to me."

"You never spoke to him?"

"No."

I looked at Jack, who was taking it all in. It felt weird to lie to him, not to mention scary, given that he was practically a human polygraph machine. I had little choice, though. As much as our conversation was privileged, at that point I wasn't about to tell my boss why the detectives had every reason to be suspicious.

"What next?" asked Jack.

"I thought that was the end of it," I said. "Apparently not. The two of them were back this morning."

"What'd they tell you?"

"That they had more questions for me and wanted to do it here."

"They've got something."

"I can only assume."

"No clue what it is?"

I shook my head. "Whatever it is and whatever they think it has to do with me, I have no idea."

Jack stared into my eyes. Knowing him, he wasn't concerned so much with whether or not he believed me. It was more like he was gauging whether or not the detectives would believe me if need be. That was the law right there in a nutshell, really. The truth was irrelevant. It was only what people believed that ultimately mattered.

Jack stood up and walked to the far wall. He turned and leaned against it, arms folded across his chest. "Did you kill him?" he asked flatly.

"What?"

"Is that a yes or a no?" Jack asked, undaunted.

"It's a no," I said, pretending I'd never been so insulted.

Jack looked at his pocket watch. "Okay, then. I've got a three o'clock conference call back at the office. Let's see if we can't wrap this up beforehand."

"Shouldn't be a problem," I said.

A minute later, Hicks and Benoit returned. Benoit had his mug of coffee. In addition to a folder, Hicks was holding a bulky tape recorder under his arm. He dropped the machine onto the table with a noisy *clang*. "Do you have any objection to our recording this conversation?" he asked.

Without skipping a beat, Jack opened his briefcase and pulled out a microcassette recorder, placing it on the table as well. "I don't if you don't," he said.

Hicks shook his head as if to say it figured. Benoit grinned. I sat there and prepared to hear what curveball was about to be thrown my way.

Hicks pressed play and Benoit started in by stating the day and the date, as well as who was in the room. He would be asking all the questions. "Mr. Randall, how long would you say you knew Tyler Mills?" was his first one.

"About fifteen years," I answered.

"How would you characterize your relationship with him?"

"We were friendly, though for the past ten years we rarely saw each other."

"Was there any specific reason for this?" Benoit asked.

"You mean why we rarely saw each other?"

"Yes."

"Nothing specific. As we grew older, I think we simply had less and less in common," I said.

"You previously told us that the last time you talked to Tyler Mills was about a month ago out at a restaurant; is that correct?"

"Yes, that's right."

"At the same time," said Benoit, "you are aware that the last phone call Tyler Mills made before he died was to you at your office?"

"Only insofar as you told me so."

"Are you reconfirming your earlier statement that you didn't speak to Tyler Mills that night?"

"Correct."

"Nor did you receive a message from him?"

"Correct."

Benoit was done setting the table. He reached into his folder and took them out. Dinner was served.

"Have you ever seen these photographs before, Mr. Randall?" he said. As he asked the question he spread them out neatly in two rows. They were the same pictures Tyler had taken of Jessica and me walking in and out of the hotel. The same pictures that Tyler had promised he didn't keep a set of. Not that I ever believed him.

I sat there and looked them over as nonrattled as possible.

"No, I've never seen these before," I said.

"That is in fact you, isn't it?" said Benoit, pointing his finger at the shots that were clearly of me.

Jack interceded. "Gentlemen, before we go on, I think you need to clarify where you got these pictures from. Without that knowledge, I'll advise Mr. Randall to cease answering any more of your questions."

"Fair enough," said Benoit, taking a sip of coffee from his mug. "One of the items we found in examining Tyler Mills's apartment after his death was a safe-deposit box key. When we identified the bank, we found these photos inside the box."

"So you don't know that Mr. Mills actually took these photos," said Jack.

"That's correct. We don't know that the former photo editor of the Deerfield yearbook actually took these," said Benoit.

Jack backed off. Another attorney, more prone to caviling, might have desperately claimed "fruit of a poison tree" at that point, meaning that the photos were illegally obtained, having not been first placed in the possession of Tyler's estate. Jack knew better. I had no standing in Tyler's reasonable expectation of privacy, and any judge would admit the photos into evidence no matter how they were obtained. To pretend otherwise would be bush-league.

Benoit resumed. "As I was saying, Mr. Randall, this is you in these pictures, is it not?"

"It certainly looks like me."

"Do you have any recollection of having been to the Doral Court hotel before?"

"Yes, I've been there."

"Do you recognize the woman next to you in this photo, and alone here in these others?"

"Yes, I do."

"Is she a friend of yours?"

"She is," I answered.

"Is she maybe more than a friend of yours, Mr. Randall?"

"Jesus fucking Christ," said Jack. "Don't tell me you guys roped one of my attorneys to accuse him of having an affair!"

"We're just trying to figure out why Tyler Mills would possibly have these photos," said Benoit. "That Mr. Randall was, or is, having an affair is not only plausible, but it raises some interesting questions. Perhaps in the area of motive. Throw in the fact that Mr. Randall was the last call Tyler Mills made before being killed, and it makes it that much more interesting."

"No," countered Jack, "what's interesting is that you guys actually think you're starting to piece something together, when in reality everyone and your mother would tell you that you ain't got shit."

"My mother's dead," came the voice of Hicks. He must have thought he'd been silent for too long. Per-

haps he saw his comment as a clever way to derail Jack.
Silly detective.

Jack looked at Hicks, momentarily befuddled.
"What?"

"I said, my mother's dead."

Replied Jack, "Oh, and I suppose you want to interrogate Mr. Randall about that death as well?"

Hicks went back to being silent.

Benoit: "Listen, Mr. Devine—"

Jack cut him off. "No, you listen. You've asked your
questions; now it's my turn. Let's start with that last
phone call, shall we? I presume the call was made from
Mr. Mills's apartment?"

"Actually, it was made from a cell phone. It was
routed through the tower that covers his apartment, so
we think he called from home, though we can't know
for sure."

Jack scratched his head. "A cell phone, huh?" He
placed both his hands on the table and leaned in toward the detectives. "I'll bet you any amount of money
that when you checked the records for it you saw that
the call lasted a minute, two tops. You know how I
know that? Because you never would've asked whether
or not Mr. Mills left a message if the call had lasted
any longer."

"That's very quick thinking," said Benoit. "However,
that the call itself may have lasted only a minute doesn't
rule out Mr. Randall's having talked to Tyler Mills or
gotten a message from him."

"No, but what it does do is allow for the possibility
that Mr. Mills called and got my client's voice mail, listened to the outgoing message, and hung up before leav-

ing one. Thus giving substantial credibility to Mr. Randall's claim that he never got any message."

Point taken, apparently, as Benoit said next, "Let's move on, shall we? You told us that you were at your office that evening, Mr. Randall, is that right?"

"Yes, I was working late."

"Could any of your coworkers substantiate that?"

"Offhand I can't remember."

"As for the pictures, do you have any idea what they're for, or why Tyler Mills might have had them in his possession?"

"Honestly, I don't," I said.

Benoit stood up and walked a few steps away from the table. He had his back to me. "Do you think your wife might know?" he asked into the air.

With that, Jack's patience ran out. "That's it, guys, this little Q and A session is over. I don't know what the story is with those pictures, but here's what I do know for damn sure. If you expose them outside of this room and it costs this young man his marriage, you better pray a hell of a lot more turns up in your case against him. *A hell of a lot more*. Because his case against you will be the likes of which this city hasn't seen for quite some time. And if you think I won't fucking make that happen, try me. Because when you do, it won't be my ass and pension on the line, I assure you."

At the very least I expected Hicks to pull some Johnny Bravado routine in return. He didn't. As for Benoit, he watched as Jack picked up his recorder and motioned for me to get up.

"This isn't over," said Benoit.

"It sure looks over to me," said Jack.

The two of us walked out of the room without so much as a nod good-bye. When we got onto the elevator we were alone.

The doors closed.

"So they can't fall in," said Jack, staring ahead.

I looked at him. "What?" I asked.

"Why manhole covers are round . . . it's so they can't fall in."

THIRTY

The phone call to Jack came three days later. It was from a "friend" of his who was familiar with the comings and goings at the precinct that Detectives Hicks and Benoit worked out of. Don't ask how, said Jack to me in my office while lighting up a cigar, just listen.

"Yesterday morning," he began, "a drifter type was arrested for a robbery committed in your friend Tyler's building two weeks before his death. It would seem the hapless fellow had tried to sell some of his booty to a local pawnshop, not realizing that thanks to our good mayor's vigorous crackdown on passing hot property, it was akin to turning himself in." Jack pushed a slender puff of smoke out the side of his mouth. "I must say, that's the problem with life on the lam. It's hard to stay current on every city's new crime initiatives.

"Now here's where it gets interesting. When the detectives ran a check on the drifter, it turned out that he was wanted in Miami for killing a man after, of all things, breaking in to his apartment. With the obvious similarities, it wasn't long before the drifter was asked where he was the night Tyler died. Lo and behold, he had no plausible alibi."

I started to smile. Jack stopped me.

"Wait, it gets better," he said. "Are you ready for this?"

Like a kid at Christmas. "What?"

Jack took the cigar out of his mouth. "The guy's dead."

I looked at him. "You're kidding me."

"No, he hung himself last night in his holding cell."

Again with that irony thing. *He hung himself.*

"Sounds too good to be true," I said, amazed.

"That they had their man? You're probably right," said Jack. "Take the evidence they have, or rather, don't have, and he no more did it than you did. Thing is, though, with him dead and buried, no charge against you will ever stick."

"How do you figure?"

"Easy. We, of course, would never claim to have heard anything about what I just told you. Instead, if need be, we would trace the crime history of Tyler's building and claim to stumble upon this drifter. The extenuating circumstances of his file alone would amount to oodles of reasonable doubt. The dumbest D.A. in the world could see that, especially when he gets wind that the drifter had been questioned about Tyler's murder before he killed himself. *Easy.* See what I mean?"

I did.

Said Jack, "It all adds up to one thing."

"What's that?"

Jack reached over, picked up my phone receiver, and

placed it down on my desk. I stared at him funny, wondering what he was up to.

With a sly grin he explained, "You're off the hook."

There were no questions from him about the pictures or the prospect of my having an affair. No wondering if there was any connection to be made from my being Tyler's last phone call. Jack simply turned and walked out of my office without saying another word.

The truth was irrelevant. It was only what people believed that ultimately mattered.

That night, I removed the bandages from my hand and chest. The wounds had finally healed.

THIRTY-ONE

"Excuse me, you're standing on my penis," Dwight said to the girl in the tight T-shirt with spectacular venetian. She didn't find it amusing. She gave him the finger and walked away.

I had ordered the stretch, specifying black and making sure there would be none of that cheesy purple neon running along the interior. One by one, I had the driver pick up Menzi, Connor, and Dwight at their offices. The bar was stocked with Cragganmore twelve-year, Herradura, Evan Williams Single Barrel, Kettle One, and a bottle of Krug Brut '85. For music? Sinatra, what else? The whole shebang was my treat to the boys, for reasons that only I would ever know, and as their self-appointed doyen for the evening, I was definitely going to do it *my way*.

"Gentlemen, the night is young and so are we," I told them.

Our first stop was the Shark Bar on the Upper West Side, and after Dwight returned to the huddle after his failed penis pickup line, Menzi had a story to tell. In his larger-than-life efforts to scope the wild Betty, his latest travels had resulted in an interesting encounter. Whereas mere mortal men sporting plane tickets aimed for such achievement as the Mile-High Club, Menzi had raised the bar considerably. He called it the Admirals Club, so named for the "members only" lounge that American Airlines offered at various airports around the world.

Menzi described how he had recently been in the Admirals Club at JFK one night killing an hour delay before a flight to London. Monique, as he said her name to be, was there waiting for her return trip home to Toulouse. Between her broken English and Menzi's two years of high school French, he managed to strike up a conversation and then literally charm the pants off Monique in a sectioned-off computer area that was under construction.

Admittedly, the four rounds of tequila shots after the initial martini he bought for her had significantly greased the wheels, but all in all, it was a pretty impressive story. Had it been most any other guy telling it—say, Dwight, for instance—I would've been prone to call bullshit. Not with Menzi, though. Having seen his prowess with women firsthand, I was relatively certain of the tale's validity. Especially given the very un–*man as hero* ending. Turns out that when Menzi asked to exchange phone numbers with Monique as she prepared to leave, she popped up the handle to her luggage on wheels and simply noted, "Had I intended to keep in touch, I never would have fucked you."

"Strange," said Menzi, swirling the remaining ice in his vodka rocks. "She delivered the line in perfect English."

Next stop was dinner at the Blue Door, across the park on the Upper East Side. For sure, it wasn't a place you'd find in any restaurant guide. Three reasons. One, the Blue Door wasn't really its name, merely the color of the entrance. Two, it had only one table and there was only one seating a night. Three, it was owned and operated by two high-priced call girls out of their top-floor brownstone apartment. "Fucking and cooking, that's what they're into," said the guy, a foreign currency trader with the Bank of Tokyo, who had given me their number. He also mentioned in some detail that they were exceedingly gifted at both pursuits. *Domo arigato,* I told him. You had to hand it to the Japanese businessmen. If it took place on the island of Manhattan and involved the solicitation of sex, they knew all about it.

Alicia and Stefanie welcomed the four of us into their home at a few minutes past nine. In a word, stunning. Nice too. Model looks without the attitude. Being the polite hostesses that they were, they asked if any of us would like a blow job before dinner. Dwight raised his hand like a schoolboy. That vision alone was worth the four grand I was shelling out for us to be there.

They really did know how to cook. A homemade gazpacho fresh from their rooftop garden to start, followed by Chilean sea bass nicely blackened and not too oily. A lemon tart and some vanilla-hazelnut coffee rounded it all off. Well done, girls.

We retreated to their living room, where we drank brandy and had our choice of smokes. Cigars, cigarettes, or weed. The biggest turn-on, at least for me, was that the girls were educated, or, should I say, talked as if they were. Alicia was big into existentialism and could quote Simone de Beauvoir at will. Stefanie, to her credit, was something of an art buff. She was particularly fond of Léger and had gone so far as to visit his museum in Biot, France. Though when you got right down to it, she explained, her favorite place to be was the van Gogh room on the upper level of Musée d'Orsay.

"Really?" I said to her. "I'm planning on being in Paris myself next April."

Then came the sex. To be honest, it was my lone attempt at manipulation that evening. As I had been riding somewhat of a winning streak, I thought maybe I could do something about my guilt with Connor once and for all. If I could get him to cheat on Jessica, I reasoned, I wouldn't feel so bad about the affair. And yet, as much as he'd had to drink, he declined. In fact, when I asked him which girl he preferred, he simply shook his head and laughed.

It was a major backfire. That Connor remained faithful to Jessica even in the face—and bodies—of Alicia and Stefanie made me feel that much worse. I declined the after-dinner sex as well, making some joke about the buddy system. Instead, I refilled my snifter and further tried to numb myself.

Meanwhile, the two single guys weren't about to decline anything. As Connor and I kicked back in the living room and watched Robin Byrd on the tube, Menzi and Dwight paired off with Alicia and Stefanie in separate bedrooms. The girls had originally suggested a foursome, but such homophobes were Menzi and Dwight that they would have nothing to do with it.

When we finally said farewell sometime after midnight, the two boys were walking with the happiest limps

I'd ever seen. The lone disappointment for them came when they tried to get Alicia and Stefanie's phone number. That's when they were told about the policy: no repeat customers. It wouldn't be as special, said the two girls. Incredible. They obviously knew what kind of word of mouth they had to be turning away business.

After cruising around a bit in the limo, we made a final stop at the Whiskey Bar. You would think Menzi and Dwight had had their fill for the evening. Then again, maybe you wouldn't. As soon as we walked in, their eyes lit up at the overabundance of talent that lined the walls.

"Like fish in a barrel," said Dwight.

"You sure your rods aren't too tired?" I asked.

"Nonsense," they both told me.

After ordering a round of drinks, I announced that I had to go to the bathroom. The pay phone was in the basement next to a cigarette vending machine. Four rings.

"Hello?" she said.

"It's Philip."

"It's late."

"I'm sorry," I said.

"I was sleeping."

"Sorry again."

"You sound drunk."

"That's because I am."

"I'm hanging up."

"Wait, I'm okay. Just a little happy," I told her. "What's this I hear about tonight being your treat?"

"You spoke to Connor?"

"Yes, before he left his office," she said.

"Yeah, it's true. Tonight's my treat."

"What for?"

"No reason."

"I don't believe you."

"Can't a guy be nice to his friends?"

"You're not that nice," she said.

"Maybe I'm changing."

"I seriously doubt that."

"Are you free for lunch tomorrow?" I asked.

"Perhaps. If I'm not too *tired*."

"Very subtle."

"Thank you," she said.

"Do you ever wonder?"

"About what?"

"In another life . . . you and me."

"You really are drunk."

"I'm serious."

"I'm hanging up now."

"See, I knew you'd thought about it," I said.

"You're an arrogant son of a bitch, you know that?"

"You wouldn't have it any other way."

"What does that make me?" she said, suspect.

"Incredibly desirable."

She hung up.

I returned upstairs right in time to see the first punch thrown. I didn't need to know what had happened to know what had happened—Dwight had hit on some guy's girlfriend a little too hard. As I rushed over, I could see the guy was a jock type, dressed in shorts and a J. Crew shirt over a sinewy upper body. He landed a right cross to Dwight's unsuspecting chin.

Of course, one of the problems with these jock types

was that they confused their ability to bench-press a lot of weight with being able to fight. Another one of the problems was that they rarely, if ever, thought to see who their opponents'‾friends were. As Dwight recoiled from the blow, Menzi—the former first-team All-Ivy tight end—stepped in, folded one of his huge hands into a fist, and proceeded to level the guy with one uppercut. Indeed, chivalry wasn't dead. He was just knocked out and bleeding on the barroom floor.

Time to go.

Before the bouncers could sort it out we were safely back in the limo. Dwight raided what was left of the ice bucket and nursed the side of his already swelling mouth.

"Jesus, I go away for two minutes," I said. "What the hell did you say to his girlfriend, Dwight?"

"Nuthin'," he claimed, sounding like he'd had a shot of Novocain. "I simply told her that I wanted every bone in her body including one of my own."

Menzi threw back his head. "You asshole, I should've let her boyfriend have one more swing at you."

We laughed and we kidded. We passed around the Krug and drank from the bottle. When it was done, so was the night. Dwight got dropped off first, followed by Menzi. Each thanked me profusely for one hell of a time. With both of them gone, Connor and I put our feet up.

"Were you thinking about it?" he asked me.

"About what?"

"Getting your money's worth with our two very nice dinner hostesses this evening."

"Did I *think* about it? Yeah. In the end, though, I

guess I'd be too afraid that Tracy would somehow be able to tell."

"I know what you mean; Jessica's kind of the same way," he said. "It's like guys must emit some type of pheromone when they cheat, and only certain women can smell it."

"Notably our wives, is what you're saying."

He nodded. "Do you think we could ever tell with them?"

Like twelve cups of coffee was his question. Very sobering.

"You're not still thinking that—"

"That Jessica's having an affair? No, I don't think that anymore," he said as the limo pulled to a stop in front of his apartment. "I *know* she's having an affair." Connor opened the door and swung one leg out. "Thanks for everything, Philip. See you soon."

THIRTY-TWO

Two rings.

She picked up. "This is Jessica."

"We need to talk," I said.

"So that's what we're calling it now?"

"I'm serious; something happened last night," I told her.

"What?"

"Not over the phone. During lunch . . . twelve-thirty. I'll be the early one."

"This isn't one of your ploys to get me to come out and play, is it?" she asked.

"I wish it were."

The weather had called for a light sprinkle that day. What we got was a midday downpour. Shoulders hunched under my umbrella, I started to make my way over to the hotel at twelve-fifteen. I didn't bother with the gym bag decoy. Arousing suspicion in my office was no longer so high on my list of worries.

Connor had closed the door to the limo so quickly the night before I hadn't had a chance to call after him. I had heard what he said; I just didn't know what it meant. Or, at least, what it really meant.

"I *know* she's having an affair."

It was Jessica and her damn tell, I was thinking. It was back. She had gone cold on Connor again. It would mean revisiting a topic that had ended with her not talking to me the first time. This time, however, I'd be more careful in how we discussed it. There was too much at stake.

Yet again.

I was short with Raymond while checking in. I couldn't help it. He wanted to tell me how much his mother appreciated the money I'd given him, and all I wanted to do was get up to the room and call Jessica. The sooner I called her, the sooner she'd get there. Sensing my impatience, Raymond apologized for droning on. I explained that I had a lot on my mind. While he appeared to understand, there was no smile from him when he handed me my room key.

"This is Jessica," she said.

"Room seven-oh-two," I told her.

"Okay."

I hung up the phone and started my usual pacing. Outside, the rain was beating hard against the windows. I tried to sit down on the bed, but it was no use. I was too anxious. I got up and started to pace again. It was going to be the first time Jessica and I were together in the hotel without having sex. For about a hundred and seventy-five dollars less we could've been having our conversation in a restaurant. A restaurant, though, meant the possibility of bumping into someone we knew, and when you least expected it or wanted it, Manhattan had a funny way of doing that to you. Besides, the image of having to tell Jessica to calm down, or worse, having to tell myself to calm down, amid a throng of on-lookers was enough to convince me that it was money well spent. Public displays of hysteria were something to witness, not partake in, I always thought.

A minute later there was a knock. Thankfully, she had arrived quickly. I walked over and opened the door to greet her.

Only it wasn't her.

"Expecting someone else?" he said.

In that instant, terrifying beyond measure, I knew it to be true. The jig was up.

I was standing face-to-face with Connor.

"Yeah, I thought so," he said, looking at my expression as he walked by me and into the room. He was wearing a full-length raincoat but had no umbrella. He was drenched.

I closed the door and turned around. Connor had taken a seat in one of the chairs by the window. His narrow eyes were fixed right on me, brimming with a controlled anger that, for him, was far more threatening than anything uncontrolled could ever aspire to.

"So this is where it happens, huh?" he said, looking about the room.

I stammered. "How—did—you . . ."

"We'll get to that in a moment," he said. "Now, is this, like, your regular room, or do you two like to mix it up and have a different room each time?"

I started to say something. I can't remember what, exactly. A futile attempt to explain that it wasn't what he thought . . . the operative word being *futile*.

Connor raised his palm at me. "You didn't give me an answer. *I said, is this your regular room or is it a different one each time?* You would think you could do me the courtesy of answering my question being that you are fucking my wife."

"Connor . . ."

"Answer me, goddamn it!"

"Different room each time," I said, half swallowing my words.

"There, that wasn't so hard, was it?" he said. "I guess it makes sense, you know, having different rooms—the two of you being big fans of *variety* and all."

"How?" I repeated. *How did he know?*

Connor reached into his raincoat and pulled out a folded piece of paper. "This is how," he said. "It arrived at my office yesterday morning forwarded to me by the executor of the last will and testament for one Tyler Mills. Strange to think I only met him once. I guess you could call it a letter from the grave."

I listened in amazement. Even dead, Tyler still had it in for me.

"Would you like to hear it?" asked Connor. "Because I'd like to read it to you."

"I'd rather you didn't."

"Too bad," said Connor. Then he quoted Mick Jagger, though most likely not on purpose. "You can't always get what you want."

He unfolded the paper, cleared his throat, and read:

Dear Connor,

I can't tell you how disappointed I am that you're reading this letter. That's because if you are . . . I'm dead.

If you don't already remember me, I met you and your wife out at Balthazar one night when you were eating with Philip and Tracy Randall. I was the one bearing champagne.

While it may not have seemed that way at the time, my being there at the restaurant was far from happenstance. In reality, it was part of a little underlying drama that you were unwittingly a part of. I think it's time you learned what's been going on.

Simply put, I knew something about Philip that he desperately didn't want anyone to know. You, especially. And because one of the few perks of being dead is never having to worry about being blunt, here goes . . .

Philip's been screwing your wife.

But by all means, don't take my word for it. Find out for yourself. He and your wife meet up at the Doral Court hotel in midtown two or three times during the week. You'll see that Philip usually, if not always, arrives first.

As for why I felt the need to write this letter? I'll let Philip try to explain that one. I'm sure he'll have some good story all worked out by then. I suppose that's why lawyers are lawyers. Like I said, though, I knew something about Philip that he desperately didn't want anyone to know. And now— presto!—I'm pushing up daisies.

Rocket science it ain't.

Revenge is sweet,
Tyler Mills

*P.S. When you do confront the son of a bitch—
and something tells me that you will—be sure to
call him Philly. He hates that.*

Connor finished reading. I watched as he slowly
folded up the letter and tucked it back into his raincoat.

"You knew the entire time last night?" I asked in
complete disbelief.

He chuckled. "Incredible, huh? But I figured, innocent until proven guilty, right? Sure enough, when I followed you yesterday, the only place you went for lunch
was a deli. So I held back last night, bit my tongue—
except for that little part in the limo at the end. Forgive
me, I couldn't resist."

"He was blackmailing me, Connor."

"So you killed him?!"

"I didn't kill him," I said. "I wanted to kill him, I
planned on killing him, but I couldn't go through with
it. Tyler actually died trying to kill *me*. It was an accident."

"An *accident?*" said Connor. He shook his head with
total incredulity.

I started to say something else. Again, I don't remember what exactly. It probably had something to do
with Tyler being a complete psycho with an overactive
imagination. For sure, I was rambling.

"Don't do that," Connor told me. "It's only going to
make it worse."

As if rock bottom had a basement . . .

So there I was, the initial shock of it giving way to
a kind of sustained panic that allowed me to see the situation for what it was. The sheer magnitude of it. Caught

having an affair with his wife and implicated in someone else's murder to boot. He knew it and I knew it.
We had the truth and it was far from irrelevant. What
remained to be seen were the consequences.

"Now what?" I asked.

"Now we wait."

"For what?" I said, though I understood.

"Not for what . . . for whom."

Jessica, naturally. Connor would need to see it with
his own eyes. Her walking into the room to meet me.
Me! Of all people. That she was having the affair he
had suspected; that she was having the affair with me—
the guy with whom he had shared those suspicions . . .
who had told him not to worry, that it was just a phase—
well, like I said, he would need to see it with his own
eyes.

As if on cue, the knock came.

"Allow me," said Connor.

He stood up from his chair and walked to the door.
I took a seat on the bed. Pacing seemed to be pretty
moot at that point. Oddly enough, if it hadn't been actually happening to me, the whole thing would've been
pretty entertaining. But it *was* happening to me; and it
was about to be happening to Jessica as well. I couldn't
look.

I heard Connor open the door. He didn't say anything. I figured he didn't need to—for a married couple
such a crossroads seemed appropriately beyond words.
As for what sound I did hear first, it could best be described as the yelp of a wounded animal. High pitched
and sadlike from her. It was followed by something that

I might have predicted, for the simple fact that I briefly entertained the same notion myself.

Jessica ran.

She didn't get very far. I could hear Connor catch up to her in the hallway. Amid her sobbing and pleas of "No!" he practically had to drag her back into the room. I never felt as helpless in my life as I did right then and there.

We're only human in the end, and for that reason alone, I imagine there was a certain measure of satisfaction for Connor in all this. Despite the grief, despite the bitterness, he had managed to create one hell of a Waterloo for Jessica and me. This was his chance to deliver the comeuppance of all comeuppances.

He threw Jessica next to me on the bed and sat back down in the chair by the window. Jessica remained facedown on the covers and sobbing. I had known her to be a strong-minded person—the native New Yorker, after all—capable of rolling with the punches when need be. At the same time, I had come to realize that everyone has a melting point. This was hers. She was no match for such a turn of events.

"Okay, shall we get started?" said Connor.

I looked at him. *Started on what?*

"Do you guys talk first for a bit, or do you get right into it? I'm going to guess that you get right into it, but what do I know?" he said with the kind of laugh that had nothing to do with humor. "What did I ever know?"

"Connor, you can't be serious," I said.

"I simply want to see what I've been missing, that's all," was his response. "Now, c'mon, you can pretend like I'm not here. That shouldn't be too difficult."

Ridiculous, I thought. Understandable, maybe, but still ridiculous. His behavior could've been a lot of things at that point. Serious, though, was not one of them.

Or was it?

"You think I'm kidding, don't you," said Connor to me.

"I don't know what to think," I told him.

"I mean it. I want you to go ahead and fuck my wife."

"Jesus, Connor. . . ."

"What, is she not good enough for you now?"

"Connor, please—"

"Don't please me, please her, buddy. You are my buddy, right?"

"This is fucking crazy. You know I'm not about to do what you're asking," I said.

Connor started to shake his head. He reached into his raincoat again. A repeat performance of Tyler's letter for Jessica's benefit was what I assumed.

I assumed wrong.

"I'm not asking," he said, pointing it at me.

It was shiny. It was silver. It was a gun.

I hadn't thought it could happen. It had. Risk Factor 10.

The things you forget and the things you remember. Connor and me, alone at the table at the Gotham Bar and Grill. He's telling me about what he'd do to the guy having an affair with Jessica. *I'll kill him. I'll get a gun and shoot the motherfucker right in the balls!*

I looked down the barrel of the gun and up at Connor. I looked back at Jessica. I was right in time to see her pick up her head and realize that there was perhaps a little bit more at stake.

"Connor, what are you *doing?*" she cried out.

"What the fuck does it look like I'm doing?" he roared back, approaching maniacal.

Reason with him, I told myself. Deep down he was always a reasonable person.

"Connor, listen to me," I said, as calmly as I could. "I think it's safe to say we're all having the worst damn day of our lives right now. There's one thing that can make it a hell of a lot worse, though, and that's if you pull that trigger."

"This coming from the only person in the room who's actually killed someone," he said. "Isn't that right, *Philly?*" He craned his neck around me. "Oh, by the way, did you hear that, honey? I think your lover killed Tyler Mills because he knew about your affair. What a hero!"

"I told you I didn't kill him," I said.

I glanced back at Jessica again to see that her fear had been joined by a rush of confusion.

Connor cocked the gun. "Now, are you going to fuck my wife, or what?"

To hell with reasoning. The Connor I knew, or maybe thought I knew, was nowhere to be found in that room.

From there on out, all bets were off.

"You want me to fuck her?!" I yelled. "I'll fuck her! I'll fuck her like you've never been able to!"

"Stop it!" cried Jessica.

My words seemed to echo as I watched the anger in Connor's eyes overflow, his face gushing with a fiery red complexion.

"Shut up!" screamed Connor at me. He got up from the chair. His elbow locked as he whipped his arm into a straight line, the gun swinging out and jolting into place that much closer to my body. "Shut up!" he screamed again.

But I wouldn't.

"Why do you think she was coming here, huh, Connor?" I said. "Because you just didn't do it for her, that's why! That's what she told me. I did it for her, though. Over and over, week in and week out. And don't you know she kept coming back for more. She couldn't get enough. FUCKING INSATIABLE, SHE WAS!"

It was a tirade, a vicious tirade on my part. It was also something else. A ruse. A way to distract Connor . . . to get between him and the gun via the very dark place that was now his mind. He just needed to get a little bit closer to me.

"SHUT UP!" screamed Connor again.

Behind me I could hear Jessica trying to catch her breath. She wanted to yell but couldn't. It was like she was suffocating—the shouting filling up the room until there was no air left to breathe. In front of me I could see Connor rocking side to side while inching forward. The gun wobbly, his emotions crumbling. Was his face still wet from the rain? No. Those were tears coming down his cheeks. Another foot or so and I'd have my one and only chance.

Connor lurched forward, his demons fully in charge. "I SWEAR TO GOD I'LL KILL YOU!" he yelled.

I lunged. My hands reaching, eyes wide and focused on the shiny metal in his grip. His finger fumbled on the trigger, and I reached him before he could squeeze. A gun sandwich, we made. The two of us struggling toe to toe, moving left and right, back and forth, with the gun between us. To Jessica it must have been the scariest dance she'd ever seen.

Later they would come to me in full. The details. Too small to register at first in the blur that was the moment. The damp smell of Connor's raincoat, soaked through around his shoulders. The way his nostrils flared and let out these quick, loud snorts. The cold feel of the gun's nozzle in my hand, smooth and substantial, as I fought to push it away from my body and by default toward Connor's.

One of us would have to give.

I could lay claim to a lot of things in my life up until that point. Being shot was not one of them. While the blast itself was piercing to the ears, it was the heat against my stomach that really threw me. More so than the piercing shriek that Jessica let out as Connor and I froze.

The gun dropped to the floor as the two of us stood staring at each other's eyes. Neither one of us was blinking.

I don't know how long it lasted, the two of us there like statues. I'm sure it wasn't as long as it felt. But when Connor's eyes did begin to flutter—when he finally blinked—I looked down. I saw blood . . . blood on both of us.

More blood on Connor.

The gunpowder igniting behind the bullet. A pulse of hot gas. That was the heat I felt on my stomach. There would be no entry wound for me to discover, though. That grim task belonged to Connor. It was his turn to look down, and inside his opened raincoat he saw the same blood that I saw. Only by then it was clear that all of it was his. It had been Connor who caught the bullet.

His legs gave out from under him, and I caught him as he collapsed. The final dip of our hideous dance. I eased him to the floor as a line of deep red began to trickle from his mouth. He didn't look at me; he looked through me. His gaze was far off, and getting farther with each passing second.

"I'm sorry," I told him, whispering. So very, very sorry.

I'll never know if he heard me.

The rain continued to beat down against the windows. Fingertips tapping at random hard against the glass. Outside, beyond the rain, I could hear the occasional blaring of a horn and the other sounds that were the city.

Inside, Connor lay dead on the floor.

Jessica wailed with denial, pounding her fist on the bed again and again. She had watched me feel for a pulse, and when I looked back at her with nothing more than a blank stare, she knew he was gone.

I went to her and she pushed me away. But if I couldn't console her, I knew I still had to coach her. That's what always got me about that day. As bizarre and devastating as it was, I never for one moment stopped being a lawyer. I couldn't help it.

"Listen to me, Jessica, because we've got maybe a minute before this room gets very crowded," I said, trusting that she could hear me. "When the cops come, the first thing they're going to do is separate us. They'll ask us both what happened and check to see that our stories match. They have to match, Jessica, do you understand? Our stories *have* to match."

I knew what she might be thinking. How perverse it was that I could be so collected after what had happened. I didn't care. I literally had Connor's blood on my hands. There was a lot of explaining to do, and I could ill afford to have Jessica recollecting one thing and me another. She could ill afford it either. Though at the time it was probably the furthest thing from her mind.

Never for one moment stopped being a lawyer ... couldn't help it.

I laid it out for her. Points one and two: it was a jealous husband bent on revenge. He had a gun and what ensued was self-defense. As hard as it was to talk to her in those terms, the real hurdle was that little bit having to do with Tyler. Connor had more than implied that I killed him.

"Was there anything else your husband said, Ms. Levine, anything at all?" I could hear the cops asking her.

I reached out gently to turn Jessica's body toward me. I needed eye contact for point three. Maybe I was getting through to her or maybe it was nothing more than her being flat-out exhausted. Whichever. All I saw was that she didn't resist. She didn't push me away.

"Jessica, there's one more thing and I know it must have confused you," I began. "Connor, I think, accused me of killing Tyler. He said something about it before you arrived, but I have no idea what he was talking about. I had nothing to do with Tyler's murder, Jessica. I don't know what would've possessed Connor to say something like that. The important thing is that we can't mention anything to the police about it, do you understand? Otherwise, it would implicate both of us."

She was still in shock, shaking and pale as could be. "Do you understand?" I asked her again.

She gave me the slightest of nods.

All I could think was thank god Connor never read her that letter.

The letter!

It was bad enough there was one smoking gun in the room. I wasn't about to let there be another.

I leaped off the bed and over to Connor. As I did I could hear footsteps running down the hallway, voices coming toward the room. Kneeling down, I dug inside his raincoat, feeling for the piece of paper. I saw him put it in there, so why couldn't I find it? *Damn it, where was it?*

Frantically, I kept searching. The voices and feet were drawing closer. Not good, Philip, not good at all. Without that letter you can kiss your ass good—

There it was.

With no more than a second to spare I felt it, grabbed it, and stuffed it away in my pocket. Later I would burn it.

Ally-ally-in-come-free.

When I looked up, it was Raymond I saw first. He had rushed into the room along with another hotel employee, a guy in a dark business suit. Behind them, I could see two onlookers, tourists probably, poking their heads in from the doorway. They would definitely have a good story to tell their friends back home.

I watched as Raymond took in the room, his eyes ricocheting from me to Connor to Jessica and back to me again. One girl, two guys, and a fair amount of blood. Knowing what he already knew before that day, I was almost sure Raymond had put it together instantly. My affair had ceased to be a secret.

"Is he . . . ?" asked Raymond, his voice tailing off.

"Yes." I nodded.

He was.

THIRTY-THREE

There was a time when I liked the word *aftermath;* liked the ring of it, liked what it stood for. It usually applied to a court case, a court case that I had won, and the aftermath was what fell under the heading "To the victor go the spoils." Back slaps, high fives, and the ridiculing of opposing counsel for their ineptitude. All of that on top of a huge fee or settlement being deposited into the firm's bank account—the same account from which I drew my bonus.

How things change.

I no longer like the word *aftermath.*

When the police arrived they did exactly what I had told Jessica they would do. They immediately split us up and questioned us separately.* Yellow tape got strung up across the room's entrance, and a bunch of middle-

---

*The manager on duty at the hotel was accommodating enough to make two additional rooms available to the police. The one that I was escorted to turned out to be a room that I'd previously been in with Jessica. I knew by the water stain left by an ice bucket on the bedside table. Jessica had pointed it out to me as being an example of how sloppy the hotel was with its upkeep. I believe she was on top at the time.

aged, out-of-shape men showed up. One with an evidence bag, one with a camera, and one who appeared to do nothing more than stand there and smoke a cigarette. They were offset by two young and fit paramedics wielding a stretcher and a white sheet to pull over Connor's head.

That I was shaken up I didn't have to fake too much. I told the truth and nothing but the truth, all of it in short, measured sentences that suggested a ticker tape. My only sin was that of omission. Yes, I was having an illicit affair. Somehow the husband found out. (He must have followed me, I conjectured.) He had a gun and said he was going to kill me; those exact words, in fact. Fearing for my life, I charged him and we struggled. The gun went off accidentally. I was lucky and he wasn't.

"Did you know the husband personally?" asked one of the cops.

"Yes, he was a frie—" I started to say. I caught myself. To finish that last word would've raised an eyebrow or two. *Some friend,* they would've thought. "Yes, I knew him personally," was my rethought answer.

More questions followed, most likely the same questions that had already been asked of Jessica in whatever room they had taken her to. Had she stuck to the game plan? With each nod of the cops' heads to my answers, I grew more confident that she had.

Way to keep it together, Jessica.

They would need my fingerprints, of course, to match up with those from the gun, as well as a sworn statement from both Jessica and me back at the precinct— not the same precinct as that of my detective friends, Hicks and Benoit, thankfully. (Talk about making their day.) I called the office from inside the hotel and got hold of Jack to meet me. While there was no "here we go again" underpinning to his voice, I knew the repercussions this time would quite possibly sink my career at Campbell & Devine. If not my entire career. To have thought otherwise would've been nothing short of delusional.

As I walked through the lobby heading for the Doral Court's revolving door, the same revolving door that I had spun through so many times after being with Jessica, my thoughts turned to Tracy. My soon-to-be-ex wife. I wondered how I was going to tell her. What words I would choose. Or would I just spew, not choosing any? I glanced at my watch. Three twenty-five, it read. If everything continued to go smoothly at the police precinct, I figured I'd be arriving home around the same time I usually did after work. I'd walk into my soon-to-be-ex loft, and Tracy, as she had done a thousand times before, would ask, "How was your day today, honey?"

I'd pause for a second, extract a deep breath, and maybe, just maybe, I'd begin, "Funny you should ask. . . ."

It seemed as good a way to start as any.

But all of that became terribly irrelevant by the time the *whoosh* of dank air hit me as I stepped out onto the front steps of the hotel. There waiting for me were three local news camera crews, each fronted by a charging piranha sporting capped teeth. Amid the slight drizzle that lingered after the earlier rain, the reporters jostled for position while thrusting their microphones in my face.

"What happened in there, Mr. Randall?" shouted one.

"Is it true you were having an extramarital affair?" shouted another.

"Did you always meet Ms. Levine here at this hotel, Philip?" shouted a third.

They would take their footage of me and my "no comment" stare and, along with the facts they'd been able to gather or guess at, piece together breaking news segments for their five o'clock broadcasts. Were Tracy not actually tuning in on her own, someone was sure to be picking up the phone to call her about it. I'd be surprised if she hadn't already changed the locks by the time I came home.

Jessica and I remained separated at the precinct. For a fact, I never saw her the whole time we were there. Just as well. I was sure she had gotten in touch with her mother, and I'd be loath to have to look Mrs. Levine in the eyes. All along the poor woman had thought she had only one problem child. In light of everything, her boy, Zachary, didn't seem so bad.

Jack showed up. A different Jack from the one I knew. This was not the kind of spotlight he lived for, and his incredibly subdued manner was one that I'd never seen from him before. His expression somewhat reminded me of my father's when I took his Volvo without permission and crashed it my junior year in high school. It was the desire to make sure I was all right fighting mightily with the desire to wring my neck. A bitter pill that strangely resembled a quaalude.

With Jack spotting me, my defense of self-defense held up. The powder residue on my hands was also found to be on Connor's, proving that the gun was in both of our hands when it went off. Throw in the state of New York's rather liberal guidelines for the use and interpretation of deadly force when your life is in jeopardy, and it became clear that for the second straight time in a week I would avoid the prospect of being gang-raped in jail.

Praise the law.

The last thing the police wanted to know was whether or not I had any plans to leave the country. As questions went, it was kind of like when they ask you while checking in for a flight whether or not your bags have been in your possession the whole time. Purely perfunctory.

I was a free man.

The reckoning, however, was just beginning.

When Jack said good-bye to me as we left the precinct via the back door, he told me to take a couple of days off. "Then," he said, "we'll talk."

I thanked him for his help and apologized profusely for the circumstances. I wanted him to throw me a bone, to say something along the lines of it not being as bad as I thought, or that these things happened. I knew better. While these things did happen, they were supposed to happen to the clients we represented, not to us. The only thing Jack told me in response was, "Get some rest."

Not much of a bone, I was afraid.

My key to the loft worked. Tracy, on the other hand, was nowhere to be found. Also missing was her large Tumi suitcase and a decent chunk of her wardrobe. Gone to Greenwich, I presumed.

I didn't want to stay in the loft either. Nonetheless, the alternative—a hotel—was something I'd had enough of for one day, thank you very much.

Besides, maybe it would be me who would change the locks. I'd claim squatter's rights and turn the place into my own fortress of self-pity. Come and get me, Lawrence Metcalf, if you dare! I'm not afraid of you and your army of lawyers! I have Patton with a legal pad on my side, and he'll slap each and every one of you silly when all is said and done.

With that I looked down to see that my glass was empty again. I went to pour myself another scotch. Was that four glasses or five in the past twenty minutes? Ah, fuck the glass. Who needed it? Straight from the bottle seemed to be far more efficient.

I passed out by maybe ten o'clock.

Though instead of everything going black, everything was white.

White everywhere.

There was a big white room with a big white table, and me dressed head to toe like I had raided Tom Wolfe's closet. Around the table were seated various women, women that I knew or recognized. There were Tracy and Jessica; the prostitute-restaurateur duo of Alicia and Stefanie; Rebecca, the hostess from the Gotham Bar and Grill; and finally Melissa, last seen throwing a drink in my face at Lincoln Center. They were all laughing, having an uproarious good time, and when they weren't laughing they were eating, stuffing their faces with what looked to be a glorious feast of food laid out in the center of the table. They ate with their hands— no forks, knives, or spoons—and what they ate was whatever you could imagine. Roast pig, game hens, and chateaubriand. Lobster, oysters, and tuna sashimi. Peaches, plums, and nectarines.

I was sitting there and watching them while they paid me no mind. At first, all the food—the way they were ferociously devouring it—was making me ill. However, the more I watched them, the way Tracy was licking her lips and Jessica sucking her own fingers, the way juices were rolling down Alicia's and Stefanie's naked breasts, trickling over their fully erect nipples, and how Melissa was feeding Rebecca little shreds of meat, dangling each morsel over her beautiful face and deep-set eyes, the more hungry I got. I wanted to join them, to partake of their feast, to know what it was that they were laughing about and to laugh with them.

But I couldn't reach anything. The food looked so close, and yet when I would extend my hands, each and every calorie was always a few tantalizing inches out of reach. I stood up, determined to get something for my mouth, except the more I walked toward the food, the farther away it all appeared. Tracy and Jessica, Alicia and Stefanie, Rebecca and Melissa. Their food and their laughter. Everything beginning to fade from view and slip to quiet until I saw nothing and heard only the sound of my own breathing, fast and heavy. I was running, trying to catch up to them, to sit down at the table again. I was trying and trying, and failing and failing. Exhausted, I fell to the ground gasping for air, rolling on my back and gazing up at the huge expanse of white that hovered above me.

Out of nowhere, I saw another woman. She was older looking and tall, thin as a swizzle stick, with alabaster skin and white hair pulled back tight behind her ears. I had never seen her before in my life, and there she was standing over me. She was neither happy nor sad. I was looking up and she was speaking to me. I could barely hear her.

"You must be Philip," she was saying.

"Yes," I answered.

The woman reached out her hand to me, and there was something tucked between two of her fingers. It was also white, and it was small and rectangular. Slowly, I took it out of her hand.

"My name is Evelyn Simmons," the woman said, her voice echoing, "and I've been retained as the listing agent for this apartment."

I was no longer dreaming.

In fact, I had awakened to a nightmare.

I was lying there in bed wearing nothing but my boxers and unable to remember ever taking off my clothes. Rubbing the sleep from my eyes, I gradually focused on what turned out to be her business card. It announced Evelyn Simmons as a real estate agent with the Pickford Group. They were a Manhattan outfit that dealt strictly in two-comma properties ($1,000,000 and up).

Evelyn jiggled a set of keys in her hand. "Sorry about letting myself in like that," she said, "but I was instructed to do so."

She didn't say by whom, nor did she need to. I knew all too well whose name was on the title to the loft.

She continued: "I've come to look around the place so we know what to list it at. It shouldn't take too long."

She had to be fucking kidding me.

More or less, that's what I was thinking. As groggy

and hungover as I was, it quickly occurred to me that that was exactly what Lawrence Metcalf would hope I'd be thinking. He was probably sitting snug in his Greenwich home at that moment, looking out on the water, a big Bloody Mary in his hand and his Precious still lying comatose in her old bedroom upstairs from the two Ambiens she had needed in order to fall asleep last night after crying her eyes out. Yes, Lawrence Metcalf wanted me to throw a fit, wanted me to toss his real estate agent out on her bony ass. He knew perfectly well that an angry man dug his own grave that much faster.

I wouldn't give him the satisfaction.

I looked up at Evelyn Simmons after finishing with her business card. "Take all the time you need," I told her with a disingenuous smile.

She nodded and stole a quick, uncomfortable glance in the vicinity of my boxers. That's when I saw that I'd been hanging elephant the entire time.

I got up, put on some pants, and did my best to ignore my morning houseguest, who was walking around with a clipboard and making notes. When she was leaving ten minutes later, I was pouring myself a cup of coffee.

"You had a nice place here," she said, strolling by me. "Too bad."

Too bad?

Had Lawrence Metcalf really told her what had happened? I doubted it. Her line was spoken more like someone who had seen a news broadcast. Or, perhaps, had read the morning papers.

Ah, yes, the tabloids.

After showing Evelyn Simmons of the Pickford Group

out, I threw a sweatshirt on and headed to the nearest newsstand, eyes down all the way. There was a chance the story had fallen through the cracks, I tried to tell myself.

I was far from convincing.

"Affair Turns Deadly" was how the *Daily News* put it. Other than spelling my first name with two *l*'s instead of one, they essentially got the facts right. Accompanying the brief story was a picture of the entrance to the Doral Court. While I didn't think such publicity would damage the hotel's reputation irreparably, I did surmise that it would put a real crimp in their extra-marital-affair business.

Meanwhile, the *Post* had their own unique spin. "Fatal Love Triangle" was their headline. What's more, they had managed to scrounge up photographs of all three of us, positioning them, accordingly, in a triangle. How ingenious. While Connor's and Jessica's pictures looked to be recent, mine was apparently lifted from my Dartmouth yearbook. To the casual observer, it must have looked as if Jessica had been robbing the cradle with me. As for the story itself, it said that she and I had "reportedly" been caught in the act by Connor. Given that *the act* was what Connor had actually wanted us to do in front of him, the old adage seemed proven once again. Truth was always stranger than fiction.

I had taken the papers back to the loft and read the stories there over a breakfast of aspirin and more coffee. The lone consolation was that in both papers' opinions, I wasn't front-page news. That distinction went to Donald Trump, who, as the pictures of him showed, had fallen down while dancing with some supermodel at a swank benefit. "Thump Goes Trump!" declared the *Post*. "The Fall of the Donald" announced the *News*.

I was steps away from throwing both papers in the trash when I got to thinking about my parents—how they had kept a scrapbook of both me and my brother while we were growing up. Any time either of their two boys made it into the local paper, the entire article would be clipped and pasted into this brown fake-leather album that they proudly kept on display in our den. From time to time I'd catch one of them flipping through it when they thought no one was around.

I wondered if it had ever occurred to my parents that the news wouldn't always be good.

Eventually, I'd have to break it to them.

THIRTY-FOUR

Sitting around in the loft while trying to avoid every mirror was starting to take its ignominious toll after two days. A truck would backfire out on the street and I'd hear the gunshot. See Connor falling to the floor. Feel the weight of his body in my arms.

While I had always thought of my life as anything but routine, oddly enough it was the absence of the little things that were, in fact, my routine that underscored the severity of what had happened. The morning shave. Picking out a suit. Matching a tie. All so mundane, and yet all so reassuring. I never would've guessed. Not having to do any of it had become one of the more unsettling indicators of how much my life had suddenly changed. And would keep on changing.

I decided to call Jack.

Maybe I was forcing the issue. If I was, I didn't care. Should my days as a senior associate at Campbell & Devine be numbered, I wanted to know. Sooner rather than later.

Like I said, I was a terrible waiter for things.

I could picture Donna sitting outside of Jack's office

when I dialed. As she spoke to me she was pretending not to know anything and doing a lousy job at it. The giveaway, in between her gum chewing, was that she was far too polite.

When she told me to hold the line, I expected the next voice I'd hear to be Jack's. Instead, Donna came back on. "He wants you to come in at the end of the day, around six-thirty. Can you do that?" she asked me.

I could, I told her.

For not having actually talked to me, Jack had managed to tell me plenty. The first thing he had told me, by scheduling our meeting after hours, was that he wanted there to be as few people around the place as possible when I arrived. That seemed to jell with the second thing—that the nature of our discussion was such that he didn't want to get into it over the phone.

At six-fifteen I caught a cab up to the office.

There was no wink this time. When I got off the elevator and passed the portrait of Thomas Methuen Campbell, his serene gaze seemed a little more on the forbidding side. I could feel his eyes following me. I thought about what Jack had once said and I wondered if he had indeed "consulted" Campbell about my situation. Surely it met the prerequisite of being a tough decision.

The floor was nearly empty. What sounds I could hear were from offices far off the main corridor that led back to Jack. As I got closer I could see that Donna's desk was vacant. By then, she was most likely on the "Big-Hairy Ferry" back to Staten Island. I knocked on Jack's partially open door. "Come in," he told me.

The same leather-inlaid desk sat between us, only

now—pardon the symbolism—it felt a lot wider. Screw the small talk. Jack wasted no time in doing his shuffling of some papers and getting down to business.

"I've always been straight with you, Philip, and I'm not about to stop now," he began, retaining much of that same subdued expression from when I had last seen him. "It's simple economics, that's all, and as if I couldn't figure that out on my own, Lawrence Metcalf was all too pleased to spell it out for me. In a nutshell, it goes something like this. If you stay, a lot of business goes. If you go, a lot of business stays." Jack shook his head. "That's some father-in-law you have there."

"*Had* would be more like it," I corrected him.

Jack nodded in agreement and went on. "I like to think that I'm capable of standing on principle. As for what that exactly means, I don't know. What I do know is that I'm responsible for the livelihood of every person at every desk out there behind you. That said, it doesn't leave me much of a choice . . . doesn't leave me much of a choice at all."

I realized the other day that we're all at the age now where we can really only rely on our instincts and intellect in order to succeed.

"Are you firing me, Jack?" I asked.

When you think about it, from the ages of, like, twenty-eight to . . . oh, let's say thirty-four, we're all kind of just out there without a net.

"Only if you don't resign," he said.

I mean, when we're older than that, odds are we'll have collected enough experience—personal, professional, what have you—to get our asses out of almost any jam.

"I guess that doesn't leave me much of a choice either," I said.

And when we were younger, let's face it, nothing really too significant was expected of us, precisely because we didn't have any experience.

"No, I guess it doesn't," he said. "I'm sorry, Philip."

But those in-between years—right now—that's when we're really on our own.

"So am I," I said softly.

We traded our good-byes, brief and stiff lipped, and I was about to leave when I realized that there was one more thing. A small favor from Jack—that he would keep Gwen on at the firm, find a slot for her no matter what.

"Of course," he told me.

I walked out of his office, seeing no one as I headed toward the elevators. Then, around the last corner, I heard it. The low-pitched machinelike buzz. I recognized it instantly. Shep and his wheelchair.

There was no long, drawn-out conversation. No awkward silences. No pitiful attempt at compassion. Shep simply rolled to a stop and peered up at me.

"Look at it this way," he said. "At least you can fucking walk."

We both smiled.

I shook his hand and told him that I'd keep in touch. "Bullshit," he said with a chuckle.

I knew I always did like him.

The next morning, with the pantry and Sub-Zero near empty, I ventured out of the loft and walked to the corner deli for an egg sandwich. On the way back a short man tapped me on the shoulder in the middle of the sidewalk. He had *disinterested third party* written all over him.

"Philip Randall?" he asked.

"Serve 'em over," I said.

Which was precisely what he did. Divorce papers. Tracy had wasted no time in filing for the dissolution of our marriage. Outside of maybe paying the electric bill, our assets were to be frozen from that point on. What would follow was sure to be the bulldozer approach, named appropriately for how no legal stone would be left unturned in order to render me broke. All engineered by that same guy holding a Bloody Mary out in Greenwich. By the time the discovery phase alone of the divorce was completed, my legal bills would rival the gross national product of a third world country.

"Have a nice day, Mr. Randall," said the short man with a smirk.

"Fuck you very kindly," I replied.

THIRTY-FIVE

Fact: the moment a guy gets kicked in the balls is not the moment he begins to feel the pain. There's a slight delay. A period of limbo during which the brain is almost in denial. It's receiving all the messages, but it seems unwilling to respond in immediate fashion.

I was aware of all that had happened. I simply wasn't processing it. As I walked back home with those freshly served divorce papers in hand, however, everything seemed to register at once. It was life catching up to me. Life telling me—shouting, if you must know—that upon further review I was nothing more than veneer. Coating. Spread thin and destined to wear through. I was wifeless, jobless, and if Lawrence Metcalf had his way, soon to be penniless. There were no two ways about it.

I, Philip Randall, had lost my shine.

And it hurt like hell.

I wanted to blame Tyler. Without him this whole damn mess would never have happened. I wanted to blame Connor. Why on earth did he have to take out that gun? But in the end, what I wanted and what I *needed* were two very different things. Because what I needed was to accept the truth. There was no one to blame other than myself.

Oh, to be young, humbled, and hung out to dry in the city that never sleeps.

———————

Another day came and went.

I picked up the phone and put it back down maybe a half dozen times. *Jessica.* Forget what I would say to her—would she even take my call? That she had kept it together throughout the police questioning was one thing. That she would have anything to do with me after things settled down was entirely another. I had no business thinking that the two of us could remain involved, let alone live happily ever after. Absolutely no business. But Jessica was all that I had left, and I'd be lying if I said there wasn't a part of me holding on to the hope, no matter how slight or therapy worthy, that our relationship could somehow go on. I couldn't deny the fact that I still cared for her. If anything, at that point I cared for her even more.

So that's what it feels like.

She would have her questions, and I would be honest with her when I could, less than honest when I had to be. It was that or never see or talk to her again. That I couldn't imagine. Eventually, I picked up the phone and began dialing.

The first attempt was to her and Connor's apartment. The recorded voice told me the number had been disconnected.

The second attempt was to her mother's apartment.

The same recorded voice told me that the number had been changed. I grabbed a pen to take down the new one. The new one, said the voice, was unlisted.

The third attempt was to Jessica's office. I knew it would be too soon for her to be back at work—at least I could leave a message. Instead of her voice mail, however, I got some receptionist. Jessica Levine was no longer employed by *Glamour* magazine, she told me. Not what I had expected.

I had run out of attempts. For the next two days and nights I drank, puked my guts out, and drank some more. Next stop, oblivion.

That's when the phone rang.

It had rung before in those few days. Plenty of times, in fact. Calls from Dwight, Menzi, and other people who had our unlisted number, and each time I would stare at the answering machine and listen as they left their messages. Some sympathetic, others just pathetic. But this call changed everything.

"Philip, are you there? It's me."

There was no mistaking the voice, nor the fact that there was only one *it's me* left in my life. Jessica was calling.

I hurried to the phone and picked up. "I'm here," I said and repeated. "You knew I'd be alone, huh?"

"I figured as much," she said in a quiet voice.

"Where are you?"

"At my mother's."

"I tried to call you there," I said.

"The reporters were relentless. She had to get a private number."

"So I found out. I also tried to leave a message for you at your office. What happened?"

"I quit," Jessica said. "I wouldn't be able to go back, at least not there, not with everything."

She was probably right.

"You know, I wasn't sure I'd ever hear from you again," I told her.

"You weren't going to."

"What changed your mind?"

"Lack of sleep," she replied. "Every time I close my eyes I'm back in that hotel room. I guess I was thinking . . ." Her voice dropped off.

"That talking would help?"

"Maybe—I don't know. I thought so; that's why I called," she said, though sounding increasingly hesitant. "Only now I'm not so sure if it's such a good idea. I think I should go, Philip."

"Wait, Jessica, don't," I implored her. "Listen, I know how hard this must be on you. It hasn't exactly been easy on me either. The thing is, the more I dwell on it, the more I realize . . . for us to face what happened I think we first have to face each other."

"I can't do that," she said, afraid.

"I know it seems that way."

"No, really, I can't."

"You have to try, Jessica. Otherwise you're never going to be able to leave that hotel room, and neither am I."

She said nothing. She was thinking about it. A good sign.

"Do you want to come here?" I asked, and waited.

More thinking. "No. It would be too weird," she finally said.

I understood. It was, after all, where Tracy lived, or at least had lived. "How about a restaurant?" I suggested. Of course, had our *last* get-together only been at a restaurant . . .

"Maybe," said Jessica.

"It would have to be somewhere out of the way," I said, "if you know what I mean."

"All too well," she replied. "Some things never change."

"No, they don't, do they?"

With that, Jessica acquiesced. We picked the place and the time. Nadine's in the West Village at eight o'clock.

THIRTY-SIX

At two minutes of eight I walked into Nadine's and turned down the first table offered to me. It was near the front. The one in the back, I explained, would be much preferred. *Whatever*, shrugged the guy with the menus. I was happy to see that not only did he not recognize me, no one else seemed to either. There were no double takes, nor anyone leaning over for a whisper and nod my way. I sat down and waited for Jessica. It was quite fitting that here too I was the early one.

As for how I looked, the difference was truly night and day. That afternoon when Jessica had called I was going on seventy-two hours without a shower and even longer without a shave. That's the thing about an alcohol binge. It doesn't leave much time or desire for hygiene.

That night, however, I was all cleaned up. Looking pretty good in my chinos and Ted Baker shirt, if I do say so myself. A ponytailed waitress came by and asked if I wanted a drink while I waited for the other person to show. No, thanks, I told her. I was pretty sure that I'd already had my quota for the rest of the decade.

Jessica arrived. As she walked toward me and sat down, I felt a twinge of nerves.

"Hi," she said.

"Hi," I said back.

She appeared tired, quite understandable given the circumstances. Minimal makeup, her brown hair tucked behind her ears, black slacks and a lime green cardigan buttoned up over a simple white T-shirt. Granted, it wasn't the most inspired of ensembles, but it was far from suggesting any early onset of Widow's Surrender.

Initially, it kind of felt like a first date, albeit a first date with someone I'd slept with many, many times. There were a few pauses and hesitant moments that stalled the conversation. We were tiptoeing around the subject, not knowing exactly how to get into it. Headfirst, I finally decided.

"I thought you would hate me," I told her.

"In a way I do," Jessica said. "Though not any more than I hate myself."

"Those things I said to Connor at the end, the yelling and screaming, I was only trying to—"

"Distract him . . . I know."

"I didn't mean a word of it."

"I understand."

"Do you know where the funeral was?" I asked her, assuming all the way that she hadn't been exactly welcome at it.

"Back in Providence, with his parents," she said.

"I guess that makes sense," I said, nodding.

The ponytailed waitress returned. Jessica asked for an iced tea and I remained fine with my water.

Said Jessica when we were alone again, "Did Connor ever mention to you that his father was very religious?"

"He may have, why?"

"Because his father called me before the funeral and said that he wanted me to come to it. He quoted the Bible and proclaimed that he was willing to forgive me for what I had done to Connor. Can you believe that?"

"You didn't kill him, Jessica."

"But still . . ."

"Yeah, I know."

We dropped the subject for a bit, read our menus, and ordered. Jessica asked me about my job. I explained that, like her, I had also quit—the difference being that in my case there was no other choice. She wanted to know if I'd be looking to work for another firm in the city, or perhaps be moving out of town. I told her I hadn't thought about it.

"How about yourself?" I asked. "Will you try to get with another magazine?"

She hadn't thought about it either.

We both had the pasta special. Penne with shrimp and broccoli. Jessica hardly touched hers.

With the table cleared, we lingered over coffee. I was stirring in some cream when I looked up to see Jessica staring at me. Her expression said it all. We were about to get back into it.

Jessica: "That day, when you first called me, you said we needed to talk. What happened?"

"It was something Connor had said," I began slowly. "We were alone together in the limo the night before. He was about to get out when he told me that he knew for sure you were having an affair."

"How could he have known for sure?"

"He didn't say. Of course, he didn't want to say because he knew I was the one. I thought maybe you would have an idea."

Jessica shook her head. "I don't."

"Nothing at all?"

"Not that I can think of," she said. "So how did he find us?"

"Simple. He followed me to the hotel."

Jessica took a sip of her coffee. It was an oversized mug, and she held it with two hands. "There's something else, as you might imagine," she said.

"What's that?"

"The stuff about you and Tyler Mills. Connor said he thought you killed Tyler because he knew about our affair."

I didn't flinch. "I'm still wondering about that myself," I said. "What's so weird is that you two didn't even know Tyler, so where Connor would ever get that idea I don't know. It certainly wasn't from me. The only possible explanation I can think of is that Connor was so angry he was saying anything to strike back at me. I mean, you saw him; you heard what he wanted us to do there in front of him—he was delirious."

Jessica put down the mug. She looked at me and tilted her head. The words were deliberate. "I think you can do better than that," she said. I stared at her blankly as she folded her arms on the table. "There's something you're not telling me, isn't there?"

"What makes you say that?" I asked.

"Oh, I don't know," she replied, a quick edge in her voice. "Maybe it was the two visitors I had yesterday. I think you've met them—Detectives Hicks and Benoit? They said they had questioned you about Tyler Mills. Then they showed me the pictures."

Easy now, Philip.

"What'd you tell them?" I asked, struggling for poise.

"Nothing, you'll be glad to know. It was both of us in those pictures, and I was pretty sure they thought both of us had something to do with Tyler's murder. Besides, I wasn't about to tell them what Connor had said without first giving you the chance to explain. That much I owed you. Though not much more. Just *please* tell me that you can explain."

"It's not what you think, Jessica."

"The point is, I don't know what to think. You never told me anything about those pictures or the detectives. You hid all of it from me," she said. She leaned in over the table, her face illuminated by the light fixture overhead. "I did my part; I kept our stories straight. Now you have to do your part. You have to be straight with me."

This was not the Jessica rendered helpless in that hotel room. This was the Jessica I knew. The Jessica that I used to take to bed. My kissable ambition. The girl who knew how to get what she wanted, and at that particular moment—with considerable leverage, I might add—what she wanted was the truth.

So, fuck it, I told her.

I told her because she had me. Because it was time
the lying stopped. Because after the price she had paid,
I thought she deserved to know. I told her because if
she could be there with me in the wake of Connor's
death, she could also understand my motive with Tyler,
that he had been blackmailing me. Blackmailing *us*,
when you thought about it. Surely she would understand.

So I told Jessica about that first lunch at the Oyster
Bar and how Tyler had been following me. The head
games that ensued, culminating in his surprise visit to
Balthazar. "My, you look familiar," Tyler had told Jessica. Yes she did, and he had the pictures to prove it.
There was the meeting in the park and Tyler's upping
the dollar amount, and there was my thinking that I had
no other choice. It was either him or me.

I described the plan. Then the night itself. My change
of heart, my fit of conscience. The empty couch and
Tyler with the knife. His throwing himself at me, and
ultimately, that horrible *clank!* of his head hitting the radiator.

I told her everything—all the way up through Tyler's
letter, and when I finished, I asked Jessica with all my
heart if she believed me.

"Yes," she said.

"Do you understand why I could never go to the police?"

"Yes," she said.

But by then her eyes had begun to well up. A lone
tear making its way down and past her cheek. She leaned
back against her chair, shoulders slumped. She had no

idea how bad it would feel. And I just had no idea, period.

I should've taken Tyler's advice.

The park. That little box he was waving over me. "It also picks up wires," he had said. "You ought to look into getting one."

You ain't kidding, Tyler.

THIRTY-SEVEN

There is no Zagat guide to New York–area prisons. If there were, I'm afraid the Butler Correctional Facility in Wayne County wouldn't rate very well. Bad food, bad decor, bad service.

The charge was second-degree manslaughter. The plea bargain was for criminally negligent homicide. The interesting thing about the wire they had Jessica wearing was that it came down to an all-or-nothing proposition for the district attorney's office. Meaning, that to believe any of it was to believe all of it. They couldn't point to my actions regarding Tyler as intent to kill without accepting the fact that I couldn't go through with it. That I was selectively telling the truth was something they knew they could never prove. There were no witnesses and there was no murder weapon to speak of. It was my word against . . . well . . . my word.

Meanwhile, Jack had offered to represent me. Instead, I asked for and took his recommendation of a hotshot attorney over at Burnham, Burnett, Redway & Ford. In the end, I was simply too crestfallen to be around Jack. I think he understood.

As for Jessica, what can I say? I guess she would've made one hell of a poker player after all. Not once did she tip her hand. Nor was there a single tell. She played her cards perfectly.

She played me perfectly.

She never did stick to the plan. The cops had gotten to her and her conscience right from the start. She told them about Tyler—what Connor had said in the hotel room—and it didn't take too long for the connection to be made. Word got back to my good buddies Detectives Hicks and Benoit that their lawyer boy was in trouble again. Gee, maybe that drifter didn't do it after all.

Yet, with all that on the table, they still didn't have a case. There were two people who could've sealed it for them: Connor and Tyler. Thing was, they weren't exactly around to testify.

Their last hope was Jessica. Maybe they had to bear down on her a bit, coax her into wearing that wire, or maybe she had it in for me the moment that gun went off and Connor fell to the floor. Either way, by the time we met at the restaurant, she knew her part cold. Ice cold. The groundwork of trust had long since been laid. All she had to do was exploit it. *I wasn't about to tell them what Connor had said without giving you the chance to explain,* she had led me.

Like the fly to the spider.

She listened while I delivered the whole story and what she did was stare. She was looking right into my eyes and I was looking right back into hers. I thought I saw understanding. What I was really looking at was revenge.

———————

"Randall!"

I had a visitor, the guard announced.

I wasn't expecting anyone. My parents had already made their one visit, flying in and out within the span of a single day. It felt very much like they were paying their last respects. I couldn't blame them. Their son, who had long before grown apart from them, was no longer anyone they could remember. I had hoped, however, that they wouldn't blame themselves. I tried to tell them that it was nothing that they had done or not done. Mom never made me wear a dress. Dad never shot the family dog. Sometimes people were the way they were because that was simply the way they were.

When I asked the guard who my visitor was he gave me the fool's grin. "What do I look like, your fucking secretary?" he cracked. Of course, to see his fat body, balding head, and pockmarked face staring back at me was to realize that, yes, he kind of did look like Gwen.

Maybe that's who it was. Jack had told her about my request that she keep her job and this was her way of saying thank you.

I walked the long stretch of low-ceilinged hallway down to the visiting area. Though she had her back to me, I could tell immediately that it wasn't Gwen.

It was Sally.

Sally Devine had come to see me.

She hugged me real tight and gave me a kiss on the cheek. She followed that by taking a step back and looking me over. "Blue denim is just all wrong for you," she said, shaking her head.

I couldn't agree more.

"I brought you something," she announced. She peeled back a foil cover from a plate. "Flourless chocolate with raspberry ganache."

Sure enough, Sally had brought me two slices of her favorite cake.

"Were you able to fit the file in them?" I joked.

"No, but I couldn't believe that the guards actually poked at them to make sure. I could've killed them!"

"Not so loud," I said, mostly kidding. "The walls have ears."

She laughed and hugged me again. I thanked her for coming. I also ate the pieces of cake rather quickly. They were the first things to taste good in a long while.

"Does Jack know you're here?" I asked.

"He thinks I'm shopping at Woodbury Common. I don't think he'd really mind, except I didn't want to take the chance of telling him. Besides, I kind of like the idea of having a guy on the side."

"It's more like on the *in*side, Sally."

"Oh, god, I know," she said. "I can't imagine what this must be like for you. Have you been all right?"

"For the most part, yes."

"Jack did tell me that with good behavior you should be out in a year and a half."

"Let's hope so," I said. "And you thought *you* had problems."

She smiled. "You were there for me and now I'm here for you."

"I appreciate it."

"I'll have you also know that I'm still not drinking," she said proudly.

"Congratulations."

"Thank you. One day at a time, as they say."

I glanced at the cinder-block walls. "I know the feeling."

We talked some more and after an hour or so had passed, Sally told me that she'd be back again in a month—if that was okay with me.

"More than okay," I assured her. I added that while I may have known a lot of people, few would ever make a trip like this for me, let alone on a regular basis.

She accepted the compliment by grasping my forearm. On that once heavily bejeweled hand of hers I saw now only a simple platinum band.

"You were smart not to wear a lot of jewelry here," I said to her.

"Actually," she said, looking at the band, "this is all I've worn for the past month. Call it the new me. I found all that sparkle was getting too damn heavy."

"I like the new you," I told her, giving her a kiss on the cheek good-bye.

I watched as she left before going back to my cell. *My cell.* Give or take, my new home was only 3,420 square feet smaller than my old one. It would take some getting used to. So too would the rest of what had become my life.

In looking back I practically had to convince myself that it all really took place. I had been blackmailed and I had plotted murder, and although I had killed no one, two people were dead because of me. The woman I had married for money ended up taking nearly all of mine. And the woman with whom I had betrayed my wife was the woman who, in the end, betrayed me.

It was, like, defining moment a-go-go.

There were no more cases for me to prepare for, no more hotel rooms to rendezvous in, and no more restaurants to have reservations at. As for guys' night out, the television was turned on in the prison lounge from eight to ten.

What there was for me was just time—time taking its time before I could start over. New and improved. Safer for the environment. It wasn't going to be easy. Then again, maybe that was the problem all along. Everything had been a little too easy.

The temptation was to be bitter. The resolve was to let it go. Holding a grudge would've simply been me, once again, elevating my interests over everyone else's. A nasty little habit there for a while. In any event, I took some comfort from the fact that Jessica had learned I wasn't the monster of her worst fears realized. Merely a guy in over his head.

I picked it up and read it again.

My brother's letter, which had arrived a few days earlier from Portland, Oregon. In it, Brad mentioned nothing about my misfortune. Instead, he chose to recall the things that used to mean the world to us as kids. Little possessions. Our ticket stubs from Wrigley Field. The silver dollars sent to us by our grandparents. The volcanic rock we found while digging in the backyard. He wrote that he couldn't remember when it was exactly that these things had stopped meaning so much to us.

Only that whenever it was, it was surely the saddest day of our lives.

HOWARD ROUGHAN is a formed Manhattan-based advertising creative director who swears his main character is nothing like him. An ex 212, he's now a 203—as are his wife and son. This is his first novel.